And Twice as Twisted

A Dark Mafia Series

Agostino Crime Family Book Four

DAHLIA REIGN

Dear readers,

Dark romance is my specialty. Therefore, triggers lie within this book. You have been warned. Xoxo, DR.

ABOUT THE BOOK

The Italian Grim Reaper was stripped down to the most innate and basic of instincts. Then *they* killed him. Until all that was left was an animal in human form.

Back from death's doorstep, he was a shell of the man he once was, while his hunger could only be sated by revenge—feeding on *their blood. Their pain.*

The same enforcer, turned brother, who was once the salvation of the Agostino Crime Family was now their greatest threat. No longer trusted with the task of protecting the eldest daughter of the New York City crime boss, Apollo succumbed to his inner demons—promising to destroy her body and her heart. Sienna Agostino was his obsession, tainted by his past sins and broken by his present indifference. She was a smart woman, until like so many before her, a man became her greatest downfall.

DEDICATION

If your answer is no, this is for you.

*Riddle me this: is it really toxic if
you fucking love it?*

Pointer finger, meet trigger. Boom.

PROLOGUE
SIENNA AGOSTINO

pollo was alive.

Well, if you could consider the *body* they pulled from the Hudson River—riddled with gunshots and succumbing to hypothermia with a gaping wound across his throat—any semblance of living. His chest would rise and fall with every intake of breath, his heart pounded, and blood filtered through his system. But that was it.

Dead. Vacant. All life was extinguished from behind his eyes.

My family blocked me from seeing him, referencing the still-present brutality marring my skin. They'd assumed it would send him over the proverbial edge and we'd lose him forever. However, he didn't speak or acknowledge anyone who came to visit.

Not my father. Not Lucky.

His silence was slowly destroying the family and none of us had a clue as to how to pull him back from the hell that consumed him.

That day, those bastards had given me everything I'd wanted, while simultaneously stealing it all away. I saw it in his eyes, the revelation, his need for me. Now, I had nothing.

And as I was known to do when it came to anything Apollo, I made another huge mistake when I snuck into his hospital room by myself. When I'd demanded he look at me, a part of me died too—a serrated knife brandished and quickly puncturing my heart. His head turned and he stared at me. Through me.

He hadn't spoken until that moment. Not a word.

"Get out! Leave!"

I had to be forcibly removed from the room by the doctors, while their attempts to calm him only inflated his anger. Towards me. His snarled hatred echoed down the hallway, and I fled from my heartache as it nipped bitterly at my heels.

I resented all the love he'd stolen from me and never reciprocated. We were in this position because of something in his past, not mine. Yet, even after he came home to the compound, he had nothing to give. He continued as Lucky's right hand. A soldier, silently following orders.

He'd proven to me what I'd already known. Even after the egregious crimes enacted against me, my heart still beat for him. While his was nothing more than an organ that pumped blood through his system.

What happened to the girl who demanded respect? I barely recognized the weak woman staring back at me in the mirror.

"Where are we?" I asked my driver. I was so lost in my own misery that I hadn't noticed we were on the side of the road. It was raining, an absolutely miserable night that matched my miserable mood. I couldn't make out much besides the trees to our right and the dreary sky looming above us.

I was forever cloaked by the dark cloud that followed me.

Usually that thought was metaphorical, but now it was physical as the car was pelted by a sudden flood of torrential raindrops.

"Sorry, miss, engine problems." My driver slid out of the car before I could respond. The hood raised and blocked my view of the road ahead of us. Pulling out my cell phone, I started checking emails before an odd noise caught my attention. Dread settled into my gut, but I swallowed back my nerves and opened the door, stepping out into the storm. In more ways than one…

"Everything okay?" I shouted as I approached the front of the car.

"Sienna." My name was called out from behind me.

Haunted. Distant. And *fucking* angry.

"W-what're you doing here?" I hated the weakness in my voice but the animosity in *his* rattled me.

"I've come for you. Isn't that what you wanted?" He took a step forward and I took two back, calling for the driver. "He's dead." The words came without remorse. "He was going to hurt you. I saved you, Sienna. Just like in one of your fairy tales." He was mocking me, his vacant eyes burning with cruelty.

"What do you want from me?" I rushed forward. Fuck self-preservation. I always knew my temper would be the death of me. "Tell me!" I slammed my fists into his chest, my pain and guilt driving each blow.

"I find it absolutely insulting that you haven't thanked me yet."

My heart was lodged in my throat as he pulled me closer. "No." I tried to push him back but all I could do was continue to flail my arms. He ignored me, grabbing both of my hands in one of his and slamming my body against the car. He pinned me in place, his much larger torso rubbing into mine. I could feel his arousal against my stomach and dread cemented my limbs, stalling my fight as if I were somehow locked in his palpable animosity.

"Fine. I'll *make* you thankful." He wrapped his free hand around my throat and tugged me forward. His muscles flexed and the tattoos on his arm seemed to dance with the movement. Mocking me.

I latched on to his wrist, scratching his skin as he opened the back door and threw me inside the car. When my pencil skirt hindered my legs from widening, he shredded it down the center and stepped between them. His fingertips roamed from my thighs, up to my panties, and rubbed me through the fine silk. He hummed his appreciation before traveling north, groping my breasts and pinching my nipples through the material of my shirt.

I managed to wrap both hands around his wrist and tug. Then, using all the force I could muster, I bent it backwards. He reached out on instinct, slamming his meaty fist into my cheekbone. My brain bounced around my skull for a second before my nails found his face, embedding into the flesh until I could feel the trickle of blood.

"I fucking hate you for what you've done!" I screamed, kicking out at him. He was temporarily taken aback, and I sought my moment to attack with everything I had. He fell out of the car and I climbed across the center console, trying to get into the driver's seat. Before I could, he grabbed my ankle and jerked. My face slammed into the gear shaft and blood erupted from my nose.

"You know you want this. I saw it in your eyes when you came to visit me. You wanted me to use this body, so there would never be anyone else after I was done with you." He kept pulling me.

I tried to catch myself as my stomach slid off the seat and my shoulder took the impact as I plummeted onto the concrete. "No, please. Don't do this."

He dumped my body into the overgrown grass and ripped off his suit jacket, dropping it beside me before reaching for his zipper. His hand was heavy against the center of my chest, pinning me down and making it hard to breathe while the rain coated my face and soaked my remaining clothing, chilling me to my bones.

"Please don't," I begged in a half whisper as I felt him tug my panties to the side and settle his erection at my entrance.

"That's it, baby." He licked along my jawline. "Give me those filthy lies. Pretend you don't want this."

My brain was foggy, my fight dwindled, and the blood in my veins stalled as he slammed into me. This was it. This was the moment I died. It didn't matter if I physically survived his assault. Because, either way, Sienna Agostino was dead. He pulled back and slammed into me harder, the wet grass slicking my spine and gliding me through the mud.

I turned my head, unable to look at the traitorous bastard so keen on destroying me. I prided myself on the fact that I was strong. That I'd overcome the stereotypes of being born a woman in the mafia. Then shattered my image by believing it somehow made me worthy of love, a ridiculous ideology that women were given at a young age.

And, in the end, it ruined me.

He was so large I couldn't see past his body, unable to beg the stars for reprieve. But God must have turned his back on me long ago. It was the only explanation I had in this moment. There was a time when

I believed people were given trials and tribulations in order to teach them a lesson. A message sent from a higher power to tell us something. There were instances where it took a while to understand while others seemed to slap you in the face without much thought. I needed God to tell me what this was supposed to mean. What lesson I was meant to learn. Instead, it was the devil who heard my please and showed me the way out.

And I understood. I saw it.

The handle sticking out from under his discarded jacket. Just within reach. I looked up and his eyes were filled with lust, devoid of the man who'd once protected me. There was no redemption after this. Not for him and not for me. I was done with my heart getting broken again and again. My body was overwhelmed with agony as he pounded into me. Harder and harder with each thrust.

My chest ached but I knew I had to do it. My arm stretched forward, my fingers digging into the mud until I felt the cool, hard metal. It was slippery in my grip, but I managed to pull it closer. He dropped onto his elbows, his face inches from mine as he panted against me. "You fucking love it. You love everything I do to you." His breaths became faster, harsher.

"Lies. It's all goddamn lies."

He stopped thrusting for a moment to stare down at me in shock.

"You may think you've *ruined* me. But I'll fucking end you." I raised my arm.

"You don't have the balls…" He stopped when I pressed the barrel to his temple. My heart was beating out of my chest, and for a moment, I thought he was right. I thought… *I can't.* I can't do this to *him*—but this man didn't deserve anything from me. Nothing but hatred.

"Your tiny balls smacking against my ass are nothing compared to the ones in my designer panties." It was raining harder now. "Fuck. You." And I pulled the trigger.

His blood sprayed in the air, mixing with the rain and pouring down over me like a hailstorm of carnage and brain matter. I could taste it in my mouth and was overcome by the sudden urge to dry heave. His large body dropped onto mine, and an agonized cry expelled from somewhere so deep within me that my throat burned as I extinguished it. All the pain, anger, sadness, and guilt transformed the scream into a crescendo of despair.

I did it. I fucking killed him. I didn't know what I expected to feel after pulling the trigger, but this wasn't it. I was numb. A huge part of me died along with him, and there was no coming back from it.

"Look what you made me *fucking* do!" I hissed into the air, the numbness fading as a fresh wave of guilt tore at the shattered remnants of my heart. I needed to leave. To go far away. From my family and their city before it was too late. There was already nothing good left of me and seeing *their* hatred would only make *me* hate myself worse. I knew if I stayed, I'd never survive.

Not after what I'd done.

Headlights pulled up behind the car and heavy footfalls echoed in the distance. Charging towards me. "Sienna!" my brother shouted as I struggled to shift the body off me. "Sienna! Fuck! What did you do? How could... Sienna!" he grunted my name. Bella sounded from behind us, and the realization had me choking on air. "No! Bella, baby, stay back!" Lucky helped roll the dead weight to the side, pulling me to my feet and wrapping his suit jacket around me.

"No..." Bella whispered, and my gaze snapped to hers. The look she gave me added to the torment I'd already inflicted on myself. There would be no reparations for our relationship. I'd ruined my family. "What did you do?" Tears filled her mismatched eyes as she tried charging forward, but my brother pulled her into his arms, holding her tight as she broke.

"I can't believe you fucking did this." Lucky sounded distant, a radio static filled my head, and I barely felt the harsh bite of the pavement as my body slammed into it.

It wasn't all that long ago that I had begged this man to give me everything I wanted, everything I thought I deserved. I thought he'd be my savior in a world built by men and against women. I wanted to be the queen on the arm of the mad king. Instead, he broke me beyond repair—something I thought I already was, but quickly realized I wasn't. Not even close.

Until now.

I rolled onto my side, pulling my knees to my chest, and stared at his motionless body. I did it. I killed him. I thought I'd feel better. But his lifeless eyes stared back at me, forever cemented in my brain. Left to haunt me.

They were the last thing I saw before everything went black. That one thought playing over and over in my mind.

I killed him. I killed...

CHAPTER 1

SIENNA AGOSTINO
SEVERAL MONTHS PRIOR

"Now I lay me down to sleep, I pray to the Lord my soul to keep." I stared out into the mesmerizing night sky above me, one arm tucked behind my head, the other resting on my stomach. "I have spent so many years asking—no, begging to hear him say those three stupid words. Words that mean nothing if he isn't here."

I wiped at the silent tears pouring from my eyes with a humorless laugh. I didn't survive the insanity that was my life to end up here. Tomorrow just wouldn't be the same *without him*.

"If you're listening, please grant me this. I begged you for his love and now I beg you for his life…" I rose to my feet, stumbling twice before righting myself again. "Fucking mud!" I grumbled, kicking off my heels.

"Your mama is gonna beat that ass if you stomp in her gardens!" Al taunted, stepping around a rose bush. "Oh, no, Sienna. Not the red-soles." He chastised with a sad smile, his eyes focused on my destroyed shoes.

"How long have you been listening?" I bent over, face-planting when my foot slipped.

"Long enough for you to rip my fucking heart out." He reached down a hand, and I stared at it for a moment before I allowed him to help me up.

I raked a palm over my face, feeling my mascara clump. "Any word on Octavia?"

"No. Nothing since Mario's call." Al pulled me to his large chest, my head slamming against the wall of muscle. "We'll find her, and Apollo will come home."

"When?" I tugged from his grip, only to fall back on my ass, and rolled to my knees with my head in my hands. The cold mud seeped through my pants as my sobs filled the open air. We'd found Apollo and lost Octavia, simultaneously. There had been no demands, no more calls, and no information as to her whereabouts, while her pleas for help, for us to rescue her, served as a haunting reminder of how we'd all failed her.

"She is stronger than we think." Al's large hand warmed my back. "She..." He stopped, knowing nothing he said mattered.

"Why're you playing in the mud?" my brother's reprimanding tone called out amidst the darkness.

"Fuck off, Lucky!" I steadied my feet before charging forward. "You were supposed to protect her! You let her down!"

"We'll find her, Sienna. Use your head, not the bottom of a liquor bottle." He lifted the empty whiskey container from the ground. "Apollo's gonna be pissed that you drank his expensive shit."

My neck snapped in my brother's direction. "Well, he ain't here to stop me, now, is he?"

"Sienna." There was that tone again. And I wouldn't allow it. My entire family was acting as though my pain didn't matter. As if I had no right.

My heart thumped in my chest, beating against my rib cage, and a red haze settled over my consciousness. A rage like nothing I'd ever felt before. He had the audacity to come here, interrupt my meltdown, and act like I was wrong for seeking a moment of reprieve.

It was true. The booze did little to heal me, and in all honesty, probably made my anxiety worse. But I was on a mission of self-destruction, and if I wanted to get tanked and play in the mud, then fuck anyone who tried to stop me.

I shoved at Lucky's chest, screaming all my pain into his face. "He doesn't want me! He never wanted me!"

"You need to rest, Sienna. You're exhausted." My brother ran a thumb over the bruises that still colored my neck. "He needs time."

"Time. Right." I rolled my eyes. And the moon twinkled in response, mocking me as it prepared to drop and allow the sun to rise again. "And Octavia, does she have time?"

"Sienna." He was losing his patience.

"Tell me, dear brother. As the future-fucking-king with no *mietitore* to do your dirty work, how do you plan to save your little sister?" I could feel his anger burning at my back. "Handed the fucking city, just because you happen to have a dick swinging between your legs, yet you do nothing with it."

"Boss, I got her," Al interjected, but Lucky's grip on my arm was already spinning me around.

"Fuck you, Sienna. Don't you pin this on me!" His tight hold on my shoulders was the only thing keeping me from falling. "I'm sorry he hurt you, but Octavia isn't my fault."

Liar. We all knew *il diavolo* was just as guilty as the rest of the family. Forever surrounded by flames, it was our turn to burn.

"Boss, let me." Al pulled me from my brother's grasp. "Breathe, Sienna."

It was too late. I could already feel myself slipping, succumbing to the darkness. Whether it be the booze, the sleepless nights, or the mental fatigue, the shadows just didn't offer me the same peace. Instead, I was plagued by the images of Apollo in that hospital bed.

"Sienna!" Numerous voices drifted in and out in the distance, but they faded quickly.

"I'm so sorry. I should've fought harder," I cried and squeezed his cold hand, begging him to wake up. His fingers twitched, forcing me to look up into a pair of honey-brown eyes that seemed to watch me curiously. "You're awake!"

He'd been shot six times, stabbed twice that. Though the worst injury was a long gash from ear to ear. They'd cut his throat before throwing him into the river. The team of doctors had no idea how he'd survived all of it and *the freezing temperatures.*

He'd come back for me.

The hopeless romantic in me fantasized that it was fate bringing us together. I was an idiot. God, I had never been so wrong in my entire life.

"Don't talk. The nurses said it could be painful. But, Apollo, I'm so glad you're going to be okay. I love—"

"Get. Out." Cold. Dead. Not pained or whispered.

"What?" I was taken aback by the venom leaking from his lips and licking at my sanity.

"Out!" He repeated the command, punctuating it with a new wave of hatred.

It startled me, forcing me to my feet as I stepped away from the bed. Left to bear witness as Apollo began throwing anything he could get his hands on. He tore the IV from his forearm, splattering blood along the white walls and linens before sending a chair flying across the room. I watched, helpless, as it shattered against the wall.

My legs moved of their own accord and I ran for the door, fleeing as doctors and nurses stormed in behind me. My cries seemed louder in the silence of the hallway as I ran along the tile flooring with my newest guard following in my footsteps. The elevator doors closed, shielding me from Apollo's screams but doing little for my broken heart.

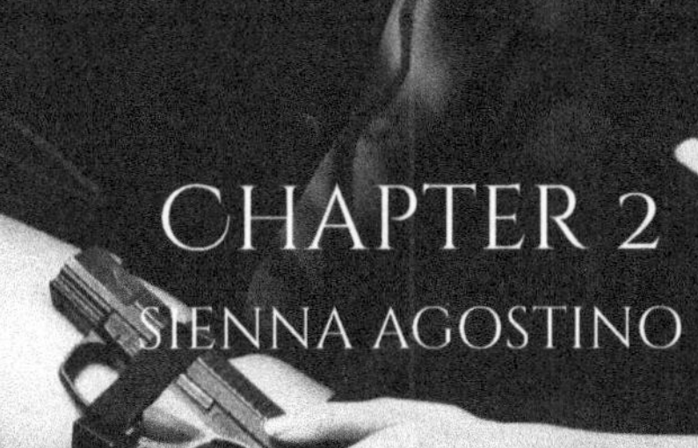

CHAPTER 2

SIENNA AGOSTINO

There was something almost calming about the chaos of a packed dance floor. People lost to their vices as they swayed and moved to the beat of the music. I threw my hands in the air above my head, bringing them down slowly as they traced over each curve of my body. I could feel *their* eyes on me. The dirty thoughts as they wished my hands were their own.

They wanted me.

Those who knew my name kept their distance. We didn't exactly advertise that *Danza* was mob owned, but people weren't stupid. Thanks to me, my brother wasn't just king of the criminal underground; he was also a productive member of society. A business owner. And he thrived in the spotlight *I* gave him.

Whatever. No one gave a shit about what I'd done. Not for Lucky. Not for my family. It didn't matter. *I* didn't matter.

The beat was a constant thumping sound as the dancers twirled on the lifted platforms above the dance floor. Their glittering costumes and feather head pieces matched the fantasy the room was creating. A fantasy where my pain didn't exist.

"It's hot as fuck in here." Rocco positioned himself between me and a group of rowdy college girls.

"That's the point! It adds to the fun." I spun in a circle, my hips moving sensuously until I lost my footing, and I slammed my back into his chest.

I was a teensy bit drunk. Okay, I was *hammered*. But I was allowed to indulge in a little self-induced pity party after everything I'd been through. My makeup covered my physical trauma and my dress forced your attention to anything but my bruises. Much to Al's dismay.

"What the fuck is that?" He gestured to my outfit.

"A dress." I motioned a hand down the expensive garment. "Roberto Cavalli to be exact!"

"Like fuck that's a dress." His face was pinched in obvious displeasure. "Trying to show everyone what gender you are?"

"Well, of course." I did a little spin, my pregame shots making me woozy. "Let them know what they're missing."

Al grumbled his agitation over stupidly selecting a white shirt when protecting me always led to bloodshed.

He was going to kill someone.

As the lights pulsed above us, I leaned backwards. And Rocco grabbed my shoulders, pushing me away from his body. "Sienna. Gross."

"I can practically see your... your..." Al appeared at my side, looking at me with disgust as he waved a hand in my direction.

"Pussy?" I chuckled, placing my hands on his chest to brace myself. Rocco was still at my back, holding me at arm's length.

"Sienna!" Al gagged as Rocco shouted, "Ew!"

I opened my mouth to repeat the offending word when Rocco covered it, shoving me forward and following Al through the crowd. I struggled to get up the stairs and Rocco had to practically carry me. My red-soles were doing me dirty tonight.

"Fuck. Shit. Goddamn it," Rocco moaned out and practically tossed me into Lucky's VIP room.

"Oh! Rocco! I'm sorry." I threw a hand to my mouth at the sight of blood soaking through his white shirt. I tugged the material free of his pants, dropping to my knees to inspect the wound over his kidney. It was only a slight tear; the stitches were holding together well but it didn't diminish my guilt. We'd gone through hell together, neither of us coming out unscathed.

"Where's the line start? I want my turn!" A slurred voice came at my back, Rocco's attention snapping in that direction. "Yeah, baby!" The guy chuckled as Rocco helped me to my feet to tuck me behind him.

"What did you just say?" A chill filled the air as a new menacing side of Rocco rose to the surface. Since the accident, my brother's enforcer seemed to be slipping away in front of our eyes. My light-hearted friend and guard had been replaced by someone tainted, crueler. With Apollo gone, Lucky and Al didn't have much time to keep an eye on him. And Rocco refused my help, clamming up anytime I tried to comfort him. "Say. It. Again."

Goose bumps lined my arms, his biceps flexing as I tried to hold him back.

The guy appeared to finally realize the threat and moved backwards, bumping into Al, before his eyes flicked between the two men. He quickly dribbled a slew of fake apologies with his palms up in a defensive posture. My brother's men were playing with the bastard now, preparing him for a fate worse than death at their hands.

"Enough." I stepped between Rocco and his would-be prey. "You're bleeding, and he isn't worth it with all the witnesses," I hissed, my gaze scanning the crowd.

"Yeah, listen to the bitch!" The jackass stared at me with a mixture of lust and loathing.

"You stupid mother—" I cocked my fist back, the blow to his nose jarring my arm. "Fucker! Ow!" I cradled my wrist to my chest for a moment, feeling the ramifications of my poor form.

I knew better than to throw a punch like that.

"Time to go." Al put the guy in a headlock and dragged him to the door. "Stay with Sienna. I'm just gonna throw the trash out." He boasted it loudly, too loudly. Which meant the son of a bitch was going to be taken to the basement of the hotel, under our apartments. As much as I hated my status, being *the* mafia princess *did* have its perks.

I escorted Rocco to a chair by the bar and called the bartender over for another glass of champagne. I needed the bubbles.

"Hey." A random girl gestured towards the row of shots before her. "Want one?"

I nodded, wanting to keep the happy nothingness in place to avoid my real feelings. Her friends were on their way to my level of drunk, but a few were also coked out of their minds. I tossed back the shot, watching two of the girls step from the group and approach a small table in the corner. My eyes focused on them and I knew I had a death wish.

"Come on." One of the girls motioned me forward, waving her hands above the white lines stretching across the table. "Here, Sienna."

Had I told them my name?

As I stepped closer, one of them whispered in my ear. "It makes everything better." Her tone was rushed, hyper. I took a hundred-dollar bill from my bag and rolled it.

Sienna Agostino would never snort coke with a fiver.

I looked back and forth between them. Something didn't feel right, but I was too committed to my self-destruction to give it a second thought. One of the dancers had stepped closer, but for the most part, we were secluded in the corner. I made quick work of snorting a line, allowing the stars to burst behind my eyes. I was momentarily stunned, unsure what to do except stare at the wall behind the bartender. He handed me my whiskey neat, eyeing me with confusion until I felt my normal smile slip back in place.

"Another!" a girl called out, though it seemed forced as she tugged me to her. *I shouldn't.* But, oh, how I wanted to.

"Bitch!" A dancer slammed one of them against the wall, smashing the woman's cell phone to the ground. Her glittery flapper dress shimmered in the light as she moved, the feathers in her hair swaying with the swift motion. I was momentarily stunned as I watched her flip the table of cocaine and grip the second girl by the throat. "You know exactly who you're messing with, don't you?" She glanced between the girl she was choking and the other one shaking on the floor. "Thought you'd get your fifteen minutes of fame with that video?"

Video? I flicked my eyes from one woman to the other, appalled by my own actions but furious with theirs.

Magazines were always looking for a way to ruin my family. They'd sell their images and tabloid stories to the highest bidder, assuming their anonymity was protected as they soiled the reputation of the mafia princess. However, I always found my mark. One way or another, I'd hunt them down. Just ask Sebastian Santoro…

If you can find him.

"How much am I worth?" I bent down into the girl's face. "Tell me!" I grabbed a chunk of her hair, pulling her closer.

"I-it was just a joke!" she cried.

"A joke! Oh!" The dancer started laughing uncontrollably, shaking the woman in her arms. "Why didn't you tell us?" And before I could move, she smashed the girl's face into the wall. Twice. I watched on as blood poured from the cunt's nose. The dancer smiled at me, as if to say *I got this*, and pulled the other girl to her feet, bracing her against the wall with an arm to her neck. "Never come back here. You didn't see anything. You don't know anything."

The woman nodded, her head bouncing up and down like one of those bobble dolls.

"You're lucky it's me and not her brother, *perra tonta.*"

The girl left her friend and scurried out of the room, and all I could do was watch with unattached amusement as the dancer adjusted her costume. She righted her dress, pulled a feather from her breasts, and dabbed at her makeup, before glancing at the clock on the wall and cursing.

"Sorry for getting involved." She had a slight Spanish accent, her caramel skin flawless against the shimmering gown and her green eyes alluring— they seemed to change color in the dim lighting. "You looked like you needed that first line. That's the only reason I didn't step in sooner."

"Thanks." I extended a hand and introduced myself. "Sienna."

"*Lo sé, princesa.*" Her smile revealed perfect white teeth. "Gabriela." The way her lips wrapped around her own name was near sensual. And I stared in awe as she sashayed towards the door.

My little brother blocked her way as he walked in, glancing at me before eyeing Gabriela like she was his next meal. His growing smirk told me all I needed to know, and I stepped to the dancer's side.

"A new girl." He took her hand and spun her out, before pulling her back into his chest.

"Nope. You can't have *this* Spanish princess too, *muchacho.*" She shrugged him loose before turning to me. "Let's dance." Then Gabriela grabbed my wrist and dragged me down the stairs. I glanced over my shoulder on the way out and took note of how Marco appeared rattled.

Interesting.

As we headed to the dance floor, the crowd shuffled slightly, letting us through. I closed off my mind, let the rhythm take control of my body, and the heavy beating of the bass erased all thoughts of my evening. Of my life. I knew what I was doing would cause more harm than good. But after all those years spent playing the picture-perfect image my family wanted, I was owed this. To fall apart at the seams until I was ready to put myself back together again.

I just wanted my friend back. The same man who always remembered my birthday and gave me the most thoughtful gifts. He noticed things, details, and he remembered them. Then, of course, there was the fact that he could make you orgasm so aggressively you swore you'd never survive. Apollo Deluca was the type of man who wouldn't just kill for you; he'd enjoy doing it.

And I missed him.

As I moved around the floor, beads of sweat dripped down my back. My limbs were exhausted and my calves ached from my shoes, but I didn't stop. The crowd was diminishing but I was far from done for the night.

"Sienna."

I sensed his presence before I felt the wall of muscle at my back, his rough tone causing the butterflies in my stomach to take flight.

"Enough."

I couldn't help but smile as I pressed my spine into his chest, his protective arms coming around me as his warm breath tickled my ear. *I knew he'd come back for me.* I just had to send the right message and he'd snap out of it.

"This self-destructive behavior is unbecoming. It's time to go home."

I nodded, my head tilting backwards and resting in the crux of his neck. "I need you."

Apollo's hands gripped my arms, preparing to spin me to face him when Al's glare appeared in front of me instead.

"Look at me." Al gripped my chin, staring at me with accusatory eyes. *And I was screwed.* "Are you fucking kidding me, Sienna?"

I swallowed the lump in my throat. The disgust I saw reflected back at me was so unlike him. His hand shook as he pinched my jaw harder, and his expression all but eviscerated my high, the coke long forgotten as my stomach swirled with threats of vomiting.

"Fix yourself, Sienna. I fucking mean it, or I'm telling Lucky."

I nodded at Al, unable to speak.

"And burn this fucking thing you call a dress."

"Al…" It came out choked, tears streaming down my face.

"I don't want to hear it. You're better than this! I've never seen you so *weak*." And in that moment, I felt like he'd slapped me. "Where is *the* Sienna Agostino? Because this *girl*, I don't like her. Rocco, take her home." Al dismissed me with a wave of his hand.

I was stunned silent. *He was right.* This path only led to death. I turned to Apollo, confused when I realized it was Rocco at my back. My chin wobbled, and I hated this feeling of complete helplessness as much as I couldn't stop it. My mind was messing with me, the cocaine obscuring the lines between reality and fantasy. I wasn't just seeing things. I was feeling them now too…

I swore it had been *him* holding me. But just like every other instance, when it came to Apollo, I was dumb as hell.

"Come on, Si. Let's get you home." Rocco pulled me to his side and escorted me to the back door.

"N-no. Take me to my office, please."

He walked me to my car, helped me slide in the back, and paused to stare at me.

"I don't want anyone else to see me like this tonight."

Rocco nodded his understanding before closing the door and climbing into the front passenger seat.

Weak. Women were presumed to be weak. That's why they had no place in the mafia. In one night, I'd given up everything I'd worked so hard to earn—respect at the top of that list.

Men were allowed to make mistakes. The dick swinging between their legs ensured those mistakes were forgiven. Forgotten. That same sentiment didn't exist for women. The moment our emotions seeped through our tough façades, our power was stripped away. No matter how long we'd fought to earn it. It was a hard, fast truth that surpassed corporate America. The world was changing. Women were fighting for equality because we sure as fuck were a lot stronger than men gave us credit for.

And, normally, Sienna Agostino was in the trenches. Until my stupid heart took everything from me. Not anymore. I'd swallow down all the bullshit and move on. From him. From my family's shadow. And from this city.

Because this mafia princess didn't take shit from anyone. Including myself.

CHAPTER 3
SIENNA AGOSTINO

"You will be home for dinner," my mother ordered over the phone, but I was barely listening.

He was going to be there.

I wasn't weak, nor was I stupid. I'd become resigned to the fact that I was never going to get what I wanted from him. So now I was going to hold my head high, steady my feet in my red-soles, and become the fucking queen of Philadelphia.

Maybe.

Romano had been amazing since the day I met him—through contracts, murder plots, and my confessed love for another man. He was still so patient with me, when there was absolutely no reason for his kindness. As the Philadelphian Don, he could very easily call my father on the engagement and force my hand. But he didn't.

I needed to rid myself of these irrational feelings for Apollo. For a man who didn't deserve me. Even if it felt like I'd ripped my heart out and left it in that hospital room.

I hung up without a word to my mother.

"What part of *you're fired* did you not understand?" I questioned the man behind me.

I was standing in my office, overlooking the city I used to love so much, which was now nothing more than ash from the fire that destroyed everything I'd cared about. My head was pounding and my mouth was dry; the coke and whiskey were dissolving but one hell of a hangover was left in their wake. I slept in my office, wearing the Balmain sheer-panel bodycon dress from last night.

"If you'd answered your phone, I wouldn't have had to hunt you down." Ander—I mean Alexei barked.

"Funny how I never noticed that Russian accent before." I tossed a glance over my shoulder, glaring at him. "Judas." And I only wished my tone was as biting as the rage I felt.

"I was trying to protect you when I learned what my family was doing. I was never a part of it."

I laughed, leaning my forehead against the floor-to-ceiling windows.

"You fucking poached me, Sienna!" he attempted to counter.

"Sienna." Rocco stalked into the room with a slight limp from the accident. "Do you need *anything*?" He stared at Alexei as he emphasized the word.

I thanked him but declined. Alexei was my problem. I needed to *handle* him.

"How's the leg?"

I could tell Alexei's question burned Rocco, his glare showcasing his disdain as the enforcer pivoted on his heel and exited the room but not before slamming the door.

"Listen Ander—shit, Alexei. Whoever the fuck you are." I didn't turn around. "I don't want to hear whatever lies you tell your pillow before you drift off to a nice, remorseless sleep."

"Goddamn it, Sienna." His hands gripped my shoulders, spinning me to face him. "I tried protecting you the entire time!" He released me and turned away, giving me a chance to really look at him.

It was almost comical how much he had changed now that his true character was on display. Proudly boasting his *Bratva* persona. He was in a full suit, including a tie, something he wouldn't be caught dead in previously. He even *looked* Russian now—there was no other way to describe it. If you knew, you knew.

"I don't want to hear it. Any of it." Enough tears had been spilt for all the lies and betrayals. I had nothing left. "Leave."

I walked to my desk and sat behind it, staring at my emails but not really paying attention to anything in particular. For the first time in my entire life, things were falling down around me. I used to see it coming, but now it broadsided me, forcing me to sit amidst the damage it created. A phoenix rose from the ashes, while a miserable excuse for a woman like me burrowed inside them.

"Are you listening to me?"

"Not really." I sat back, rubbing my irritated eyes.

"I thought you'd want my help finding Octavia." He turned towards the door, stopping when my stapler hit the wall next to his head.

"Don't you fucking say her name," I screamed, releasing my pain, anger, frustration at the closest target in sight. "Why would I want your help, huh? You and your fucking Russian assholes probably took her!"

One second, he was across the room. The next, he was looming over me. I was forced back in my seat, staring up at him and daring him to do something. Anything. A sick part of me wanted the pain, wanted him to lash out verbally and physically. But he didn't rise to my challenge.

I wanted to rip someone apart, but there was no one worthy enough. No one who would satiate my rage until my sister was found.

As much as his presence enraged me, I knew Alexei was working tirelessly to bring Octavia home. She was last seen at Bella's *funeral*, getting into a car with an unknown security detail. And then she vanished. We had nothing on her, not a single sighting since the moment they pulled out of the parking lot. Lucky was apparently exhausting all possibilities, but every lead came up empty. Without Octavia... without Apollo... Sienna was nothing. I was an empty, tarnished shell.

"Your brother is worried about you," Alexei interrupted my pity party.

"The king has time to worry about little old me? How darling of him." I walked over to the newest addition to my office, my beautiful cherrywood bar.

"Seriously?" Alexei shoved to his feet and snatched the whiskey from my hand. "You've lost clients, you're drinking in the middle of the day, and passing out in clubs at night! *Blyad',* Sienna!" *That's it.*

"Get your traitorous Russian ass out of my goddamn office! You've already been fired!" I tossed back my drink, hating that the sweet burn of the whiskey was already gone.

"I *will* find her, Sienna." He stared for a moment longer before turning and leaving.

Once the door closed behind him, I collapsed onto the floor. Crawling over to the window, I leaned my back against the wall and stared at the city as I continued to drink, watching the sun go down over the horizon. I was a total mess, obliterated and depressed. I couldn't get a handle on anything and allowed the booze to drown out the voices in my head.

"Go away!" I yelled when someone knocked, a bottle of whiskey later.

"Miss Sienna," a small voice called out around the door. "I... I'm sorry. I just wanted to give you this."

"Evelyn! Please, I'm sorry," I muttered or maybe slurred. "Come. In." I hiccupped out the words. Evelyn Campbell, my little protege, was a quick rising asset in my legal department.

"I'm sorry to bother you. I just..." She stepped closer, looking down at me with nothing but adoration. "Here."

I took the paper from her hand, and after a few minutes of concentration, I could finally make out the words. It was an invitation. I swallowed back the tears it invoked.

"I'm graduating and would love it if you could come. I know you're really busy and all, but I wanted to ensure you got the invitation. I wouldn't be graduating at all if it weren't for you and everything you've done. And I—"

"Evelyn." I stopped her nervous rambling. "First, I am *beyond* busy with the many, many things an important CEO like me has on her plate."

"I understand. I just—"

I cut her off. "I wasn't done. I am very busy… *clearly*." I waved at my drunk ass sitting on the floor. Snatching her wrist, I pulled her to the ground beside me. "I will never be too busy to celebrate all *your* hard work."

We smiled at each other as I poured her a glass and we sat back, watching the sunset side by side. Then we cried together, over another glass of whiskey, discussing all the men who had done us wrong.

"I hope I'm not out of place here, but you're the strongest woman I know and whoever did this to you… well, I know you'll make them pay." She gave me a sinister grin, and I couldn't help the choked snort-laugh combo that left me.

"Sienna!" Al shouted, his heavy footsteps stomping off the elevator.

"I meant to tell you your bodyguard said he was on his way." She smiled sheepishly. It hadn't escaped me that Evelyn had developed a little bit of a crush on my big-ass best friend.

"Can you please tell him I am on a call and will be out shortly."

She nodded, placing her glass on the bar and squeezing out the door, as I watched the cars below. Normal people finishing their workdays and heading home to their uncomplicated families. Exhaustion swept over me. Placing my forehead against the cool glass, I shut off my mind and eyed the building across from mine. Lights were turning off and people were leaving for the night. Curiously, I looked to see if there was someone as pathetic as I was in that building too.

"Are you kidding me? That's the fucking dress I told you to take off last night!" Heavy footsteps charged towards me.

"I don't like you like that," I mumbled, as his large hands reached out and pulled me to his chest.

"Please, like I'd ask to look at what's practically falling out of this *scrap* of fabric." He jostled me around. "Basically incest in a thousand-dollar dress."

"More like two thousand." My stomach sloshed with each step.

Placing me on my feet for a second, Al straightened my dress and then threw me over his shoulder. He spoke softly to Evelyn, confirming she had a ride home before walking into the elevator.

"If you're gonna puke, you better warn me," he grunted.

"Then put me down. This doesn't feel good." A descending elevator was painful enough, but this position made it ten times worse.

A second later, I was on my feet and tucked into his side as he attempted to get me out of the building without everyone staring. "Sit." He tossed me into his car with little care for the jostling, and my stomach continued to jar with the sudden movement.

"Take me… to… my apartment." I curled into a small ball, my ass on the floor and my head resting against my arms on the seat.

"Nope. Compound." The car lurched forward as he pulled away from the curb. "Mommy's orders."

"Alvin. No. Not doing this. Not tonight." Everyone needed to back the hell off me.

"Sienna, you just need to put all this behind you. He isn't going to leave the family, so you might as well get over it."

Because it was that goddamn easy!

"I'm astounded that I've never realized how much of a prick you really are." I kept my face pressed across my arms. "I almost died thanks to him. My father is in agony over Octavia's disappearance, knowing it's his fault. Add my brother's bullshit into the mix, and it sounds like a terrible fucking dinner party. No thank you."

"Grow up, Sienna." He sighed, as if *I* were the problem.

"Run along and do your master's bidding, lap dog. I was stolen, beaten, stabbed, and almost died because the man I *love* has a past. Now he's treating me like a pariah. I'm *sorry* that I can't just wake up and act as if Apollo *cutting me* out of his life is so simple!"

"Sienna!" His anger didn't come close to my own.

"Hey, Al?" When he looked down at me, I smirked. "Fuck you." And then I proceeded to throw up the entire bottle of whiskey, and the remnants of my lunch, all over his front seat. I barely heard the sounds of him yelling over the noise of me purging my soul.

If it were that easy, don't you think I'd heal myself? *Se solo.*

CHAPTER 4
SIENNA AGOSTINO

"Stop sulking." Two words. That's all I got. Several weeks had passed since I threw up in his car, but Al was still barely speaking to me.

"I'm not." I rolled my eyes and crossed my arms.

He liked to pretend he didn't dry heave the entire way home. I did destroy his fancy new Audi, and I am pretty sure he'll never be able to drink whiskey or eat salami again. He wanted me to buy him a new car, but I told him he could get fucked. I did, however, tone down my drinking and spend all my time split between work and the gym.

And finding Octavia.

Her second call since her disappearance turned all my focus to finding her. It was Octavia, for all intents and purposes. It was my baby sister on the other end. I knew the resigned, submissive tone that started the call. But by the end, she was unrecognizable.

"Sienna, please stop looking for me," Octavia whispered into the line.

"Octavia! Oh, God! Where are you?" I rambled on, kicking off my heels and running for my office door.

"Sienna!" she barked and the confident, angry tone stopped me in my tracks. *"You don't get it. I don't want to be found."* Gone was the

meek and mild sister I knew, and in her place was someone who sounded... a lot like me.

"What're you talking about? Octavia, tell me who took you and where you are?" I sobbed at the end, unable to hold it back as Alexei and Al darted towards me.

"Sissy, please," she whispered. "I love you. No matter what happens, please remember that. But I need time to heal... from..." Her words died in her throat.

"Octavia, I will help you," I urged.

"No one can help me but myself. Move on with your life, Sienna. One day I will be fine. One day I will come back. Until then, take care of yourself and be happy. Even if that means leaving the family, the life."

"Octavia, please." My voice cracked. I needed my sister, and I hated how she sounded so sure of her choices.

"I'm fine, Sienna. Or... at least I think I will be." Her tone was empowered until she whispered the last part. "I won't be weak anymore."

"Little doll, end it," a deep voice commanded in the background, almost recognizable but not quite.

"Who the fuck is that? Let me talk to the bastard—"

"Doll! Now!" His command sent me over the edge, while my sister's matching tone halted my rage.

"Enough, Sienna! I love you, but back off. I'm not as weak as you all think." And then the line cut out.

We hadn't heard anything else and I couldn't trace the signal. Whoever had her was smart, or had the funds to ensure someone intelligent was on his books. If I was going to find her, I was going to need help.

That bitter truth tasted pretty salty on my lips.

"Yes," Alexei answered on the first ring, but I couldn't speak. This was harder than I thought. "Sienna. Open the door." A knock had me dropping the phone and reaching for the knob instead.

"How the hell did you get in here?"

Alexei casually rested his shoulder against the doorframe. "Seeing how you've been working out, I won't lie to you and risk being on the receiving end of your knuckles." He squeezed my toned arm. "Lucky asked me to find Octavia and this is the best place for me to do that." He stepped back, obviously concerned over my response.

"Then why isn't she found?" I turned on my newest red-soled heel and stomped back to my desk. "And my brother doesn't run my company, by the way."

"Will you tell me about the call?" He appeared amused by my deepening scowl.

"You motherfucker. You tapped my cell?" I sputtered but stopped when he didn't say anything, motioning for him to get to work.

We spent the afternoon reviewing everything he had on my sister's disappearance. It turned out he was able to trace her movements throughout the city for a short time until all circuits were shut down. At once. It was as impressive as it was infuriating. Twenty minutes was all it took for every trace to turn up empty.

"They must have left the city. The blackout included the private sector of JFK."

I rubbed at my temples. "Maybe. I don't know." I sighed, mentally fatigued.

"Let's stop for the day." Alexei closed his computer. "We can continue this weekend, wherever you want."

You could only burn the candle at both ends for so long before nothing was left. Till the fragrant scent was reminiscent of burnt flesh and tears.

I slipped into my jacket as we walked into the lobby. I opted to not discuss my weekend plans with my Russian friend. Alexei had lost the ability to comment on my life the moment I'd learned his true identity.

The elevator doors were just closing when Farrah, my secretary, shouted, "Have fun in Philadelphia."

I kept my gaze forward, stepping into the elevator. "Sienna. *Iisus Khristos.*"

"Not your concern, *Alexei.*" I accentuated his name and closed my eyes.

"Stop calling me that."

"Isn't it your legal name?" The doors opened and I didn't wait for an answer, walking to the front entrance as two of Romano's men flanked my sides. They took my bags, motioning me towards the SUV idling at the curb. I smiled at the line of armored cars that surrounded the vehicle. Romano was taking my safety seriously after my last *attempted* trip to his city.

"Sir, back, please."

I glanced over my shoulder and froze. Alongside one of Romano's men was Apollo. The rest of the world faded away as we stared at each other. The stitches were gone while the twisted strings left a barely visible scar on his tattooed neck, with the bruises and cuts now a distant memory. Silence stretched between us and the city disappeared. We were lost in each other's gaze, far removed from our current predicament. Apollo ignored Romano's team. Then, slowly, he turned to look each man in the face. Memorizing them. He knew who they worked for. Knew where I would be going with them.

My heart raced as a moment of guilt spread through me. The skin across my chest blossomed red and my face heated. There was no reason for me to feel this way, but beneath the weight of his gaze, I felt it all.

Suddenly Rocco was at his side, whispering in his ear, and a second later, Apollo disappeared into the crowd. "I'll handle it," Rocco said into his earpiece, waiting for me to enter the vehicle.

"Ma'am."

I turned towards the guard and slid inside, where the men reported to the remaining transports, and we took off into the city traffic. I closed my eyes and tried to breathe through the panic and guilt that had settled on my chest.

I had nothing to feel guilty about. His choices forced me to make my own.

"Traffic is light, ma'am. We should arrive in less than two hours." The same guard spoke to me from the front passenger seat and introduced himself as Romeo—Romano's right hand.

Staring out the window, my eyes burned with unshed tears. Why now? Why would he show the moment I decided to take my life back?

It didn't matter. It was over and there was no going back. Too many years. Too many tears.

As we approached an accident scene, my heart lodged in my throat. Everything around me turned to white noise as my ears pulsed, sweat broke out across my skin, and my stomach turned violently.

Romeo twisted in his seat. Grabbing my wrist, he pressed his thumb against my pulse point. "Deep, slow breaths." His command allowed me to focus on his voice as he gave me random facts about Philly. After a few minutes, and seemingly satisfied with the rhythm, he released my hand.

"How long have you been with Romano?"

Romeo was an attractive man, roughly in his early-thirties, with thick dark-brown hair and jade-green eyes. He had a playful disposition and a smile that melted your heart with two proud dimples on display. He'd been with Romano for several years, following him from the streets and becoming his right hand when he took over. He claimed Romano was earnest yet demanding—he treated those he cared about like royalty. I didn't bother to ask about his enemies because I'd already heard the stories. Romano's rise created a power struggle, one he'd climbed over countless dead bodies to win.

"Wow," I muttered, staring at the city skyline now looming on the horizon.

"It's not New York, but sometimes change is just what the doctor should've ordered." Romeo pulled his phone from his pocket. "Romano wants you to head directly to dinner if you're not too tired, ma'am."

"Whatever the boss wants." A heaviness lifted from my chest as things fell so easily into place.

We stopped outside a nondescript brick building. The armed cars in the front and rear of us cleared the sidewalk before I stepped out. There was nothing fancy or appealing about the place, just a glass door next to a simple sign.

Romeo opened the door for me and offered a hand. "Welcome to *Fetta di Paradiso*, home to Center City's most sought-after desserts." He placed my arm in his and escorted me into the building.

The moment the doors opened and I smelled the scent of fresh cakes, pies, and other baked goods, I understood why it was called *slice of heaven*. The outside was boring, but the interior was opulent with white marble floors, gold display cases, and large chandeliers with diamonds.

"Pick whatever you like. The boss will be here shortly." Romeo disappeared as the additional security details spread throughout the room.

"Parli Italiano, bella?" An older, round woman appeared from behind the case, smiling at me as I nodded. *"Cosa posso portarti?"*

She wanted me to pick something from one of the displays, but each shelf was better than the last. Cannoli, tiramisu, panna cotta, tartufo, *sfogliatella*, panettone and so much more were spread through the cases. I was practically drooling, my hands and nose pressed against the glass like a kid in her first candy shop. When I couldn't choose, she told me she'd make me a sampler and I clapped my hands, hopping up and down on my stilettos.

"Sweets are what gives me the most beautiful smile?" Romano's raspy voice sent chills down my spine as he stepped alongside me. "Sampler, Maria!"

"Hush!" *Maria* shouted from behind the case, making us both laugh as he steered me towards a table.

Ever the gentleman, Romano pulled out my chair before unbuttoning his jacket and sitting across from me. As if memorizing my features, he took in every detail until I squirmed. The scar near his chin danced as he fought a smile.

"How was the ride?" he asked, leaning back in his seat.

The question was so simple and so… normal… that I couldn't help but laugh. All the tension and stress of these last—God, it felt like years—lifted for a brief moment and I laughed. Hard. So hard I hiccupped as I wiped away tears and tried to rein in my emotions.

"I'm sorry. This is all just so…" I paused, unsure how to finish.

"Romantic? Thoughtful?" His smirk was approachable, boyish almost.

"Normal." I laughed, and he frowned.

"I'm unsure how I should feel about that." Before I could answer, Maria approached the table, depositing a large variety of treats. "Thank you, Maria." His eyes didn't stray from mine.

Glancing up, I realized Maria was staring at me. "Those eyes," she whispered. Only, judging from the way she spoke, it wasn't a compliment. She glanced back and forth between us before glaring at Romano. With a flick of the wrist, he waved off whatever silent conversation she was having with him. "*Prego, è troppo magra.*" Maria bounced back into the kitchen, making me laugh again.

"I think you look incredible." Romano eyed my lean torso, ignoring Maria's statement about me being *too skinny.*

And then we were off. We explored every treat on the tray and went back for more cannoli. Maria was a wonder in the kitchen and I had no doubt this was a very successful venture for Romano. After the bakery, we toured Center City and South Street, as he showed me all the artistry, shops, and dining options *his* city had to offer.

"Everything okay?" I asked when we had to stop for Romano to take yet another call.

"Of course. Business." He didn't look up from the screen when he answered me.

"Sir," Romeo interrupted. "She's causing issues."

She? Romano's shoulders tensed as he apologized to me and stepped away. Romeo watched me, probably assuming I'd bombard him with questions. But it wasn't any of my business. Romano's conversation was short and edgy.

In our world, mistresses were a common practice. Hell, he knew I was in love with another man and yet here we were. I couldn't dare accuse him of anything when I had my own guilt to carry. Though I couldn't help but wonder if he would keep her after we got engaged? *If* we got engaged? That would be a question for another day.

We ended our evening early, as Romano escorted me to my private suite at the Four Seasons. The view was breathtaking. It overlooked the art museum, and boathouse row was lit up against the water. He kissed my hand and wished me goodnight. I was thankful he didn't push for more, unsure how I would feel if he aggressed.

I changed into comfortable *Gucci* track pants and stepped into the bathroom. The reflection in the mirror was one I hadn't seen in a very long time. I no longer looked broken, lost. The predatory gleam was back in my eyes as I felt myself become whole again.

"Screw this." It was still early and I knew sleep wouldn't come. Not for a while. So I changed into a pair of Joseph black stretch leather leggings, a Burberry off-the-shoulder white sweater, and a black studded pair of red-soles. I twisted my hair into a high messy ponytail, freshened my lipstick, and headed for the door.

Then stopped.

Normally, there'd be no second thought to take off on my own. But after my abduction, I learned some things. Instead I sent a text, and within minutes, there was a knock at my door. I opened it and my mouth watered at the scene before me.

Romano had changed from his fitted suit into a pair of designer jeans and a grey button-up. Untucked, collar open, and his tanned chest on display. His hair was ruffled on his forehead, tousled like he kept running his hands through it. Without saying a word, he extended his arm and I wrapped mine around his bicep as we took the elevator down to the hotel bar.

"Wow." My eyes scanned the change in scenery. Only a few people mingled around the white granite bar top. The lighting was muted because the square seating area was enclosed by floor-to-ceiling windows. The room was lit up from the outside spectacle dancing across boathouse row.

"I agree." When I turned to look at him, he was staring at me. "Are we talking about it or just drinking about it?"

When I didn't answer, he pulled me towards the bar and ordered me a drink. The conversation was light, just two people getting to know each other. He was a disarmingly charming and sophisticated man. Yet so simple and laid-back.

With all the information and history he shared with me, I couldn't help but think he was hiding a part of himself. Then again, I didn't have any room to talk, since I was hiding in his city to avoid my truths.

But his presence was still nice, a piece of solace away from everything my family and company entailed.

And just like that, before I knew it, the weekend was over.

"I'm sorry I can't take you home." He walked with me from the hotel to the idling car. "Business calls."

"Not a problem. I want to thank—"

His calloused hands gripped my face and pulled me to him. His lips slammed against mine and stole my breath, my mind startled and lost to the sensation. It was over far too quickly as he helped me into the car and I was on my way home. I read through a few text messages, learning nothing new about Octavia. Al let me know he was going to meet me on my way to my proverbial prison. My brother had planned to lock me down to avoid any further concerns over my well-being.

"*Meritavo di meglio,*" I muttered to myself, garnering Romeo's attention.

"You do deserve better. The question is… what're you going to do about it?" Romeo's retort nestled deep in my gut, settling like a rock.

That *was* a good question.

CHAPTER 5
ROMANO BIANCHI

This woman did things to me. Things that were both enlightening *and* debilitating. What was supposed to be an alliance turned into a game of cat and mouse. Her perfume aroused me and her playful shoves made my dick hard enough to shred through steel. I wanted her. Just one fucking taste, but I couldn't.

Too many things were going on behind the scenes for a woman to ruin it.

When I'd received word of Sienna's accident, Romeo had concerns about the proposed alliance with New York. Her brother was known for being brash when it came to his family. A war, I could handle. Just not right now. I needed to get all my chess pieces in play before someone flipped the board.

In traditional mafia circles, someone like Sienna Agostino was supposed to remain pure, untouched. I wasn't an idiot. She was hiding in my city to avoid another man. There was no assumption when it came to the woman's virtue. Romeo had texted me about Deluca's unexpected arrival right before her departure. He owned her.

Why would you want something shiny and new, when you could have more fun after it was broken in?

I hid behind polite smiles and gentlemanly behavior. But like the scar on my face, my demeanor was jagged and twisted. I chose which version of myself I wanted you to see, so knowing the woman as I did, I gave Sienna her Prince Charming.

Suits and pleasantries were forced on me as the veritable mafia king of Philadelphia. However, crawling out of the gutter and growing up how I did made it all a joke to me. I'd gotten to where I was by taking someone else's weakness and making it my strength. Which was exactly what I would do with the Agostinos.

New York was a thing of the past. The city of brotherly love was the goddamn future of *il familia*.

I didn't want anything from her, other than hearing her scream my name as she raked her nails down my back. Everything else was paperwork between me and her father. Once we scrawled across that dotted line, I'd pull the trigger.

Then it would be too late. She'd have signed her life away to me and there wouldn't be anything her father, her brother, or her little toy —Apollo—could do about it. Unless they wanted to start a war. And if they did, they'd fucking lose.

"Something on your mind?" Romeo asked, leaning against the brick wall in my office.

I came from nothing and didn't hide behind fake affluence. Even now. Where the former boss sat in a high-rise in Center City, I ran my shit from a warehouse in South Philly. In the middle of the old Italian neighborhood. Its original brickwork made it a beautiful space, but the outside reeked of squalor and despair.

It was how I never forgot where I came from. How I never forgot the blood I'd spilt to get here. Because it didn't matter the amount of money you made or the image of wealth you portrayed. It mattered how quickly someone could take it from you. And I fucking dared someone to try.

"Think this plan will be their breaking point?" I traced a finger down my scar, following the path of uneven skin.

"She'll never forgive you." It seemed Romeo was growing rather fond of my Agostino prize. "And, yes, I do. One daughter missing, the other broken, and then…" He didn't have to say the rest. We both knew what was coming.

"Perfect." I smiled, a true, honest smile. "Before we know it, Mario will lose his entire family and Lucky will be begging me to save them all."

"He's going to be a problem." Romeo tapped the image of Apollo we'd taped to the wall.

We'd dissected their entire organization, studying every contact, every business, every secret, and every lie that family'd ever told. They were dripping in deceit since before they could crawl. Mario's lies would force all the Agostino children to turn their backs on him.

Once they learned the truth, I'd be untouchable.

"Elaborate." I sat back in my seat, cracking my knuckles and breathing deep.

"He's a loose cannon. Always has been. But a few more screws shook loose after that most recent attack." Apollo's fall had the potential to fuck up my plans. "He showed up at the pickup. The bastard isn't going to let her go without a fight."

"Good. I want to see if the devil's right hand bleeds." I stepped to the barred windows of my office, staring out at my empire.

Philly had been my home my entire life, an amazing city that cultivated the man before you. Born half-Italian, that's where my roots in *il famiglia* had ended. I didn't have the glamour and education the Agostino children were given. I fought tooth and nail to get to where I was. I pissed off a lot of people when I took over the succession from the current boss—a decision that painted the streets red.

Now I would do the same to New York, starting with Mario's precious children. I would take everything from him. This plan assured my protection once the final pieces fell into place. Sienna's signature was just step one. Part two had already been secured.

The agitated voice started shouting again. The sound carried down the halls and bounced off the walls before falling on deaf ears. *She* hadn't stopped since we brought her here. There was a long road ahead of us until the big reveal. But, in the meantime, I needed to get this situation under control.

"Go shut her up," I commanded Romeo. "I need silence."

I'm coming for you, New York. And I won't stop there.

CHAPTER 6
APOLLO DELUCA

old. So fucking cold. Potential hypothermic chill.

Everything hurt and the goddamn water was like a thousand knives assaulting my body. The nerve receptors just under the surface of my skin reacted quickly, my heart rate and blood pressure expeditiously sharpening. Your body temperature dropped twenty-five times faster in water than air of the same temperature.

I could barely keep my head above the surface. Fatigue set in as my limbs would slow and my head would submerge. I opened my eyes and let the saltwater burn, staring at the black abyss that enveloped me.

It was thoughts of Sienna that reinvigorated my fight. I'd catalogued the wounds they'd given her, and I felt peace, believing someone would get to her before she bled out—while my own future didn't seem as likely. If I survived, only one thought would be on my mind.

Revenge. And I'd get it.

My lungs were taking in water. I was drowning on the inside long before I would on the outside. I closed off my mind to the innate panic. It was funny how the same instincts that were meant to keep you alive, only helped to quicken your demise in a situation such as this. God— not that I believed in him—was one fucked-up son of a bitch.

In my head, I screamed for help, but never made a sound. No one would hear me and no one was coming, much like my childhood.

The thought of death wasn't terrifying. Not like it should have been. It never was. My rage was the only thing that kept me going. But the idea of letting go was nearly as gratifying. Peaceful. Her face was the last thing I saw as I succumbed to exhaustion, knowing Lucky would burn down the city to avenge me. To avenge Sienna, if they were too late to rectify my mistake. My inability to protect her.

"Wake up, Apollo!" Small hands shook my body.

"Bella, back up! He could hurt you," Lucky bellowed.

"Open your eyes, Apollo. Please, you're safe!" Bella's voice was filled with such emotion that I forced my dry gaze to hers. She ran a soft fingertip down my face, her mismatched eyes dripping with tears. "You're safe now."

I turned away from her. No one was safe around me. From my godforsaken birth to my near death, I'd destroyed everything I touched, and the Agostinos were unwilling to see the truth.

Reality crashed back into me as I shook off the memory of my time spent in that frigid water. My purpose was reinvigorated.

Cassandra was dealt with but the other two… I was still owed their blood. Their pain. Their deaths. It was mine to control and deliver. They couldn't hide from me forever. Focus and commitment was all I needed to get the job done.

Sienna was my blind spot. Whenever she was near, she was all I could see. That first taste of her had been my undoing. I was a crazed man, driven by obsession rather than duty. I'd become complacent, clouded by the misguided dream that I could have more.

Death was my only companion. Not her. Never her.

That didn't mean Romano-fucking-Bianchi was for her either. Watching her get into his idling car, I'd been ready to start a war. Instead, I shut my mouth and let her leave with them.

"Go, Lucky." Bella shoved him towards the door. "Homer and I will keep Apollo company." She lifted the large book for reference. If I weren't so apoplectic, I'd be entertained by my best friend's discomfort.

Lucky was concerned. That much was made obvious, if not by the expression on his face, then by his whispered warning to his wife—the one I'd overheard in my dreamlike state. I'd lost my mask of control in the Hudson, but not my ability to read people.

I lay in bed, staring at the ceiling. Bella's reticence as she read her book at a safe distance stifled the room, while her audible sighs and random glances made her need for attention all too apparent. I would have mocked her lack of subtlety if I had any semblance of humor left within me.

"I know you're attuned to my sighs. Can you please put me out of my misery?" Her tone reflected her evident displeasure.

"You're the one who decided to read that poor example for historic literature." The book was horrendously overrated.

"How do you not like the *Odyssey*? Even the damn movie was good! Great soundtrack too." She nodded, as if her argument bore any merit. It didn't.

"Never saw it." I shoved the blankets aside and stalked to my bathroom.

"That doesn't surprise me." Bella charged to her feet. "What does is your lack of concern for Sienna. You both almost died, and now you've cut her out of your life." The tiny woman slipped her arm through the small opening in the door, forcing me to keep it ajar.

She kept rambling, claiming that my ignorance was morally inept, my actions self-absorbed. I removed my shirt, noticing the obvious change in body language when my hands crept inside the waist of my sweatpants. I waited for her to catch on.

"Oh." She guffawed, turning to face the door. "But don't you think, after everything, maybe you were brought back together for a reason?"

"Bella, turn off the incessant Romeo and Juliet complex." I stepped under the showerhead and my muscles immediately relaxed. Hot water expanded blood vessels and opened circulation, a natural vasodilator I found comforting. "Rationalizing everyone's decisions and making off-base hypotheses won't change the facts."

Her rage obviously outweighing her decorum, Bella spun on her heel to face me, with an accusatory finger aimed in my direction. "So, let me get this right. You *fucked* before you both almost died, and now you dismiss her! You can't be that fucking stupid!" By the end of her tirade, she was yelling, her pale cheeks brightening with the exertion.

"How far along are you, Mirabella? By twenty-seven weeks, the fetus can hear sounds outside the body. If you continue with these antics, your offspring will come out the womb saying *fuck*," I mocked, gripping my cock to add to her discomfort. "*Sono sgomento, Bella.*" Then I tsked my tongue for good measure.

Frankly, I was tired of all these little girls insisting on going toe-to-toe with the boys. If she wanted to sit at the table with the men, I would treat her like I treated any one of them.

"*Gesù Cristo!*" Lucky appeared in the doorway like an apparition in the night. "I hear the word fuck ten times and come to find my pregnant *wife* in the bathroom with a naked man."

Bella gasped, Lucky's tone forcing her to assess the situation. She twirled on an angry heel and stormed from the room. Beneath the mock irritation, my best friend was amused by his wife's lack of social awareness.

"She's something else." He chuckled before turning his silent glare on me.

"You're as relentless as your wife. I assure you I will not sever the radial artery in my wrist, nor will I spontaneously combust." My jaw worked over the words as I spoke, each syllable taut as it clung to the air.

"I'm asking because I am me… and you… are you." He paused, and his patronizing tone had me teetering on the ledge between insanity and blinding rage. "I have something that needs to be handled and I need to know if I can trust you with it."

"The fact you have to ask is downright disrespectful. I may not be the same man you knew, but I have never given you a reason to question my loyalty." My palms twitched, forcing my thumb to stroke each finger as I counted in my head.

"Sienna is on her way back from Philly. I need someone who can handle her… reluctance. I've already texted and informed her of the imposed lockdown."

I swallowed past the bile that was lodged in my esophagus at the mere mention of her name. "I'm not her fucking babysitter." I turned off the taps, grabbing for a towel and wrapping it around my waist. "*Piccola puttana.*"

He refused to respond, opting to give me orders he knew I'd be pleased about instead. "Then I need you to head to the docks for an extermination."

I took the information and slipped into a navy-blue Brioni suit. The same material that once made me feel whole was now clawing at my skin, strangling me.

Philadelphia. Romano-fucking-Bianchi.

Sienna's lack of cognitive reasoning was the catalyst for all her problems. Instead of recognizing her debilities, the woman fucking doubled-down. She was looking for a shoulder to cry on; though I'd bet she'd find more than that with that cocky excuse for a Don.

"*Cagna insensibile,*" I muttered in fast Italian as I descended the stairs several minutes later.

"You picking up Sienna? She should be back in the city shortly." Pieces of banana mixed with saliva projected from Al's mouth as he spoke.

"Practicing?" I lifted a brow, my palm clutching the handle to the front door as a banana peel launched across the space and landed against my back.

"You've always been a real prick, but it's not funny anymore." Al's whining devolved into white noise as I began to formulate a plan.

We had another wannabe thug sniffing around the docks and I needed to ensure he wasn't working for anyone... prior to his disposal. These types of jobs kept me busy, my mind focused on anything other than the man I used to be.

Suddenly, I found myself pulling up to the penthouse and standing just inside the lobby. A quick glance to the side, and the bar was already calling to that disastrous part of me that needed to drown my soul in whiskey. However, I knew once I started, I wouldn't stop until I was either doused in blood or smothered in pussy.

Perhaps a mixture of both...

Just as I was about to tell myself to walk away, three-tinted SUVs stopped at the curb. In perfect succession, two sets of doors opened and several men slipped out and onto the sidewalk, attempting to clear the area. Their skill set was lacking, and within moments, they tapped the window and Romano's second-in-command emerged.

The bright sun made her dark hair shimmer as I caught my first glance. She was flawless in her designer loungewear and lack of makeup. This was the Sienna I used to love seeing, the unpretentious girl who wasn't hiding behind that self-made entrepreneur façade.

Romeo nodded and Romano's men surrounded Sienna as Lucky's crew stepped out to meet her. *He touched her.* My teeth rattled as I clenched my jaw. I tapped each finger to my thumb, but I kept losing count.

He fucking touched her. She let him taste her.

Romano was practically begging for a slow, painful death. Each liter of blood exiting his ventricle chambers to coat my hands. A weekend of him tasting something that didn't belong to him.

Romeo handed Sienna's bag to one of the Agostino enforcers before dipping his head in farewell, and she *smiled*, the expression pleasant, intimate.

My count was long forgotten as I stepped into her path. "Leave." The one-word command sent the rest of our men in the opposite direction. I snatched Sienna's bicep and tugged her away.

"Remove your hand," Romeo barked at my back, but I spun to face him with my gun raised to his forehead.

"This isn't your city."

Romano's men circled us. Whether it was a show of force or to prevent curious onlookers from getting a better view had yet to be determined.

"And right now blowing your fucking head off seems like the best way to prove that."

"I'm okay, Romeo. Thank you." The moment the words left her mouth, I dragged Sienna towards the elevators. It was pure agony ignoring her heaving breasts as she attempted to shrug loose from my hold.

"Another dog at your command. What did you give him to make him heel?"

She ignored the comment. "You're hurting me," she hissed out instead, as the elevator doors closed in front of us.

"You don't know real pain." An image of her bleeding out in that warehouse flashed in the forefront of my mind. I shook my head in an attempt to clear my thoughts.

"Fuck you." Her left hand shot out, striking my throat and opening the wound. "Oh fuck."

I squeezed her arm harder, refusing to loosen my grip, even as my body's natural pain receptors screamed at me to react. To stop the bleeding and apply pressure to the gash.

The elevator door opened and I shoved Sienna into her apartment. She dropped her bags and stared at me, unshed tears brimming along her blue eyes. I unclutched my fist, releasing her wrist and taking in labored breaths, as we glared at each other in equal measure.

When her resolve gave way and she attempted to step towards me, I growled and took another step back. If she touched me, if she got too close, I'd hurt her. I knew she'd smell like him and it would send me spiraling over that ledge. I'd be murderous.

"Did he fuck you?" Her head snapped back as if I'd struck her. "Did you fucking like it?" I hissed the accusation.

"You son of a bitch!" Her sweet tears beckoned me to lick them, to trace the trail of venomous lies down to her jaw. "You cannot talk to me like that!"

I knew she wanted to hit me and I dared her to do it. "You did." I laughed humorlessly. "You're not permitted to leave this apartment without an escort." I turned to the door, shrugging her loose when she grabbed at my arm.

"What the fuck is wrong with you?" She faltered when I forced her backwards, not stopping until she was pinned to the wall.

"Me? Have you looked in the mirror? A pitiful little girl hiding behind such a beautiful face. How long did you cry on his shoulder before his dick made it all better?" My nose was less than an inch from hers as I slammed her arms above her head with one hand and gripped her neck with the other. I spread her legs with my knee, holding her torso in place with my body.

She coughed and shook, trying to fight me off but she was too weak. Sienna was always too weak. She was no match for me. In more ways than one.

"What the fuck?" Al beat his fist into my back, but the fear in Sienna's eyes was intoxicating. I took a breath to break the enchantment, dropped my hands, and whirled around before aiming two fingers at Al's trachea.

"Whore," I mumbled, spitting at Sienna's feet and storming from the apartment.

I powered off my cell, unconcerned with the repercussions if Lucky tried to reach me, and headed outside. My Maybach Exelero was still parked at the curb, my keys inside—no one would dare touch it. I was losing my control and needed an outlet. Preparing to find a fight or someone to kill, I stopped in my tracks when my eyes lifted to find Rocco leaning against the car.

"I got a gift for you." The bastard stared at his nails, as if bored. The man pulled from the wreckage wasn't the same man I'd known for a decade. "*Gifts,* I should say."

My hands clenched into fists as a surge of rejuvenated energy entered my bloodstream. I craved the sound of bones breaking, flesh splitting, and muscles tearing. I needed it more than I needed air to breathe and food to function.

We took the elevator down to the basement under the penthouses. The smell of bleach did little to hide the death in the air. Inhaling deeply, I felt a sense of peace settle over me. As my boot hit the last metal step, I noticed a whimpering female chained to one wall and a disoriented male grunting over the drain in the center.

"What? Al and I had our fun." Rocco shrugged, indifferent, as Al narrowed his eyes at me, clearly still a little peeved by my throat punch.

"And her?" I stalked towards the girl. "And what of you?"

"I-I... I wasn't going to do anything. It was a joke, but I'd never!"

Her words were cut off by the sound of heels clicking down the staircase as a woman I'd never seen before appeared.

"She handed your princess a line of coke and then videotaped it." The newcomer was gorgeous, her voice measured as she spoke with a hint of a Spanish accent mingled with disdain.

"Apollo, meet Gabriela." Al motioned to the girl. "Lucky hired her to tail Sienna."

My eyes snapped to the woman in question as she stood tall, her frame lithe, but as she flexed under my gaze, I could see the defined muscles throughout her body. Her hair was in a braid, shaved at the sides, and her posture deemed her dangerous. Her stance spoke of her specialized training, one that proved she was up for the job.

"*We* don't kill women," Rocco stated simply. "Seeing as we usually rely on Sienna or Bella, both of whom are indisposed at the moment, we got creative."

"And him?" I nodded to the male on the floor.

Al relayed the story of how the fucker had assaulted Sienna at *Danza*, before I quickly turned my attention back to him. As I approached, I couldn't help but enjoy his cry of pain when the restraints on his ankles pulled tight.

He had nowhere to go.

"I-I was drunk! I didn't mean the disrespect… I-I'd never have acted—" He stopped speaking when I squatted in front of him.

"Drunk." I nodded in understanding. "Changes in your neurotransmitters are often signs of overconsumption, making you susceptible to poor decision-making."

Gabriela watched on with a sense of enthralled detachment, before turning to the female dry-heaving by her feet. "Vomit. I dare you." Gabriela addressed the girl, but her eyes remained glued to our male captive. "You make a mess on this floor, and I'll make you eat it, then lick it clean."

Rocco's expression contorted in to a large grin, the first I'd seen since the accident.

"Long-term chronic or excessive alcohol abuse has significant consequences. I mean, behavioral changes, clinical depression, personality issues, and suicidal tendencies." He flinched as I snipped a pair of scissors through the air. "Clearly, the reason you're in this predicament is related to the latter. I cannot fathom another reason you'd disrespect *la nostra principessa.*"

"Pura stupidita." Al laughed from the corner, staring at his phone for a moment before pivoting on his heel and leaving.

"Fallo male, Apollo." Rocco stepped closer to Gabriela, but his eyes were lit with excitement as he stared at the soon-to-be corpse in front of us.

"Solo en la muerte hay justicia." Gabriela's Spanish had me faltering.

"Only in death is there justice," Rocco repeated, smirking at Gabriela's shocked expression. *"Soy fluido en espanol e italiano."* They grinned at each other and I withheld my eye roll.

"You asked her to suck your dick?" I questioned, as Rocco made quick work of pinning the bastard onto his back before helping me remove his pants. "Instead, I'll give it to her on a fucking platter."

I flicked the scissors open again, and the girl on the floor released a shriek so shrill it reverberated against the concrete walls before bouncing back and piercing my eardrums for a second time. I snipped the scissors twice, easily cutting through our captive's flaccid member —not much to boast about. Blood poured from the wound as I turned my back on him. We would let him choose whether he wanted to live out his days permanently deformed or succumb to the blood loss over the next 3-5 minutes. Surprisingly or not, no one ever chose the former. I supposed they believed there wasn't much point to living a life as a man without a dick.

I made my way to the stairs, stopping to peer at Gabriela and the girl gasping in her grip. The Spanish enforcer glanced at Rocco as he leaned over her shoulder, watching the girl's fight slowly come to an end, much like her life.

"Marcisci all'inferno, cagna." Gabriela straightened, spitting on the prone form at her feet and strutting up the stairs in her stiletto heels.

"Fuck." Rocco straightened his belt before following her.

I ignored them both. I needed distance from this hotel. And Sienna…

However, like always, I wasn't that fortunate. I came to a stop outside the front doors, just as the woman herself was walking out to meet Al—I hadn't even noticed he'd followed me. Because all I saw was her. All I pictured was Romano's hands on her, her laughing and smiling at him.

He touched her. Touched what didn't belong to him.

I was unable, perhaps u*nwilling*, to stop myself as I barreled towards them. Shoving Al out of the way, I wrapped my hand in Sienna's hair and dragged her back inside. My brash actions had stunned her into silence.

For once.

She was standing upright but her neck was cocked at an odd angle, her body stiff in my grip. I didn't let go until the doors opened. I entered the code into the keypad and shoved her into her apartment for a second time. She stumbled a few steps before straightening herself, kicking off her shoes and pulling her skirt up just enough for a fighting stance. We stared at each other for a second, then I charged.

"Fucking bitch," I growled, lunging for her as she hissed and struck out at me.

CHAPTER 7
SIENNA AGOSTINO

"What the fuck was that about?" Al coughed through the swelling caused by Apollo's attack on his throat. He reached out to brace himself on the wall, trying to stay on his feet.

"How the fuck should I know?" I hated the traitorous tears that were now pouring down my cheeks, but *fuck* did that hurt.

As if the bastard's words weren't enough of a slap to the face, his disrespect as he spat at my feet sent me over the edge. What started as a slow drizzle turned into a tumultuous downpour of heartbreak. His actions hurt, cutting me so deep I'd have a permanent scar. Just because you couldn't see it, it didn't make it any less real.

"Fuck. Me," Al grunted, climbing onto a bar stool as I handed him a bottled water.

"Apparently I fuck everyone, so why not?" My laugh was forced, pained.

"Si, you know he's just…" I could see him battling himself to find the right words. "Fuck, I don't know anymore." Al's phone rang and he mumbled in response before warning me to stay put until he got back.

He took a piece of chocolate on his way out as I kicked off my heels and collapsed onto my sofa. I needed to shut my mind off and get lost in the fantasy I used to have. *Gone with the Wind* was one of my favorite movies, even if—much to my dismay—I sometimes saw myself as Scarlett O'Hara.

If I kept playing this game with him, with my life, I wondered if I'd end up like her. It took her losing all the things she said she didn't want to realize it was all she truly ever needed. I craved to be loved. I knew that. I wanted to kick Lucky off the throne, but by doing that, I'd ruin everything else.

"Yeah." I answered my phone when it rang. "How should I know? He called me a fucking whore and left my apartment," I told my brother.

"I want you at the compound. Now," Lucky commanded on the other end.

"Yeah, yeah, your highness." I hung up just as Al was walking back into the apartment. "I'm getting dressed," I grumbled, before heading to my closet.

I went right for the new Saint Laurent pieces I'd ordered from Bergdorf's—a white V-neck lace bodysuit that left little to the imagination, tucked into the leather sequin miniskirt. I grabbed a leather jacket and finished the look with a pair of Louboutin red-soled booties.

Al scowled when I walked into the room. "We're just going to the compound, Sienna." He shook his head but opened the door and escorted me out. Al stepped off the elevator first with me close behind him.

"Fuck off," Apollo growled at Al, and before I could get my bearings, he wrapped a hand in my hair and yanked me back into the elevator.

He was completely disheveled. His tie and jacket were gone, and his white shirt was soaked with blood. He looked like a maniac, his eyes wild as he pinned me in place. The elevator doors closed before anyone could come to my rescue.

I didn't speak, barely breathed as we were carried up to my apartment and he forced me inside. Once he released me, I kicked off my heels, pulled my tight skirt up higher, and prepared for his attack. My heart raced and my blood pounded in my ears. But, for whatever reason, I needed this. *We* needed this.

"Fucking bitch."

Those two words were all it took to tip me over the edge of my rage. I flung fist after fist as Apollo blocked each of my attempts at hurting him. I pushed, shoved, punched, and screamed—anything to get a reaction. I started to cry at some point, but it barely registered as I sought to cause him pain. Like he'd caused me.

"You just cut me out of your life! *Me!* No one else! What did *I* do to deserve that?" I threw an elbow, reveling in the grunt he made when it hit. "I bled for you, goddamn it!" Shoving away from him, I panted, trying to catch my breath as the shattered pieces of my heart crumbled inside me. He stood silent, his chest heaving as he watched me. I was about to start yelling again when a cloud of anger settled between us, and he forced my back to the wall.

"I almost fucking killed you!" he shouted, his face an inch from mine. "I live in the fucking darkness and the only light I see are the flames that surround me. And they will burn you to nothing, Sienna." His brown eyes turned to pools of honey, melting as his anger spiked and his sanity shifted.

"If it wasn't you, it was the devil beside you that sent me to hell. But for you… only you, Apollo." I reached a gentle hand up to stroke his face. "I'd make sure we both fucking thrived in the fire."

He didn't hesitate. His hand wrapped around my throat, his lips latching on to mine as his grip tightened and squeezed. Our mouths molded perfectly together, but our movements progressed until we were nothing more than a mess of teeth, grunts, and growls. My lungs seized, craving air, but I couldn't pull away as his hard body continued to pin me against the wall.

His bicep flexed as he lifted me off the ground by my throat until my legs were wrapping around his waist. He could kill me here and now, and I wouldn't even care. He lifted me higher and higher, my lungs bursting.

Then, when my mind was ready to shut off, he released my throat and carried me into my bedroom, throwing me onto the bed. I'd barely had a second to breathe before he was on me. His thick body covered mine, as he trailed kisses from my lips, down my neck, to my breasts. He ripped through the fabric of my lace bodysuit, his hands exploring every inch of my exposed skin.

"I need you," I moaned, my plea barely above a whisper.

His eyes softened, turning into pools of delicious nectar I wanted dripped all over me. His caresses were gentle and kind, unlike any part of him I'd ever seen before. He pulled my skirt and panties down my legs, placing a kiss on each thigh before slowly pushing inside me. And as he continued to make love to me, I couldn't help but want to scream at him to fuck me instead. I knew how to handle his hatred, how to fight against his anger, but his tenderness... I was certain it would be my undoing.

"Sienna," Al shouted, startling me. I looked up to Apollo and his face was blurry. "Sienna, open your eyes," Al continued to urge me.

"Apollo," I moaned.

"Sienna! Take a deep breath," Al soothed, as my vision of Apollo disappeared and I was left staring into my brother's concerned eyes.

"There she is. Nice and slow." Lucky helped me sit upright before leaning me against the closest wall. "Is this your blood or what was on him?" he asked, forcing me to look down at myself.

I tried to blink away my confusion, the cloud that seemed to block my vision. What the fuck happened? We were making love one second, and the next...

"He fucking strangled her, Lucky," Al hissed, worry evident in his tone but the malice was more prevalent.

My clothes were still on and I was in my living room. It hadn't happened. I... passed out because the motherfucker choked me! Unwanted tears tipped over my lash line, as a pained shriek parted my lips until my voice went hoarse. Al moved, picking me up and holding on to me.

Apollo had tried to kill me...

"What the hell is happening?" I asked Al, but he just shook his head. "Lucky, we need to find him. He isn't okay." I needed my brother to understand.

"Sienna, right now if I find him, I will fucking kill him for touching you," Lucky growled, locking my door behind us as Al carried me out of my apartment.

We drifted down the elevator in tension-riddled silence, none of us knowing what to do next. Apollo was shredding himself at the seams and no one seemed to know how to handle him. The elevator door opened and about twenty men I recognized surrounded us. I felt like the President's daughter as I was shuffled into the center of a group of armed and imposing bodyguards. Four cars idled at the curb, but it was Romeo leaning against the rear that gave me pause.

I didn't deserve Romano's loyalty.

"Are you all right, *mio amore?*" Lucky answered his phone on the first ring. "What! Where are you?" he shouted, while Al and I shared a concerned look. "Haul ass to the compound," my brother ordered the driver. He listened for a few more minutes before hanging up with a grunt. He slammed his fist into the window over and over again as Al pulled me closer to him. We were both expecting the bulletproof glass to shatter. Lucky sighed. "Bella's okay, said he's just sitting in the garden in silence."

"I need to get to him." More tears appeared on my face. I saw them before I felt them.

"Absolutely not," Lucky growled at the same time Al grunted, "No fucking way."

For the entirety of the drive, I was forced to sit between my brother and best friend. Forced to listen to their idle threats of maiming my designer shoes and telling my father on me if I even attempted to go near Apollo. My throat hurt from where he choked me; it was the only reason I wasn't arguing with them. I was lost to my thoughts, to my own misery. Too lost to care what they were saying on either side of me.

When we pulled up to the compound, my father was waiting on the front porch, his arms crossed over his chest. The car had barely stopped before he was ripping the door open and pulling me into his arms. It was then that I finally broke. My tears were silent but never-ending while my sobs were muted, barely a rasp, as I fought to catch my breath. It felt like hours were spent standing there as I purged my soul in my father's arms. He pulled back, using his thumbs to wipe away my tears as his heartwarming face melted my heart.

Within a second, the image of my loving father was replaced by the formidable Mario Agostino. He brushed my hair away from my shoulders and stared at my neck, his glare sending shivers down my spine. He glanced between Lucky and Al in silent conversation.

"Garden," Lucky growled, turning on his heel, and we all followed in his wake.

My dad held on to my hand and tugged me along with him. I wanted to go almost as much as I didn't. I wanted to run to Apollo and protect him from my family's wrath almost as much as I wanted to unleash my own. Even more so, I wanted to stand in front of him and see if he had a semblance of concern for what he'd done to me. But both parts were equally terrifying.

"Apollo, I am not shooting you." Bella's agitated words echoed amongst the vegetation in the garden.

"Do it, Bella. Please." My heart ached at the defeat in his voice. "I've lost control. I keep fighting to maintain it, but it's gone! I. Almost. Killed. Her."

"But you didn't. Sienna is okay. We just need to get you help." Bella's tone didn't soften. She was downright pissed. "I won't kill you. Shoot you in the shoulder or something? Maybe."

As we came around the corner, our steps faltered at the scene playing out in front of us. Apollo was on his knees, Bella standing over him with his nine in her hand, which was aimed at his shoulder. They both turned at our approach.

"Mario... I..." Apollo's eyes bounced from one figure to another, skipping over me completely.

"After all I've taught you, after all the lessons on harnessing your rage, you almost killed *my* daughter." Dad's arms were still wrapped around my shoulders, but his muscles tensed and shook. "I've killed for far less, Deluca."

Apollo slowly rose to his feet, his face blank as he stared at my dad in return. He removed his jacket, withdrawing the second gun at his back and handing it to Lucky. He opened his arms wide and closed his eyes, waiting for my father to react.

No one moved as time seemed to quicken, matching my racing heart. I'd cried, fucking bawled my eyes out over this man, and now I had nothing more to give.

My dad released me before reaching into the back of his waistband, and I knew what was coming. As I looked to Bella, my brother and best friend, I hated the expressions of pity they gave me.

Fuck. This. And. Fuck. Him.

I snatched Apollo's gun from Lucky's hand, and before anyone had time to stop me, I fired a single shot. Apollo jerked back, his eyes filling with surprise when he realized it was me on the other end of the barrel. Blood started pouring from the wound in his shoulder as he reached up a hand to cover it. And I smiled as the red liquid seeped through his fingers.

The only thing I could think of was how strange it felt to be so *calm*. The tears had dried; my heart was existing in mere pieces, but I was done being pathetic.

"I've spent countless hours begging for you to see me as more than Lucky's sister. I've stitched you up, cleaned blood from your hands, and loved you unconditionally. All while knowing you couldn't return the affection. But then you gave me something, a small part of you." I stepped closer, keeping the gun aimed at his torso. "You were given a second chance, Apollo. Fuck you for taking mine from me."

He glanced behind me, at each member of my family ready to rip him apart. I stepped into his space, pressing the barrel to his heart. I was proud that as upset as I was, my grip remained steady.

"You don't deserve me. I'm *done*," I growled, clicking the safety in place before dropping the gun at his feet.

"*We* are far from done," my father countered as I walked past without a backwards glance.

He deserved my hate, not my heart. The stupid part of my brain said that if he worked hard enough, I'd let him back in. But fuck that bitch. He didn't deserve a single thing from me anymore.

I was Sienna-fucking-Agostino and I didn't forgive anyone.

Instead, I fucking made you regret ever fucking hurting me in the first place.

Two dozen red roses were perched in a gorgeous black designer vase atop my desk. I was a sucker for the classics, especially when it came to flowers. My heart skipped a beat, telling me that maybe there was a chance they were from *him*.

But I knew it was Bella's brother sending a message, an indelible one at that. Our conversation when I visited Gio in jail was one that I'd replayed repeatedly in my mind. He wanted me to be his queen, to rule beside him in the kingdom he'd built on a foundation of pain and misery. Evidently, he still had no plans on leaving me behind.

Just what I needed, more complications, in my already complicated life. It was time to end this once and for all.

I stared at the rose in shock as what appeared to be blood slowly dripped from the soft petals and began to pool on my glass desktop. I raised a challenging smirk at my assistant and stormed out of the office. When the elevator opened, I flipped off my building security and darted out the door, flagging a taxi and disappearing into the city streets.

I wasn't dumb. I was sure someone had eyes on me. But I needed to feign anonymity. The drive came to an end when I pulled up to the high fence, the barbed wire catching my attention. It was a spiraling mess of pointed pieces that promised to tear your flesh apart. And yet, here I was, threatening to climb over them.

"No going back now," I muttered to myself as they escorted me into the interrogation room.

Gio Moretti was handcuffed to the table, but he acted as if he didn't have a care in the world. His gaze seemed to penetrate me and I lifted my chin, prepared to hide my fear. He licked his lips and a wicked smile spread across his mouth. "There she is. My bleeding heart coated those roses in anticipation." His face was so complacent. He was so goddamn sure of himself.

"You're crazy, Gio. This ends here. I came here to tell you to stop." I slammed my fist into the table.

"I say when it ends!" His cuffs echoed against the metal bracket, making me flinch. "You belong to me."

Games. That's all it was. I was the unattainable, the sister of his enemy. None of this had anything to do with me. He'd spent his entire life trying to emerge from his father's weak shadow, wanting to one up Lucky.

"I'm not a chess piece you can move around the board to punish my brother. I won't allow you to hurt me or my family." I crossed my arms over my chest, his eyes hungrily following my lifted breasts.

"Oh, Sienna. Revenge against Lucky? Fuck your brother. I wanted your family to suffer, but it seems we share an enemy who plans to do that for me."

A chill traveled down my spine. "What're you talking about?" I leaned my elbows against the cold steel table, my face inching closer to his.

"Don't worry, sweetheart. I'll protect you. I protect what's mine." His arrogance was stifling, filling the small room like a poisonous gas.

"I'm not yours!" I pushed to my feet, my chair toppling over beside me.

When a person was utterly insane, there was no part of them that saw reason. A man completely lost to his own god complex wasn't someone you could bargain with. I had no idea why I came here.

Calling Gio out wouldn't stop this. If anything, the hunt… the chase was turning him on even more.

"Two choices. Willingly. Or beaten into submission." He sat back, pleased with himself. "Either way. You're. Still. Mine."

He was a predator staring into the eyes of his prey. The scent of my blood was drawing him closer and I knew there was nowhere for me to hide. He was going to get out and I would be running for my life. You can't tempt a wild animal when you are at your weakest. It only spurs on their natural bloodthirst. He was hunting me and these chains were doing nothing to hold him back.

"Did you like the roses?" The inflection of his tone was unnerving. "Painted red for revenge. My men sent them a little message about touching what belongs to me."

"You know who attacked me." It wasn't a question.

"You're welcome." He rose to his full height, fast as lightning.

His hand shot out and caught my shirt, tugging me forward so abruptly I lost my balance. Our lips connected and my gasp gave him entrance to my mouth. He had a tight grip on the material of my blouse, my hands pressed to his chest, and I still couldn't break free. Guards shouted in the background, but Gio only backed down when I bit him.

"That's my fucking queen." He howled with laughter, blood pouring out of his mouth.

The guards raised their batons, beating him back until he collapsed in his seat. And he continued to laugh throughout the entire ordeal. They were going to kill him, and he didn't give a damn. I'd given him exactly what he wanted.

Me. This visit just handed me over to yet another unpredictable enemy.

"Soon, my queen!" Gio shouted.

I'd messed up.

Gio Moretti wasn't going anywhere, and I needed to deal with him before someone else got hurt protecting me. He didn't know it yet, but I was going to be the one who took him down. Just like Cassandra.

Fucking Cassandra and those two assholes took everything from me. I was glad the bitch was dead but prayed for God to somehow revive her. Just so I could kill her all over again.

I gripped the piece of paper Gio had shoved into my hand before I'd left, staring down at two names. There was nothing redeeming about the man. Even if he did just hand me my revenge on a silver platter. And now all I needed to do was kill *them*.

They took everything from me, and it was only polite to return the favor.

CHAPTER 8

APOLLO DELUCA

This disillusion was all-consuming and I was losing my ability to think, to properly process my surroundings. The control I held over every aspect of my life, my psyche, had shattered. Leaving me floating amidst the chaos, instead of anchoring me to the present.

The scent of *another* man lingering on her skin had filled my lungs. That lack of reality was the incendiary device that led me to this moment, my relationship with *il familia* decimated.

Had I really smelled Romano on her skin? I didn't know anymore.

At the end of the day, her spending the weekend with him painted a bright-red target on Philly. *If* he'd touched her, Romano deserved to suffer in my same purgatory. I was stuck between the hell she evoked and the heaven between her thighs. Neither of us deserved her. The mere thought of them together burned my throat as I swallowed back my desire to murder *him.*

The power of these images forced my hand, and by the time I'd snapped back to reality, she was already unconscious at my feet. Lying so vulnerable and unprotected as I fled—a coward's flight.

As angered steps charged from a distance, I knew this was the end. I'd happily welcome the filicide that was coming my way. The man was like a father to me, the closest thing to a parental figure I'd known. Mario had given me a life to succeed and I'd practically spat in his face.

My refusal to look at her was solely based on my need to dismiss her, us. She needed to realize *this*, she and I, would never be. My urges for her had blinded my ability to rationalize. The desire that burned each time she was near was what incapacitated me.

Confusion rocked me as a gunshot echoed and pain lodged into my shoulder. My eyes dancing between Mario and Lucky, I saw that neither held a smoking gun. They stared to their right, forcing my gaze for the first time to Sienna.

I'd broken her.

She held no concern for the bullet she'd imbedded into my shoulder and the action was owed. Sienna was unscrupulous when it came to protecting her family but always allowed pain and sorrow to trap her soul.

Not anymore.

When the barrel of my own gun was pressed to my chest, a part of me wanted her to pull the trigger. All the adversity I had inflicted upon her warranted my end at her hands. It was the only thing I had assumed would offer her the solace my actions could afford her. There was not a word or a backwards glance as she walked away from me. An action so minimalistic and yet so… final. No matter what transpired, moving forward, the beating organ in her chest cavity had combusted. There was nothing left.

"We should take turns," Al growled, my eyes turning towards him. "You piece of shit."

Bella smiled at Sienna's ghost, my blood appeasing her. Lucky was vibrating with a barely contained rage, but when I turned towards Mario, his glare made me flinch. "I took you in because I saw *such* potential. Your loyalty proved I could trust you. And then you do *this* to *her*." His words did their damage.

"Mario…"

He raised a hand to silence me. "I knew it would come to this. Years of watching my daughter fall for you, I had no idea how to stop it. I *fucking knew* it would end badly, but she's too fucking stubborn. She thought she'd be happy with whatever *piece* of yourself you gave to her." He paused and I had to clench my jaw to keep from responding. "Now… you've broken her and I don't know if she'll ever be the same."

A fist slammed between my shoulder blades, forcing me to my knees. I could immediately feel the swelling in my upper back, overlying the coracoid and acromion processes. I didn't even try to protect myself. I deserved the excruciating sensations assaulting my large intestine—thanks to Lucky's boot. Al kicked me in the back, my thoracic curvature taking impact and causing me to roll the opposite way. He gripped the collar of my shirt and pulled me closer to him; the rage emanating from him was stifling. His right fist felt like a sledgehammer to my jaw, forcing my mandible to shake.

"Sleep with your eyes open." Al's warning trickled through the pain. "Watch your fucking back, Apollo. Because we will *always* choose her first."

Bella slapped me across my face, her open palm darkening the imprint of Al's knuckles, before Mario hauled me to my feet and Lucky kept me standing. My head rolled sideways and I couldn't gain purchase with my boots. The Agostino patriarch may have been getting older. May have *soldatos* to do his dirty work. But he hadn't lost his touch. Two heavy punches and I dropped to my knees once more. The direct blow to my lower back brought immense pain—a kidney bruise, also known as a kidney contusion. The blunt force trauma would cause internal bleeding, accompanied by sharp pain and tenderness. My back muscles and ribs took the impact; the bones were more likely cracked than broken.

"Sir." One of the guards entered the yard, addressing Mario. "Your package has arrived."

"Clean him up." And then he was gone.

Al and Lucky started dragging me towards the house, my head thumping as consciousness slipped through my fingers. But each time they purposefully jostled me, I would snap out of the haze. Grunting as they dropped me on my bed, I couldn't look at any of them.

"You got what you wanted." Bella shoved at me until I rolled over so she could place a towel under my shoulder.

And I growled as she unceremoniously dumped peroxide onto the gunshot wound. "Fuck! Bella!"

"Whoops," she said, but her tone was dry. "You wanted to push her away, and *poof* she's gone. You'll never get her back now."

I closed my eyes as Bella cleaned the wound, biting my tongue when she dug for the bullet with ill-practiced hands. She was doing her best to make it agonizing. The pain wasn't what I deserved, but I wasn't dying today.

"There." She dropped the bullet onto the side table. "Keep it. That way every time you see it, you'll remember what you've lost."

"Bella." I stopped her from leaving.

"Save it. Those words aren't for me. You need to think long and hard about your next move." She looked over her shoulder. "You've all but pushed her to Philly. I suggest you open your eyes before it's too late, because *when* she goes, none of us will get her back."

"Fuck Romano." I winced, trying to sit up against the headboard.

Without another word, Bella turned and left the room.

The four stages of healing were arduous enough. But each open wound would go through the hemostasis, inflammatory, proliferative, and maturation stages to put me back together. And as my body mended itself, I had time to search for the duo far more deserving of this pain *and* my wrath.

The near-death experience at the water's edge seemed to diminish my ability to recall events. The two *boys* thought they had gotten away scot-free, but they hadn't. My body was on the rebound and I had no doubt I'd find them. Their faces, they were right there... yet I couldn't grasp them. Until I closed my eyes and the past came throttling to the forefront of my brain. And then I realized why this was happening. *La verità ti renderà libero.* My past had come back to haunt me and Sienna paid for those crimes.

"How did it feel?" I directed my question to the slumped and barely conscious man. He was tied to the metal table and stripped bare.

"Huh, wh-what?" he mumbled, his eyes opening wide and taking in his surroundings. *"What the fuck? Who are you? What the fuck are you doing?"* he stammered, echoing the same questions screamed by my previous victims.

"Answer me." My pointer and middle finger pressed into the center of his forehead, slamming his head back down onto the table. *"How did it feel? Did you enjoy his cries of pain? Did he call out for his mommy or daddy?"* When he didn't answer, I continued. *"I know exactly who you are. Eugenio Affanad, once a member of Mario Agostino's trusted counsel. Husband to Mary and father to two sons, Carlo and Fausto. And a fucking philanderer with a grotesque affinity*

for little boys." I snarled the last sentence. "Tell me. Have you touched your sons too?"

His eyes popped open and a look of disgust marred his face as he hurled some creative words my way.

I was going to kill him and allow his sons the peace of not knowing the disgusting creature their father truly was. "You are my first kill... unassisted. I guess you should feel pleased by that fact."

Carlo and Fausto. They were the spitting images of the man who had died on my table, and clearly out for unjustified revenge. They had no clue as to their father's guilt and now we'd suffered for it.

Mario didn't want the boys or anyone to know the truth about Eugenio. He knew they'd be tainted by the memory of their pedophile patriarch. That was a mistake. I didn't hurt the innocent, but they shattered their ability to be called that as soon as they harmed *her.*

Dressing quickly with two guns strapped to my chest and a knife on my belt, I left my room. The first time since being shot. So consumed by my mission, I missed the soft body coming up the stairs, my chest shoving her backwards. She tried grabbing the railing, but it slipped from her fingers. I lunged for her, pulling her to my chest but lost my footing. As Sienna screamed, I turned us and my back took the impact as we slid down the remaining steps. The stitches in my shoulder split and the pain coursed through my body. But worse... my dick came to life with Sienna's ass pressed firmly against it.

"You motherfucker!" A click sounded above us and I looked up into the barrel of a nine.

Sienna pushed off my body to stand. "Al, stop. He didn't do anything." She stood in front of the gun. "This time." Holding my bleeding shoulder, she helped me sit up and started unbuttoning my shirt. I hadn't even realized I wasn't wearing a jacket as she pulled my arm free. She poked and prodded, inspecting the wound before nodding. "It's fine. The stitches are still mostly intact." Then she turned on her heel and headed into the family room.

"Cold." Al chuckled, extending a hand. "Where are you off to?"

"I found them." Saying it aloud appeased some of my rage.

"Office. Now." Mario stood outside the door, while his tone left no room for argument as we followed him inside. "Who are they?" The tick of his jaw proved he was mad at himself.

We never should've hidden Eugenio's past.

"Al will go with you." He stopped my interjection. "I let you fucking live because you're a son to me. But do *not* push me, Apollo." I nodded in respect to the man that helped me harness my cacodemon. "I am also bringing additional reinforcements into the city," Mario added.

Into the city. Fucking Romano…

"We need to cut ties with Philly. He's a threat to you… to Lucky." It wasn't often I challenged my boss, but I couldn't hold my tongue.

His moment of silence was deafening. "There is more at play here than you realize. Philly will stay in line. I've assured it." Mario lit his cigar, puffing a few times. "Tell me. Why do you have such a problem with Philly?"

I was mute. Unable to articulate my reasoning.

"Nothing to say?" he challenged me, but I clenched my jaw and remained stoic. "Lucky may be preparing to take over my reign but let me make something perfectly clear to you. This is *my* city. And Romano knows that." The cigar smoke puffed in my face. "Now tell me, Apollo. Is there anything concrete that points to Romano being a threat to *my city*? Or is it not my empire that he's threatening?"

I always listened to my gut and it said to put him six feet under.

"Al! Go with him." Mario's command was final and I was dismissed.

I felt the tension lightening with each step I took, the proverbial burden being lifted from my shoulders. Their death wouldn't right their wrongs, but it would alleviate some of the affliction on my psyche. It would appease the tarnished fragments of Sienna in my head. The images of her beaten and bleeding, begging me with her eyes to save her. Their deaths would serve as the recompense for her pain. And I would savor killing them.

CHAPTER 9
MARIO AGOSTINO

I destroyed my family. Me.

All the years I'd spent fighting to be the most powerful man in New York. All the blood and sweat I put into owning the mafia. For what? It was gone in the blink of an eye and my children were paying the price.

Octavia. My sweet, sweet Octavia. It was a silent agreement in the family that she was to be protected. My youngest girl was too good-natured for the world she'd been born into. Far too loving and kind to be the daughter of a mafia boss.

Each of my children inherited something from me. Each with a personality trait or strength that was a direct reflection of one of mine. Except Octavia. She had her mother's kindness and generosity. But where my wife was fierce, Octavia was submissive.

She was the good all of us wish we could be—the gentle part of our bullet-riddled lives. I'd made the tough decision to marry her off outside of *il famiglia.* I thought a normal life would be better suited for my girl, away from the blood and destruction.

Instead, she was targeted for her softness. She was targeted because anyone on the outside looking in saw she was the weakest link in the family. Without a doubt, Octavia knew her mother and I would die for her. Everyone knew her mother and I, her siblings, we'd all burn the world down to save her. And now, her abduction was causing complete discord in my ranks. In my heart.

And then there was the package.

My daughter's innocence coating the bedsheets. They'd taken what didn't belong to them. And I could only hope I got her back in one piece. My lack of sleep was messing with my head.

I'd built this empire on broken bones, gallons of blood, and a pile of enemies. All so my family could have everything. Instead, it was taking everything from me. Her bloody sheets and the broken voice telling me she didn't want to come home. Those were my undoing.

Thirty years on top of an organization such as this came with its crimes. Came with its blood, blackmail, and death. I thought my empire was untouchable. But the higher you climb, the farther you fall. The slightest misstep sent you spiraling.

They had me exactly where they wanted me. They were targeting my children and I was dancing with every tug of my strings—all while praying for them to take my life and spare Octavia. Yet it wasn't the screams or the blood that had broken me.

It was the call.

I stared at the phone, silence stretching behind heavy breaths.

"She tastes so good. Her tears are sweeter than any candy. Her cries are a soft symphony. And her blood, it's like a drug, giving me the best high with every drop I take."

The whimpers in the background sent me to my knees. "Tell me what you want!" My chest heaved and my heart felt ready to explode. "She doesn't deserve this."

"I know." There was a moment where I thought he'd return her to me. The conviction in his voice gave me hope. "That's why I'm hurting her. It's you *who deserves to feel helpless, to know your daughter is in pain because of* your *choices."*

"Do you want my city? I will hand it all over if you give her back to me... alive." I gulped out the last word.

"Funny you should say that, Mario. I'm going to take your city. I've already started to siphon your power without you even knowing

it. I don't need your daughter to claim your empire." A chain creaked in the background. "I took her because I wanted her. Your city under my control, your demise at my fingertips... it wasn't enough. I want it all. I want to watch you fall apart, knowing she's mine."

"She's not yours!" I slammed my fist into my desk, the decanter of Scotch rattling with the force.

"Now, now, calm down. You don't want her scared of you too, do you?" No, what I wanted was his blood. *"Octavia, sweetheart. Do you have something to tell Daddy?"*

I swallowed audibly. Hearing my daughter whisper to him set my heart on fire. I'd die a thousand deaths to get her back.

"Daddy." Her soft voice came on the line and everything around me disappeared.

"Octavia, baby. Are you okay? What has he done to you?" Too many questions bubbled to the surface. "I will kill him for hurting you. I know it's a lot, but you can survive this. I'm coming for you, Octavia."

"You can't save me, Daddy. Octavia is dead." It was her confidence that made me falter.

"Don't say that, baby girl."

"Say what? The truth? If it didn't happen now, it would later. I know, Daddy." When I didn't respond, panic seizing my brain, she laughed humorlessly. *"You were going to pass me off, hand me over to someone else because I was a problem you didn't want to deal with anymore."*

"No, baby girl. No. It wasn't like that." How did she know about her arranged engagement? *"I wanted to protect you. I wanted to save you from this life."*

"Because you think I'm weak. You all do. You'd rather dismiss me than believe I can hold my own." Her sigh was beyond pained. *"None of you have ever seen my strength, because I promise you I'm strong."*

Tears burned my eyes and acid swirled in my throat as I shouted my own promises to her. Promises that I'd do anything for her. I had no idea where she was or who had her, but I needed her to hold on.

"I'm not coming home, Daddy." My heart stalled in my chest. "He will never let me go."

"Octavia, don't say that." I threw a glass at the wall, the shattered pieces glittering in the light.

"It's the truth." It came out as a whisper, a sound that would haunt me until I died. "Tell the family I love them and that I will be fine. But, Daddy, I need you to let me go." She whispered in the background before disappearing.

"Don't fucking touch her." My throat was dry and ached as I shouted. "Take me instead."

"But this is so much more fun. Octavia, say bye to Daddy." He toyed with me and my palms itched to kill him.

"Stop worrying about me, Daddy. Find peace in the fact that I am strong enough to handle him. I love you."

I struggled with words as I threw out every expletive in both Italian and English. What had he done to my beautiful daughter? Why didn't she want to come home?

"Maybe you should've protected her better. And I'm not just talking about from me." The anger in his tone forced me silent. I felt as if he was trying to send me a message, but I couldn't understand it.

My daughter asked me to let her go. She'd rather stay with the enemy than her own blood. He was right. This man had wanted to take everything from me and he'd succeeded.

"That's not going to help." My eldest son loomed in the hallway outside my office. He motioned towards the glass of Scotch I'd filled to the brim. The alcohol barely took away the unpleasant memories anymore. Instead, it offered me a numbness that allowed me to detach from my surroundings. A reprieve if only for a little bit.

As my son—who was an exact replica of me at his age—glared at me in disapproval, I wanted to scoff in his face. "Just wait until all this is yours, then talk to me about my vices." I stood and made my way to the window, smiling as I watched my wife wander through her gardens.

"What was it like?" Lucky stood at my side, posing an innocuous question, but one I understood held much deeper meaning.

"Not like this." I motioned around the room. "I came from nothing, had nothing other than an Italian name. I killed, I lied, and I fought dirty to get here."

"But you had Ma's softness to protect you." We stared at my beautiful wife, the mother of my four children, the woman who had single-handedly brought me back to life over and over again.

"Even that wasn't easy. Or, back then, enough. I loved another woman, but your grandfather forced me to choose: love or power. I couldn't have both."

We never hid the truth from our children. From a young age, they all knew there was a very good chance I would arrange their marriages. Just like my own father had done with me. While I was the one to get my hands dirty to amass my power, it was my father who had built alliances. Isabella's family came from old money with even more valuable connections. Seraphina, Bella's mom, did not. We grew up together, our bloodlines fighting amongst each other to get the upper hand, but our love wasn't enough.

"I hated her for it," I whispered, watching her smile as the wind blew her hair around her. "I resented that *she* stood in the way of my claim for power."

The beginning of our marriage was anything but blissful. It was filled with constant bickering, a lot of tears from my wife, and terrible words and actions from me. When the walls came crashing down around us, she was the rock that built me back up. I promised I'd spend the rest of my life making it up to her.

I lied. I cheated. I went behind her back and brokered deals that her father would have been less than pleased with. But she protected me from him, time and time again. She knew she had as little choice in the marriage as I did. But if she was going to be forced to marry a monster and become queen, she'd do it her way. And she did, gracefully.

"When did it change?"

Isabella waved when she noticed us watching her.

"When you were born." I motioned for my son to take a seat, realizing this conversation was long overdue. "When she got pregnant, we'd been at each other's throats for months. I hated that I was building a life with her, with someone I thought I could never love. When, in reality, it was because—"

He smirked, the apple not falling far from the tree. "You did love her, but it wasn't your choice, so you fought it." He laughed, knowing all too well how that could've easily happened with him and his wife. But my son was a far better man than I ever was and would be an even better king.

"We didn't speak for months, not until the night she went into labor." I took a long drag from my cigar, handing another to my son. "Things had just really started to settle with me taking over the city. The streets had amicably accepted my reign and I'd put out a lot of fires. I had several families that were backing us and had cleared the way for me to sit on my throne. As you know, all it takes—"

"Is one bullet for someone to steal it from you." He cracked his knuckles, no doubt recalling several incidences from his youth and then again with his bride. "I'm not mad at you anymore for lying about Bella."

He was. That was a type of anger and hate that would never fade. But I needed everyone to believe she was dead to protect them. Just another check on the lists of grievances I'd caused my family.

"It was late. I'd just come home from drinking at one of the corner bars I owned back then. I was drunk, so drunk I didn't even notice the voices in the hallway." The cigar burned bright as I was transported back to that night.

"Christ, Rick, give me a hand."

Riccardo, my oldest friend, laughed as he helped me get my key in the door.

"Another fucking night locked in my prison," I slurred out and regretted my words almost immediately.

I'd spent the night at the corner bar, drinking away my problems. However, none of them were real. No, the real problem was the fact I didn't even know why I was so angry anymore. I'd fought so hard to stay away from Serafina, my true love, at my wife's request. As my son grew in her belly, her only ask was that if I sought comfort elsewhere that it not be with the one woman she knew I loved. Her blanket approval meant I cheated with any bitch within reach. So many wanted to swallow my cock to say they tasted royalty. And I let them. So many of them. Too many. I walked out as soon as my balls drained and each new conquest made me hate myself a little more.

Isabella was a beautiful woman. The sweetest soul I'd ever come across. She turned our house into a home. My men respected her, enjoyed her company. And the more time I was around her, the more my walls started to crash down around me. Which meant that the guilt began to eat at me more and more. I slowly stopped sleeping around, and to ease the guilt, I drank. A lot.

Like tonight. I could barely make out the outline of my front door, let alone get my key to unlock it. Riccardo moved fast, opening the door and shoving me inside with a laugh as I stumbled. I gave him the finger, straightened, and wandered aimlessly towards my bedroom.

I should apologize to her for everything I'd done this past year and beg her to forgive me. *That thought was running through my mind as I continued down the hall.*

"What the—" I stopped when someone grabbed my arm and tugged me into my office, closing the door and placing a hand over my mouth.

Isabella was in a silk nightgown, her large belly showing how ready my son was to enter the world. Her finger covered her full lips to silence me. She tapped her ear and pointed towards the door. It was only then that I finally heard the voices.

"I told you he wouldn't be home yet. We should've handled him at the bar," one voice muttered.

"We never would have made it out alive. Now be quiet. Let's handle the wife and his unborn spawn first."

Isabella tapped my arm before lifting three fingers—three men.

My adrenaline was coursing through my veins, slowly reducing my inebriation. They wanted to hurt Isabella and my son… because of me. *I tucked her away under my desk, telling her to be quiet as I jumped behind my door just as it started to open. I moved fast, even in my drunken state, and attacked like a madman. I'd disarmed and knocked out two of them before the third even realized what was happening.*

The last fucker refused to go down as easily. We went blow for blow while the other two started to come to. My wife and unborn son needed me. I'd already let her down so many times. I needed to protect them. Blood was coating the floor and my knuckles were torn open. It wasn't until Isabella whimpered that I came back to reality.

One of the men had her pinned to his chest. His gun against her temple. I stared at them in horror. "No!"

Isabella held on to her belly, her face twisted, pained.

"Wouldn't I be doing you a favor?" His thick accent hinted at his identity. Many were direct immigrants from Italy, but this thick brogue was particular to one group. "You don't care about this bitch."

I took a punch to the gut, then the nose, the repeated blows forcing me to my knees. I stared up at the third man in confusion. Why would they *be doing this? To what gain? Did I have it wrong?*

"We got this, boss." One of them nodded at the other two before disappearing down the hall, and the front door slammed.

"Mario, th-the baby's coming," Isabella whined, her knees buckling as she dropped closer to the floor.

"You're both fucking dead." My hands twitched, needing to kill them. "Isabella, look at me."

She peered up at my face, hers riddled with agony.

I'm going to make this right. *I silently told her we'd get through this. I'd spend the rest of my life making up for my bullshit.*

"Shoot the bitch!" one shouted as she called out for them to wait.

"Mario, I love you. I know you never wanted this, me, but I still love you." She stopped to scream in pain, and the man holding her seemed conflicted. "Mario," she whispered, before nodding at the guy behind me.

And then I saw it.

I elbowed him in the face and ducked to my right, Isabella's gun going off immediately. I didn't hesitate, charging the man at her back and slamming my full weight into him. I subdued him easily, but Isabella had other plans. She groaned in agony but continued to lean over my shoulder, the gun held strong in her grip.

"Rot in hell, bastardo." The gun discharged and his body dropped at the same time hers started to fold over.

I moved quickly, helping her to the ground and pulling up her nightgown. "Oh fuck." I called 9-1-1 first, Riccardo second.

"Whatever you do, make sure my son is okay," Isabella commanded and only then did I notice the puddle of blood forming under her.

"You're both going to be okay. And I promise you I will do right by you and this family. I'm so sorry for everything, for what I've put you through. I love you, Isabella." And I meant every word of it.

As she gave birth to our son on the floor of my office, so many images of a future without them flashed in my mind. Made me sick. It was one promise I knew I'd spend the rest of my days fulfilling. I'd love her and my family until I died. Whatever I did in life, it would be for their benefit. Because this woman owned my heart.

"That's why we named you Lucifer." My son eyed me curiously, so I clarified, "If you'd have killed a woman as tender as your mother, I would've thought you were the devil. Instead, you were really fucking *lucky* she was much stronger than that."

"Sienna needs to leave, Pops." The kid had an uncanny ability to smother my decent mood. "If she thinks we all turned our backs on her, then she'll go."

"I know. She needs to hate us to leave." I despised saying it aloud, but it was true.

Apollo was like another son to me, and if we didn't get him straightened out, he'd either die or be sent to prison. When it came to those two, their version of love was so toxic it promised to implode— at least until they got their heads on right. Once it clicked and Apollo was back to himself, I had no doubt they'd make amends.

I had Philly's alliance and offer of protection, even if my family would hate me for it. I never really understood Shakespeare until this moment. My decisions left me uneasy, since they were made because of my crown. I had to protect Sienna, and if Apollo couldn't, I'd ensure someone else could. My adopted son would never love her, not the way my eldest daughter needed him to. He'd show it in his protection, his loyalty, and his possessiveness. Once everyone realized this, everything else would click into place. I just needed to push him and get him there.

Before they killed each other.

"So, that's the plan?" Lucky asked, swallowing the same bitter pill. "He's losing control. They can't be allowed near each other."

Sienna was going to hate us.

Realistically, we didn't have many choices. We could let Apollo continue to spiral and end up in a cage, or worse having killed my daughter. We could treat him like a sick dog and put him out of his misery. Or, finally, we could force Sienna to leave. She needed to go away until we got him under control. Because letting Apollo off his leash would be the end of us all.

The ultimate betrayal could very well be the one that saved my daughter. She'd never leave on her own; she was incapable of walking away from a fight. But if we turned our backs on her and made her angry, she'd leave and actually do right for *herself.* For once, she'd choose herself over this family.

"Someone needs to take the bullets out of her gun." I took another puff of my cigar. The statement was comical but it didn't make it any less true.

Our conversation transitioned from business to family. My son was preparing to add on to his, meanwhile I was losing control of mine. We'd need to send Sienna away while we begged Octavia to come home. It was an absolute mess.

But I would save my children and pay for my sins. I just didn't expect my two daughters to have plans of their own.

CHAPTER 10

APOLLO DELUCA

"Don't be afraid of your *feelings*, Alvin. Speak your mind," I snapped.

We'd had a moment of peace between us but that didn't absolve me of his anger. My hands shook as I gripped the wheel. My shoulder throbbed from Bella's fastidious prodding, but I was far more plagued by her words.

"Do you really feel *nothing* for her?" His tone gave me pause.

"Fuck." A deep, cathartic sigh rattled my breaths and my endorphins rapidly increased as the stress of my thoughts weighed heavily on my chest. I left the car and was transported back to *that* moment.

"I love you." Sienna's choked words stalled my movements, forcing me to meet her gaze.

My eyes clenched as pain throttled my system. Grabbing my chest, I pounded my fist into it—over and over—needing the pain to dissipate. And then it clicked as I stared back at her, the gravity of the situation dawning on me.

"Oh. My. God. It took until this moment for you to get it!" Cassandra started laughing, but I couldn't take my eyes off Sienna. "Love, Apollo. You fucking love her."

"No!" The knife imbedded in her torso. The initial strike wasn't likely to kill her but it wouldn't take long for her to bleed out.

My body was on autopilot, unable to hesitate even if I wanted to. There was only one way out of this. To fucking end them all. He'd just pulled his knife out of Sienna's body when I collided with him. I quickly got the upper hand, his small frame doing little to subdue me. My hands were coated in blood as I tried to rip him apart.

One minute, I felt nothing. The next, red-hot impulses shot through my every nerve ending. Blood poured from my wounds, while the rapid pulsing of my heart forced me to my knees. I collapsed onto my stomach, staring at Sienna from the concrete.

"Si-Sienna." I couldn't lift my head but I needed to speak. "I-I do. I..."

"Oh fuck. Oh shit!" Cassandra cried, dropping the gun onto the ground.

For years, I ignored the niggling feeling that drifted through me when she was near. I ignored the smiles that tugged at my lips when she was antagonizing me. I refused to acknowledge the erection her perfume gave or the ache in my balls when she smiled. One taste, that was all I needed to become addicted.

And now it was too late.

The excessive blood loss and pain were making my mind blank. I was resolute to the fact that this was the end and I felt a strong desire to go back in time to eliminate her anguish. To stop fighting my urges to be close to her. To claim her.

Sienna screamed from a distance as the older one pulled my head back. "Here's a treat for the fishes." He smirked as he glided the blade across my throat, then shoved me off the rocks. Silencing my voice as the current swept me away.

Far too many images and scenes were replaying. There were so many moments that I had the urge to take what she was so willing to offer. But I didn't. When I finally caved and allowed myself to enjoy something that was so far above my station in life, it was stolen from me. I was going to die while dreaming for one last taste.

The waves rocked me into a false sense of security, my mind pretending I was in a warm bed with my face buried between Sienna's thighs. If by some miracle I made it out of this, I would enact my revenge. I wouldn't stop until the city was painted red. I was going to fucking kill them all.

And Sienna would be free to live her life... away from me. Away from the danger and peril I caused. See, I'd always been as clever as the devil, but if I made it out of this... I'd be twice as twisted.

"Apollo! Fuck!" Al's shout startled me back into the present, but it was too late. My car jumped the curb, and my rims screeched as I fought to regain control. We clipped the corner of a building and the vehicle came to an aggressive halt. "Goddamn it." The impact folded his door around him, pinning Al to his seat

"What happened?" I rubbed my eyes, shaking off the haze of my mental fog.

"You started fucking yelling and let go of the fucking wheel. You douchebag!" He twisted but it was no use. He was stuck. "Can you get me the fuck out of here?"

"She haunts me. Every second. The moment I close my eyes, all I see is her. All I see is the knife entering her ribs. All I hear are her screams—" I stared through the broken windshield. "I was the reason she almost died."

"You think that matters to her? She just wants you... Against everyone's better judgement." The silence stretched for a moment before he huffed at me. "You're killing her, a little bit more with each day you ignore her. She thought you died, and when you came back, your silence was another wound to her chest."

"She was hurt because of my past. Mine." I cracked my neck from side to side.

"If it isn't your enemy coming at her, it's Lucky's. Or Mario's. Fuck, or even her own. You can't protect her from it all. She's strong enough to stand at your side." He twisted in his seat. "She was stabbed seven fucking times and woke up a day later, wanting to find you. Avenge you."

"It's not the same. Darkness follows me. It always has. It's why I am who I am for this family." The metallic taste of blood filled my mouth. "She's my weakness. They'll come for her."

"Oh, get the fuck over yourself. Your enemies aren't her only threats." He shifted in his seat. "Now will you help me get the fuck out of here."

"Your elephantine condition is not my concern." I climbed out of the car, closing the door and muffling his rant.

"Don't you leave me, you motherfucker!" Al shouted, but I was already walking away.

This was my mess, a debilitating wrong I'd right on my own. As I was always meant to do.

The children didn't deserve to be punished for their father's grievances. But there was the apple and all that... I'd made an immense tactical error in not immediately eliminating the threats, as I had done with their predecessor. But that was an indiscretion of my youth. I'd learned since then. And I wouldn't make that mistake again.

I climbed the fire escape of the old building, using my knife to pry open the window. My hands were still and precise—the promise of death calmed me. As I stepped inside, I could hear voices coming from the other room, mixtures of anger and fear. One loud, one soft.

"Shut the fuck up! No, he didn't." A mumbled response. "I said shut up!"

I stepped farther into the room, closer to the voices.

"Believe whatever you want about your daddy. Those are facts, in black and white." Papers were fluttering in the air as I peered around the corner and into the hallway. No, not papers, *photos*. "You should've thanked him for ending that sick son of a bitch, not condemn him!" Sienna stood in front of the sons, a nine in her hand aimed strong and true.

My blood traveled vigorously south, my dick coming alive at the sight before me. She didn't notice me, her sole focus on the two men bleeding at her feet. They were beaten and battered; a crescendo of blood spray had erupted across the white wall. The bruising showed signs of age, meaning more than likely someone else had gotten to them first.

"Look, please. We-we just wanted to… we didn't know." It was the one who'd cut my throat. He was pleading with her now.

She squatted to meet him at eye level, staring at him for a moment. "You knew, didn't you? There was no way you would track down his killer without first learning the why." His silence was her answer. "You're just like him, aren't you? Another sick fuck."

Her words seemed to sink in as the older brother looked to the kid in disgust, but instead of responding, the younger one reached into his waistband. I stepped into the room, slapping the back of his head with the butt of my gun.

"I'd advise against that." I enjoyed their haunted expressions. "You look like you've seen a ghost," I deadpanned.

"What're you doing here?" Sienna didn't look at me; her focus remained glued to her targets. "They're mine, Apollo. Mine." She rolled her shoulders and braced, a clear indication she was ready to pull the trigger.

"You are sorely mistaken, Sienna." Her face was a shield of determination. "They hurt you because of *me*." My speech was shortened as one twitched, attempting to rise. "So they're *mine*."

The elder brother barely straightened his legs before her gun discharged. The bullet penetrated is frontal bone, tissue and brain matter spraying into the air. The sound bounced between the walls but seemed hushed over the loud thoughts in my brain.

The younger one was shouting at her, demanding she pull the trigger. Her smile was cold, venomous, filled with promise. "You took everything from me." It came out as a whisper, the sound irreparably broken.

"We thrive in the fire and cannot be burned." I ran a finger along the raised tissue that spanned the full width of my throat. "Your incompetence shows. The carotid artery runs along *both* sides of the neck. And yet, you missed." I, however, wouldn't make the same mistake.

Sienna watched me draw my blade. "Unlike my family, I don't care for games," she hissed. Her gun discharged again. And again. He took two bullets in the lower chest cavity that would ensure a slow, painful death. Then she flicked her knife out, intending to step forward but I caught her wrist.

"I know you were taught to share."

Her pulse was beating assuredly against my thumb as she stared at me with those empty eyes, closing herself off. The deep-red, sanguine fluid of our enemies coated her skin, further eliciting my erection. Her tanned flesh against the crimson color gave her a haunted glow. My palms itched to touch her, to feel her underneath me.

"Eye for an eye, *fica*." I made a precise incision to rupture his carotid, dragging it slowly across his throat.

Sienna stepped to my back, her front pinned to my arm as she wrapped herself around me. We watched in silence as every last drop of blood left him. It lasted till he stopped twitching and then she turned on her heel. "See ya." Her dismissiveness snapped my resolve and I gripped her arm, spinning her to look at me. "Let. Go!" she snarled, trying to shrug me loose. "It's over."

I forced her backwards, her heels clattering as she scrambled to shy away from my touch. Her back slammed into the wall, and I braced my arms on each side of her head, refusing to touch her. The quietude mixed with the metallic scent of blood before stretching between us. Her breasts rose and fell rapidly and I seethed at her impetuousness. The spoiled mafia princess, once again clawing her way under my skin.

"Over." My disdain dripped freely with the singular word.

"Yes." Her audacity shone like a beacon in her eyes, and I planned to show her just how wrong she was.

We'd never be over. Not even when Mario gave me an ultimatum and I left the city. She was the only woman capable of getting me to this point. So completely unhinged. From the first taste of her delicious nectar, her virgin blood coating my cock, I knew she was inescapable. She'd forever be interred in my bones, smoldering under my skin.

I breathed heavily, my body inches from hers as we stared defiantly at one another. The air was filled with the static of death. My dick was hard and my mind periled with errant thoughts of all the debauchery I wanted to enact on her body.

My resolve crumbled and I had to have her.

My mouth crashed to hers, my hands gripping her face to pin her to me. She tried to fight at first, but it was futile. She bit me, earning herself a growl that only spurred me on. She scratched at my limbs, my back, forcing my larger frame against hers, pinning her where I wanted her. My balls ached as she succumbed to the same carnal instincts that plagued me.

I kissed the seam of her lips, biting along her jawline, enjoying how her body shook. I dipped my thumb into the small streak of blood across her cheek and smeared it. A strange but perfect combination against her tanned surface.

She shoved me backwards, her chest heaved and she raised her hand with a clear need—so I let it happen. The slap echoed, and the pain impulses flared to life as my lip split open. The taste of blood erupted in my mouth, setting free the animal barely contained within.

"Fuck. Me," she whispered the command before jumping into my arms and wrapping her strong legs around me.

Our lips connected with snarls and pants of anguished need. We were toxic, the promise of ruin to each other, but both equally unable to resist. The moth knew the flame would burn, but the beauty and trance of the flames made the slow death worth it.

Her body molded to me. I wrapped my arms around her and held her tight. "I fucking hate you," she admitted between kisses, ripping open my shirt and rubbing her heat against me.

"I know," I ground out.

"Shut up and fuck me," she demanded as I dropped to my knees and laid her on the blood-soaked floor.

The buttons on my shirt were torn, more of the crimson liquid dripping down my chest, and she stared hungrily as I pulled what was left of hers over her head and drooled at the toned, bloodied sight before me. She was a work of art. Chaotic and breathtakingly beautiful. A perfect contrast of dark meeting light.

"These might as well be painted on you." Her leather pants were glued to her lithe legs. "Fuck. This." I pushed my thumbs into the seams, the material splitting when I tugged. Sans panties, Sienna was sprawled out beneath me, bloody and soaked from her arousal.

And I goddamn hated her as the river's edge flashed behind my eyes. Her current predicament reminding me of the way she lay motionless in that warehouse, the persistent ache in my chest unsettling.

"What are you waiting for?" she asked breathlessly. Her eyes were black, dead holes but her core was dripping for me.

"*This*… This changes nothing."

She flinched like I'd struck her, staring at me with pure loathing behind perfectly fanned lashes. Even when her world was crumbling around her, she shielded herself with hatred to survive.

This was merely sex. My words reminded her as much, adding yet another offense to my list of travesties. The devil was my brother, I was the reaper, and Sienna was my absolute demise.

I wanted her to suffer, to hate me. I needed her hate, yearned for it. Because when I left, left her and the city, then she'd survive without me. She'd hold on to that hate and live another day.

"Pretty little Sienna. Always used to getting what she wants."

Her eyes were aflame, burning with anger.

"Today, you'll get it." I dropped to my elbows, attacking her core with the savage strokes of my tongue, enjoying the garbled pleas that hung in the air. She was soaked, her thighs pinning my head and shaking as I found the bundle of nerves—demanding atrophy. She screamed my name and I smiled as I gave her a few lasting strokes. "My favorite flavor." I wiped the back of my hand across my face. "You want this?" My erection settled against her entrance to further punctuate my statement.

"You know I do." Her words were flat, monotone, but her body gave away her secrets. I pushed inside, the place that was made for me. Where I found sanctuary. "Harder."

I pulled back and slammed into her. She tugged my body tight to hers, latching her teeth on to my shoulder to quiet her moans. All the gunfire and yet she was concerned over her screams. Harder and harder, I gave her what we both needed.

"Shit," she whimpered. "Apollo." Her eyes opened, and I stared into a dangerous current of icy-blue water.

"Come for me, Sienna. Do it." I moved my hips back and forth while my sweat mingled with the dried blood before splattering onto her skin. My perfect tainted canvas.

Her body coiled and her muscles tightened as she came, forcing my own release to follow. She quivered beneath me as we lay in silence. Neither sure what to say. Neither wanting to break the spell. She rolled onto her side, unable to face our sad reality, before pushing to her feet. I helped tug her up.

"They were expensive," Sienna hissed out, her fingers clinging to the tattered leather of her pants.

"Send me the bill." I twisted my neck, feeling the skin pull from my scar.

"Trust me, I will." She picked up my shirt, throwing it over her head and buttoning what was left of the torn material. Then she stepped into the bathroom as I made a call to the Agostino cleaners.

When she emerged a moment later, my jaw clicked to prevent my mouth from opening. A piece of leather from her pants was wrapped around her waist as a belt, allowing my oversized shirt to give her an hourglass figure. Her long, toned legs were on display and her calf flexed as she walked towards her discarded gun. She checked the clip, engaged the safety, and deposited the nine into her clutch before tucking the bag under her arm. Back to her practical indifference, the mafia princess ignored me and walked towards the door.

"Where did you park?" I asked, coughing around the tightness in my throat.

"I managed to get here without you. I think I can manage to get home too."

My retort halted her escape. "I totaled my Maybach previously and my Audi on the way over," I confessed.

"Christ." She sighed. "Let's go."

"We probably need to get Al too."

"Fucking. Children." She turned and stomped away.

And I followed like an obedient puppy, albeit shirtless. We were most certainly a sight as the neighbors quickly slammed their doors and their resounding locks clicked into place. She ignored them as she took the hall like her own personal runway. We'd just made it to the street when my head snapped to the side, my nose erupting on impact.

"Motherfucker," Al grunted, grabbing Sienna's hand and walking her towards her car, presently parked on the street. Neither of them said another word as they climbed inside and pulled away. I stood on the sidewalk like a *senzatetto pazzo*, watching them leave. I grabbed my phone and Lucky answered on the first ring.

"I need a ride." I chose to ignore his laughter, as Bella shouted at him to hang up on me, and continued to stare out into the distance as if I could still somehow see *her* speeding away.

I'd been enamored by this woman all my youth. Sienna Agostino was whatever she needed to be to survive. She could fit into any group with a snap of her fingers and a sway of her hips. The gift of just a taste had turned into an addiction that was going to be the death of me. At the same time, my palms itched to feel her skin as I disjointed her neck and watched the life drain from her body.

On any given day, it was a battle to see which impulse would win out. And today was no different. I hated her as much as I needed her and vice versa. It was only a matter of time before one of us destroyed the other. Even knowing this, there was nothing either of us could do to stop it.

CHAPTER 11
SIENNA AGOSTINO

"Whose blood is that?" Al asked, climbing into my driver's seat.

"*Theirs.*" I peeled a piece of the dried bodily fluid off my skin before rolling down my window to flick it away.

"What the hell were you thinking going there alone?" He smacked my steering wheel, his dramatics making me roll my eyes.

I adjusted Apollo's shirt, much to Al's angry glare, and quickly countered. "Whose blood is *that*?"

"My own," he deadpanned. "Motherfucker blacked out and totaled the car. They literally had to cut the door off to get me out. And do I even want to know why you're wearing his shirt and what used to be your pants as a belt?"

"Semantics." I brushed off his concern, ordering him to take me to my apartment.

"Nope. Mario wants you home," he muttered before singing his taunt. "*Somebody's in trouble.*"

I punched him in the arm, ignoring his stupid chuckle as he drove me towards the compound. I'd kept some of the truth from my family. I could've kept it all to myself and just done what I wanted. But after my abduction, my need for self-preservation had kicked up a notch.

"Office. Now," my father clipped the moment I walked through the front door.

"I'm really tired," I said, flopping into the chair while suddenly all too aware of my limited attire. "Uncle Rick?" I dropped my feet to the floor and leaned forward with the shock. My Uncle Rick—my dad's best friend—hadn't been around in a few years.

"Hey, princess." He'd aged. A lot. And not in a handsome way, like my father.

Uncle Rick had always been around at the holidays, birthdays, and all that jazz. Then when he found a new, much-younger wife, he sort of disappeared. Speculation at best, I knew something else had gone on between him and my father. Neither would admit it, but I had a feeling it had to do with my father never taking a right hand. The king never wanted a usurper.

Uncle Rick patted my shoulder before exiting the room, and I turned to face my father's wrath. "Sienna, do you have a death wish?" His voice was deflated, and suddenly I realized how old he'd gotten too. This life—his children—were taking an insurmountable toll on him.

"After I went to see Gio, I knew I could handle it." There was no counterargument.

He wiped a tired hand down his face, his voice so quiet it gave me chills. "Sienna, I have one daughter missing… Do you really think I want to worry about the other?"

"Dad, I—"

"Silence!"

I jumped in my seat, his anger unexpected.

"Gio Moretti hates this family and you run off on your own, to do what? Fulfill some goddamn vendetta that Apollo and Al were going to handle themselves?"

"Dad, I…" I tried again, and he took that moment to notice my clothing.

"Are you. Fucking kidding me. Sienna." He leaned over his desk. "That *morto figlio di cagna* almost killed you… I almost threw him out of this family… and you." He stopped. *"Gesù Cristo. Non so cosa fare con te."* I dropped my jaw to interrupt again and he talked over me. "How can you be so stupid? I raised you better than this."

I throttled back in my seat, tears immediately forming at his verbal assault.

"You're going to Philly. Tomorrow. I'm not going to worry about two daughters, not now."

"No. I. Am. Not!" I rose to my feet, just as the damn belt came loose and I had to catch the shirt before flashing my father. *Classy.*

"Yes, you are. Or so help me God, Sienna, I will fucking take you there myself. I am making a deal with Romano."

We were back to the same reality of my future being chosen for me. I was being punished for someone else's actions. I'd just gotten myself back on track and was starting to settle into a new rhythm. Now my independence was being taken away from me. Again.

Well, this time I wasn't going to sit pretty.

"No," I said calmly.

"Excuse me?" he ground out, the vein in his temple throbbing.

"I said no. I will not allow other people to dictate my future any longer. It's not my fault that I love a psychopath! But isn't that punishment enough? Knowing he'll never love me back?" I slapped my father's desk with my fist. "She's my sister and it hurts me too! Why are you okay with losing both of us? I won't go!"

"I will." Apollo stood in the doorway and I hated that my body thrummed to life.

Since he left the hospital, his impeccable suits were things of the past. He stood shirtless with blood-tinged pants, wearing my teeth marks in his shoulder and my scratches down his arms. Normally he'd have changed already… but this new Apollo didn't care.

"You've got a lot of balls showing up here like this. Instead of killing you, your brothers and I taught you a lesson with our fists. Now you walk in my office smelling like her?" My face burned bright in embarrassment as my father added, "Did you not learn the first time?"

"Dad, I…"

He laughed loudly, stepping around his desk to get closer to Apollo. "You won't claim her, and yet no one else can have her either."

"What?" I looked at Apollo, but his clenched jaw said it all.

"Nothing to add?" My father poked the bear. "I didn't think so. Sienna, you will go to Philly. Now. I will iron out the details with Romano." He picked up his phone before dismissing us with a flick of his wrist.

I walked past Apollo, hearing him quietly close the door. I made it halfway up the stairs before I stopped myself. I turned around, my heels in my hand and the smell of Apollo drowning me. His shirt felt soft on my skin and I hated that I wanted him to take it off me.

"Tell me what Daddy meant." I knew he wouldn't answer. "No one else can have me?" His jaw worked back and forth but he was mute. "Right. Well, I'll launder this and get it back to you." I tugged on the shirt.

"Something inside me snapped when I watched them stab you. Then, all I remember is the back and forth battle between floating and drowning, fighting only so that I could find out if you survived." He stared past me. "Since I was pulled from the river, my control is gone."

"Control?" My words were barely above a whisper as I internally pled for him to go on.

"Controlling the darkness. Every time I look at you, all I see is your blood on *my* hands." He walked past me in the direction of his bedroom. "And now you took away the only thing that *could've* put me right."

Ever watched one of those women-targeted movie channels? Where it was nonstop bad acting, the same plots over and over—so bad, but you watched them anyway? That was my life. I'd yell at the female leads over how stupid they were for falling for the same bullshit. They knew he was bad for them, but they were too stupid and blinded by love to do anything about it.

Then it usually ended with someone dead…

Well, introducing Sienna Agostino. The dumb-ass female lead who would keep dealing with shit she didn't deserve. And her costar, Apollo Deluca. The man who simultaneously drove her crazy and would—more than likely—eventually kill her.

Unless she fought back…

The question now was: which one of us would end up dead by the time the credits were rolling? And by whose hands? There were so many variables spread between the two cities.

Walking into my bathroom, I cringed at my reflection. I had dried blood on my face and body, my makeup smeared and my eyes red from my internal woes seeping through any available crevice. I rubbed the heels of my palms into my eye sockets, the harsh pressure doing little to dwindle my pounding headache. My life was a whirlwind of bullshit but at least I finally put my foot down. Moving forward, I was making decisions for the betterment of myself, and not for that of my family.

"Sienna!" Marco pounded on my door.

"Christ! Can't a girl shower in peace? What!" I shouted back before opening the glass door and angrily wrapping myself in a towel.

"Someone's been trying to reach you and the fucker won't tell me who he is. He said turn on your phone," he barked, slamming the bathroom door twice because my brother is an asshole.

Mumbling to myself, I tightened the towel around me and walked into the bedroom while ignoring Marco's commentary on my lack of clothing. I powered on my cell phone and computer, smirking as my bastard brother acted so inconvenienced. My phone started ringing as soon as the service was reconnected.

"Sienna, this is important, but I need you alone," John said, as I turned to my brother and made up a lie on the spot. John was the cop who had helped Persephone in her time of need, though I hadn't spoken to him in a while.

"You fucking kidding me?" Marco punched my wall as he left.

"Your brother's a real charmer. Listen… *he's* out." John's tone was layered with worry and stress, and I felt like I'd swallowed my tongue. Surely, I had heard him wrong. "I was trying to give Persephone time to heal before testifying. They used it to their advantage." His panicked voice did little to calm me. "Almost six hours ago."

My heart pounded in my ears as unease settled in my gut. "He'll still be in the city."

"Or he has someone in the city to get *you*." I didn't like that answer. "I watched you together, Sienna. This thing he has for you is real… it's dangerous."

"Yet you didn't tell my brother."

John wanted Gio alive and he wouldn't allow Lucky to interfere. "I know how your *family* deals with police cooperation." *Aw, he was looking out for me.* "I can't let the mafia handle this."

"Allegedly," I muttered, my mind in a tailspin. My brother and Apollo would hunt him down and more than likely, I'd lose them all at once. The FBI were too close to this. Apollo was too unhinged and Lucky didn't know how to backdown. They'd both be gone because of me.

"I figured I'd run police protection by you." I was telling him no before he even finished his sentence. "Then what are you going to do, Sienna? I can't have a war. I won't sit back and do nothing."

"I will handle it." I sounded stronger than I felt. "He won't… he won't hurt me."

"You sure about that?" When I didn't answer, his impatient sigh hung heavy in the air. "Think this through, then get back to me."

"Yup." I hung up, tossing my phone onto my desk and flopping into my seat. The weight of the world on my shoulders was starting to bury me into the ground.

"Who was that?"

I shrieked, staring at Apollo in surprise. *Give me a damn break!*

He was showered, but in sweatpants, sans shirt. His hair was still dripping down his chest and into the waistband of his pants. I stared at the wet material, inadvertently licking my lips.

"Ever hear of knocking?" My breathy voice gave me away.

"Answer. Me." He ground out the words, taking a step with each syllable until he was looming over my desk. I gave him the same lie I told my brother, but this time it fell flat. His eyes flared. "Try that again."

I gulped, remaining quiet.

"Lie to me, Sienna. Do it. See what happens."

I leaned across the desk and repeated myself, without breaking eye contact. He suddenly wanted to act like my hero, stumbling back into my life as a messy, sex-oozing, tattooed god. Well, fuck him.

"Okay."

I tilted my head, surprised he'd given up that easy.

Only, he hadn't.

I didn't see it coming. He pulled me across my desk by my wrist and it immediately started to swell. My thighs ripped open when dragged across the harsh surface, my entire computer system following me to the ground. His toned body pressed me into the floor and his sweatpants did little to hide his pleasure at my pain.

His firm hand on my neck kept me in place, squeezing hard enough to bruise while daring me to lie to him again. A crazed monster set on teaching me a lesson. *Fuck him.* I let out a scream, lifting an arm and scratching down his face, unconcerned with the repercussions.

"Your audacity to assume I cannot smell your lies is astounding." He pinned my arms above my head, infuriated and shaking. "Tell me."

"Fuck you, Apollo."

He didn't relent, no matter how hard I fought. "*To thine own self be true, and it must follow, as the night the day, thou canst not then be false to any man.*" His Shakespearean quotes only stoked my fire. "Your lies will be the death of you. So concerned with proving your strength that you'll charge over the front lines alone, instead of with an army at your back."

"I don't need to prove anything anymore. I've done it over and over." I lifted my hips, but it was no use.

"When your lies catch up to you and send you to an early grave, it'll just be one less person in this family for me to worry about." His words were a knife to my heart, icy and sharp, with every intention of causing irreparable damage.

"Get off me!" When he didn't move, I spit in his face. "I can take care of myself."

"Clearly."

I was getting emotional whiplash from all the back and forth with this man. "*Clearly.* As I proved at the river's edge, when I crawled out of the hell *you* created." It was a low blow, but I was too pissed to care. "And if I can't, I'm sure Romano will take care of me."

He'd hurt me and it was time to hurt him back. Then again, this merry-go-round wasn't any less painful. He was a goddamn mental patient at this stage. Long gone was the man that protected me, the *friend* I'd grown up with.

He shoved himself off me as if my touch burned, tugging at his hair and pacing. He'd lost any semblance of composure, his appearance unkempt while he muttered to himself like a full-on basket case.

I climbed to my feet, adjusted my towel, and made the ultimate mistake—another one in the grand scheme of things really. *I turned my back on him.* I should have known better than to take my eyes off a rabid dog.

He gripped the back of my neck so hard I hunched my shoulders. "Romano will protect you?" His hold kept me silent. He walked us towards the bed, his chest to my back as I dropped onto my stomach. His heavy weight pinned me down, even as I fought him. I was beaten —black and blue—but only I could see it, could feel it. "Does Romano touch you like this?" His calloused hand ran down my body, squeezing my hip. "Do you make those noises for him?"

Suddenly, I was flipped onto my back and his warm mouth latched on to mine. I was lost to everything but us. But this moment. He ravaged my body but fucked my mind—gone from reality—and I didn't want to come back. He pulled one delicious orgasm after another from me. Apollo took each of my hate-filled speeches and laughed at my promises of pain. He drained me mentally and physically until he came. Then he shoved away from me.

"Who was on the phone?" he asked as he adjusted his sweatpants. I maintained the lie because this had nothing to do with him. *"Due possono giocare a quell gioco."* He thought two could play at my game, but I'd lose no matter what. "When you lose everything, I hope you remember that you chose this path on your own."

I wanted to run my hands through his messy hair. "As you've said, I'm not your problem." Heading for another shower, I bit my lip to hide my sobs. "Leave, Apollo."

"I dare you to go to Philly."

I froze, my heart hammering in my chest.

"I'll make you watch as I destroy the entire *fucking* city, Sienna. *Ti sfido.*" And then he was gone.

I turned the water to the hottest setting, leaving the bathroom to let it fill with steam. I sent Alexei an email about scheduling a meeting and then called John. "I'll be bait."

He didn't respond.

"Use me. Let's draw him out."

"Sienna, I won't do that." His tone told me that was a lie. "Not only will the department say no but…" *But my family would kill him if I got hurt.*

"Okay," I stated with finality.

"Okay?" He drew out the singular word.

"Uh-huh. Happy hunting." I disconnected the line, sending him to voicemail when he called right back, and dialed Alexei instead.

"Yeah?" Alexei questioned with no greeting.

"Call your uncle. One of his contacts will know where Gio is hiding." I yawned, completely depleted of energy by this point.

"No," he ground out, so I hung up on him too.

I'd do it on my own then. I wandered into the bathroom and stared at myself in the mirror, my fingers running over the bruises on my neck. Could I leave my family behind and run away with the enemy? In the mafia, my family reigned supreme, but would they allow me to live if I committed the ultimate sin? Some travesties were *unavoidable* because of our limited moral compasses.

But this… this would be *unforgiveable.*

He wanted to give me my *city. To take it from my brother.*

And I could be queen.

Maybe his desire, his affections, his drive for us to lead together… maybe it could turn into more. Maybe I could love him. Or maybe the poison Apollo injected into my veins was sending me over that edge into insanity.

After all, I'd become accustomed to a life of devastation and pain. So why not where a crown along the way?

CHAPTER 12
APOLLO DELUCA

*P*etulant *little bitch! Guard cosa mi hai fatto fare!*

My intention had been to gain answers, not tempt my inner beast. Lurking skin deep, he seemed to bubble to the surface whenever she was near. Her lies thickened the air between us with ease and forced me to shatter the brick wall harboring my rage.

And I knew what I had to do.

Her list of grievances quickly caught up to my own, drawing a line in the sand and preparing us for this battle of wills. If her games were going to be my undoing, then I was going to take her with me. The end of the road met a thick line of trees, and we barreled towards it at dangerously high speeds.

"Woah." Bella approached me slowly as I stood with my back to Sienna's door. "Apollo?" she whispered, faltering when I made eye contact.

"Leave." The word came out breathless, and I gripped the pulse point in my wrist, counting along with my rapid heartbeat. There was a strong association between anxiety and respiratory symptoms.

The smell of coal infiltrated my nostrils. The path to hell was right in front of me.

"Apollo, it's okay." Bella raised her palms as I took a step towards her. "Lucky!" She slammed into the wall, shrieking when I took another step.

I could tell her she was safe, but I wouldn't believe my hypocrisy either. I wasn't blind to the fact that I couldn't conceptualize my actions. My mouth opened as something fractured my occipital bone, forcing me to my knees. The blow sent me slumping onto my side, and I cradled my head as I curled into a ball at Bella's feet.

"Bella! Get Lucky, go!" The youngest Agostino stood above me. Tall and imposing.

Ever since the disappearance of the girl he'd been *seeing*, he'd fallen into the ranks. It was only a matter of time before the games he played caught up to him. It was unfortunate that someone else paid the cost. Tessa, his plaything, had *disappeared.* Though something about that story, that girl, never seemed right to me.

I tried to rise but Marco twisted me into a submission hold, wrapping his legs around my torso as his arms circled my neck. We became lost to the outside world, each trying to beat the other.

Several heavy steps charged towards us, the approaching shouts coming out in waves of static. Al ripped us apart, holding me to his chest with a bicep lodged under my jaw, applying precise pressure to my cricopharyngeal muscles and closing off my airway.

"Sienna." Bella's soft gasp forced us to look in her direction, only to find the woman in question standing in the doorway, her silk robe doing little to hide the bruises on her arms and her neck. I'd hurt her. Again.

I could only surmise that I was suffering from a mild cognitive impairment—the stage between normal aging and severe trauma. It was characterized by problems with memory, thinking, and judgement.

"I'm fucking done with you! I don't know if the reasonable side of you drowned in that fucking river or if it never existed at all." I couldn't blame my best friend for the assessment. "Sienna will go to Philly and you're out of this house."

"No, I won't." Her refusal was dark, stern. "This is ridiculous!"

"You will go to Philly. There is no choice in the matter," Lucky commanded.

Deadly crimson waves hardened her face as she fought against his orders. She wouldn't bow to her brothers demands; everyone knew that. However, the mere mention of Philly—of Romano touching what belonged to me—had me twisting against Al's hold.

"Why am I being forced out when this is *his* fault?" Her voice was high-pitched and devastated, eliciting a niggling discomfort in my chest.

"Get the fuck over it, Sienna. You can run *Energia* from anywhere. You just need to be away from each other!" Al released me, shoving me into the wall and knocking me to my knees again. "This fucking obsession, or whatever it is you have for him, needs to end! He's going to fucking kill you!" Al leaned forward until they were nearly nose to nose. "How dumb do you have to be to see that, Sienna!"

"Al!" Bella gasped, her expression appalled, yet she didn't offer Sienna any support.

"Seriously, sis," Marco added, staring daggers at me. "This is ridiculous."

"Again! How is this my fault?" Sienna's composure was unraveling as she stared at each of her accusers, one at a time.

"Because he's gone off the deep end, and you're *supposed* to be the smart one out of all of us!"

Her jaw dropped at Marco's insult. She was waiting for *someone* to stand up for her. But they'd turned their proverbial backs on her instead. The accusation in her eyes turned to pain as she realized everyone was siding with Lucky. With me. And not her.

"Pick!" Lucky's rage settled on his sister.

Sienna's normal complacency when it came to her family and duty was gone and an icy chill filled the hallway. It was frigid, almost painful. Slow and blank, she glared at each of her onlookers before ending on her brother. "As you wish, brother." She turned to walk into her room. "Or is it my king? Seeing as I'm still in New York... for now." Glacial. She gently closed the door and the entire hall noticed the turn of the lock.

"Something's wrong, Lucky." Bella stared at Sienna's bedroom door. "She never folds like that."

"This doesn't feel good," Marco muttered before disappearing down the hall.

"It had to be done." Lucky pulled Bella into his arms.

"She's lying." I swallowed the rest of my words, the rough skin of my scar crawling, begging me to tear it open with my nails. "About the phone call." My hands shook as I replayed each of her lies.

"I'm aware." Lucky refused to look at me. "Alexei couldn't trace it either."

She was the queen of secrets, keeping everyone in the dark. Her cowardice was almost alarming. Sienna refused to appear weak, dismissing our attempts to help. There was an army at her back, threatening decimation, and yet she marched into battle alone.

"Stay the fuck away from her." Al shouldered past me and stormed down the staircase.

Lucky walked off behind him, commanding his wife to follow suit. But as was true to her nature, Bella was yet another Agostino who was too defiant for her own good. And she fought back where she knew she'd win, and her husband handled the rest.

"It's the funniest thing," Bella whispered, still staring at the door. "Sienna is the strongest, most intelligent woman I've ever met. Except when it comes to you." Bella craned her neck to look at me.

"You heard your *husband*." My mouth watered as Sienna's scent lingered on my skin.

"Can you stay away?" she asked, stepping closer. "Answer me this: who sent you in there?"

How the fuck did I end up in Sienna's room?

"As I thought, you're confused." Bella smiled sadly, wrapping her cold, thin fingers around my wrist. "Neither of you have been particularly healthy in your pursuit of each other. But unlike my husband, I see what's really happening. Sienna is lashing out, begging someone to be on her side. To receive the same allegiance we all give you. And if we're not careful, we're going to lose her… forever."

"She won't leave."

"Isn't she already gone?" Bella's question had me turning to look at the door.

"She's not leaving." I silently dared Sienna to open it.

Her refusal to listen caused total discord, leaving us to pick up the pieces. I'd attempted to right the wrongs from my past, but as usual, Sienna was one step ahead of us. The Affanad boys' deaths were supposed to bring me peace, the tranquility my control provided. Well, that was *before* I was thrown into the Hudson.

And she took that from me.

"Fuck!" I slammed my fist into the wall, ignoring Isabella's shout of protest and disregarding everyone else, as I sped away from the compound in Al's Audi. I quickly rolled down the windows to alleviate the smell of vomit and whiskey. The man was boorish, but this was a whole new level of repulsive, even for him.

My thoughts returned to the object of my contention. Sienna's face had turned disarmingly blank. Something in her head sizzled to life—a plan I'd guess. And that was far more dangerous than her verbal threats. She was the queen of rash decision-making when she was emotional. The dismissal of her family, the arrangement with Romano, and Gio Moretti always in the background, I was curious… would she snap and turn against us all?

I stood at the window of my office at the docks, lost in the memories of floating in the frigid waters, until my phone rang.

"Sending Al with a present." Lucky hung up, and a few minutes later, Al walked in with an unconscious body slung over his shoulder.

"He was caught breaking into Sienna's apartment." Al dumped the man at my feet.

His words reawakened my nervous system. Waves of adrenaline contracted the vessels in the body, directing blood to all the major muscle groups, and mine were currently pumping more oxygen into my heart and limbs. I was invigorated, focusing my rage on the man with the death wish.

"Where the fuck's your suit?" Al stared at my bare feet and chest. It was a wonder I'd remembered pants. "Christ, you really are fucked up. Apollo, don't do this to her."

"Assumptions are made and most assumptions are wrong."

He cracked his knuckles and glared back at me.

"You're bursting bubbles of synovial fluid and reducing lubrication to your joints."

Al continued to stare at me, his expression a mixture of anger and confusion. Good, that gave me time to prepare for the punch line.

"Chronic cracking of the knuckles can lead to a reduced grip strength. And since you can *go fuck yourself,* you may want to stop that before you can't grip your flaccid member."

"You son-of-a—" He halted in his steps when the figure at my feet moaned.

"Hello." I ignored Al and addressed the man between us. "We can make this very easy. I ask a question, you answer truthfully, and I end you quickly."

"Fuck you, ya Agostino scum." He spit the words, blood coating the air when he spoke, and tried shaking the chain loose, only to howl out in pain when his ankle bent at an awkward angle.

"Deluca, actually." I turned with clippers in my hands, enjoying the way his pupils dilated with fear. "Apollo Deluca."

"You-you… you're the reaper." His whisper earned the smallest tilt of my lips.

"Indeed." I turned back to my table of toys.

"Why were you in Sienna's apartment?" Al questioned, kicking him in the ribs when he didn't answer. "You'll tell us eventually, so save yourself the pain."

He remained silent as his eyes landed on the table of devices.

"Do you know much about anatomy? Humans, which represent the most complex lifeform, all share certain requirements: respiration, digestion, and excretion. These processes are interrelated and utilize organs, mass cells, and other physical anomalies that are above your level of cognitive ability." I twirled the rope around my hands, turning to look at our captive still bound on the floor. "I think the most incomprehensible fact for individuals such as yourself is that the human body can go up to three minutes with no air and survive with little to no damage."

"This should be good." Al grinned. They called me sick, but I was merely a singular act in this demented circus of *il famiglia*.

"When we approach five to ten minutes, there is concern for brain damage. That being said, I believe we can attempt four minutes safely and see how many times I must resuscitate you until you fold." I turned to Al. "For science, of course."

"Of course." He nodded at our patient, who proceeded to fill the room with a pungent odor as he relieved his bowels.

I swept my arms over his neck, wrapping the rope around his throat and pulling tight. His limbs flailed and his fingers fought to relieve some of the tension. The rope impeded the flow of oxygen, preventing blood flow to the brain. He was unaware but the combination of pressure to the neck was also restricting his trachea, which was what made respiration impossible, eventually resulting in his slow asphyxiation.

I was counting in my head, ensuring he would suffer but not too hastily. If we crossed over four minutes, I might not get the information I needed. But his presence in Sienna's apartment assured me he possessed pertinent intel when it came to the threat against her life.

He'd give me answers. They always did.

As minutes turned to hours, I grew restless, nearly allowing our captive to succumb to brain death before he finally squealed. I was unsure, at first, if he'd be able to articulate a response. But once the oxygen fully saturated his lungs and the blood flow resumed, he sang a very interesting tune.

And gave me a name.

"Find that motherfucker," I commanded Al before ordering Rocco to meet me at the docks. "I want answers. Now."

I'd quickly changed into a suit, and shortly after, Rocco arrived, practically frothing at the mouth for a little bloodshed. Al had already pinpointed the location and put feelers out for the man in question.

Al parked outside the small Italian restaurant; several armed men stood outside, awaiting our arrival. We paid them little attention as we stormed through the front doors. The place was empty except for the two fuckers seated at the table in the center.

"I heard you were looking for me. What can I do for you, Deluca?" Romano's cocky tone was practically begging for a bullet.

"Is someone missing a check-in with you?" It was subtle, but his scar bounced just enough to tell me I'd hit the nail on the head. "Someone with a very important task?"

"Stop speaking in circles and ask the fucking question." His impatience curled my lips into a grotesque smirk. He didn't know his man was missing… until now.

"Why did you send someone to Sienna's apartment to pick her up?"

His brow scrunched, and for some reason, it gave me pause.

"Pick her up?" He nodded towards Romeo, who stepped outside to make a call. "I didn't send anyone to pick her up."

He was telling the truth. I could tell, read it on his face, hear it in his voice.

"Didn't send anyone to pick her up. But you had someone on her." It wasn't a question, and his knowing smirk proved my point.

"I did. You should speak with Mario about that."

Al turned and showed him his phone, giving Romano a glimpse of the man I'd just killed.

"It's true. I had someone watching the apartment, but *that's* not him. Though I'm assuming he's the reason one of my guys is missing."

"You're lucky I believe you." It was my gut reaction.

Romano wiped his mouth and smiled, his scar dancing with the movement. Romeo walked back in and whispered in his ear. "I gotta go. I'm heading back to *my* city and would like to stop for a coffee along the way." I wanted to give him a matching scar to answer for his feral smile. "Till next time, Deluca." And then he and the rest of his entourage left.

"You really think he didn't order it?" Al's question was one I could answer with no hesitation.

"I know he didn't."

True to his word, it appeared the Agostino patriarch didn't believe his son or his men could protect his daughter. I understood Mario's need to ensure Sienna's safety, especially with Octavia still missing. But to seek an outside source was not only a sign of weakness but an act of disrespect to those who looked up to him.

"Make that call to Lucky now. He needs to have a conversation with his father."

We climbed into the SUV, our minds consumed by the newest unanswered question. Meanwhile, the beast inside my chest was rattling the cage and all he wanted was blood.

What a fucking nightmare.

My family had officially turned on me. At first, I was beyond devastated and now I'm downright pissed. I know I have—at times—made decisions without consulting them. It made them angry. Then they saved my ass or vice versa and we moved on. But to stick up for *him* and hand me off to another man, that wasn't okay.

Far-fucking-from it.

"Miss Agostino, what a pleasure."

I set my cup on the saucer, swiping a drop of my coffee from my lips with my tongue, while Romano greedily traced the movement with his eyes. "Mr. Bianchi, I do believe you're in the wrong city," I mused as he pulled out a seat before I could offer. "And, of all the quaint little coffee shops, you just so happen to visit this one."

"There's a lot you still don't know about me, Sienna." The silence stretched for a moment as a million questions bubbled to the forefront of my brain. "Perhaps I'm just an avid caffeine enthusiast." He looked around the meager décor and outdated furniture.

"Perhaps." I sat back and crossed my legs, tapping my thumb on my thigh as I eyed him curiously.

"Or *perhaps* I was in the city on business and happened to stop by your office." I knew where this was going. "Farrah is quite pleasant."

"Farrah is a sucker for a good romance story, and a chance meeting is right up her alley." She'd have happily told him where I was.

He nodded. "My presence seemed to piss off your *bestie*. Farrah all but threw your schedule at me to get me out of there."

"Alvin?" I questioned but already knew the answer. "He's a tad protective. Now, after…" I gulped past the pain. "Af-after Octavia, he's borderline territorial."

"If you were mine—" Tucking a stray curl behind my ear, Romano stroked my cheek. "I'd be downright murderous." The conversation dropped to just above a whisper, his stare never wavering.

"Wh-what?" I coughed past the dryness in my throat, squirming a bit in my seat. "Why're you here?"

His knowing grin seemed to mock me. "You know why. Mario told me you're aware of his plans for *us*." His tongue traced along the curve of his lips. "I'm just waiting on a few minor details…"

"Lucky is increasing profits, strengthening his hold as he prepares to step in. An alliance makes sense."

His eyes assessed me as he sat back in his seat.

"You want something else before you agree." It wasn't a question.

"I'm a businessman, Sienna. Your brother may've been the face of those deals, but who was really at the helm of those negotiations."

I didn't need to answer. We both knew it was me.

At one time, I wanted nothing more than for my family to be in the spotlight. I didn't need the credit, just the overall profitability of our name. However, as of late, I wanted my accolades. They were long overdue.

And Romano was giving them to me.

"You've intrigued me, Mr. Bianchi. And I don't mean by sweet talking my assistant, in order to gain yourself a boring black coffee."

He tossed back the rest of the cup without flinching.

"Just about every legal deal this family has conducted since I was sixteen was my doing. So, I'm curious… what deal are you willing to broker for *my* alliance."

Romeo walked in with a playful smile, quickly dropping it to look at his boss and whisper something in his ear. The agitated growl that left Romano forced my thighs together.

Goddamn, this man was hot. Why couldn't he be enough for me?

"I apologize but we need to continue this at another date." Romano stood up from the table, placing a gentle kiss on my hand. "Next time, Farrah can schedule dinner for us."

"I look forward to connecting with her," Romeo muttered, garnering our attention. "To schedule that dinner, of course." He did little to hide his smirk as my hackles rose with the comment.

I crossed my arms over my chest, nodding as they both dipped their heads in respect and left. "Fuck," I hissed once they were out of earshot.

"Fuck." The sentiment was echoed back at me.

I looked at the barista who stared longingly at the door, fanning herself with napkins.

"Girl, that shit was swoon-worthy!"

I shook my head and sat back in my seat, unable to pay attention to my tablet. Another latte was dropped in front of me, but I couldn't focus on anything other than Romano's sudden appearance. My father had made it clear that he was using me to form a continued alliance with our neighboring city.

But something felt... off.

I took a sip of my latte, the caramel melting on my tongue as my mind raced. Too many variables lurked in my life and I just added Romano to that list. I dropped my tablet on the table with an agitated sigh. My afternoon was screwed. There was no way I was going to be able to concentrate now.

Nothing was ever simple in the mafia. My goddamn brother said he wanted me gone, but there was a reason outside of his concern for my well-being. Lucky for me, I knew when to call their bluff, and no one's poker face could outdo mine.

"What're you doing here?" Alexei asked as I stepped off the elevator to my office.

"Ballroom dancing, idiot."

Rocco chuckled at my back, his disdain for Alexei as evident as my own.

"Lucky said you were headed to Philly?" His innocent question shattered the wall holding back my stifling rage.

My feet pounded their way into my office, the thin heels of my red-soles threatening to crumble from the impact. My hands shook so badly I was unable to grab my door and slam it in his face. I threw my pale-blue Hermes Birkin handbag onto the chair at my desk, gripping the edges to keep me upright.

"So, about Philly…"

Twirling on my heel, I felt it give way as I started yelling. "Bastard *thinks* he controls this city, but he doesn't control me!" I shouted, not giving a damn that the entire lobby was watching my meltdown.

"Sienna." Alexei raised his hands, palms up in surrender.

"And I'm out." Rocco practically jumped from his chair and darted into the lobby. I shoved Alexei out after him and slammed the door in his face.

I stumbled for a moment, before kicking off my broken heel, and wandered to my view of the city. What was once my solace now laughed at me. It was cruel and mocking.

No one knocked, leaving me to work in peace. I found myself lost to a little perusal of confidential police files: *Released due to insufficient evidence. Lead witness incapacitated and unable to be interviewed to support claims.*

I scoured through the details of the case, the declarations from other partners and the information he turned over. Gio was good at covering his tracks… but I was better. The police needed new evidence or a confession. And I had plans to get them both.

Farrah alerted me of the time and I grabbed my bag before heading to the elevator. Alexei and Rocco rode down to the lobby with me in silence. We jumped into the SUV Al was driving and headed straight towards the college. The air was sizzling with excitement as we ushered our group inside the auditorium.

"I bet you're the proudest father in the world right now." I smiled at Evelyn's dad, shaking his hand as we approached our reserved seats. "Alvin, Alexei, and Rocco." I motioned towards my entourage, and he nodded.

Al quickly stepped forward, shaking the man's hand and offering his congratulations before kissing Evelyn's mother on the cheek. I stopped for a moment, staring at my best friend curiously. He was in a suit, not out of the ordinary, but today he wore a three-piece—gray with a matching vest. His shoes were new and shined, but even more peculiar was the fact he held a bouquet of flowers in his hand.

Rocco caught my attention; his expression matched my own as we watched the men make quick small talk. They conversed as if this wasn't their first-time meeting.

Interesting.

"Miss Agostino, we can't express our—"

I cut him off with a wave of my hand. "We've been through this. Your daughter did the work, not me." I gestured to the large auditorium presently hosting the graduation. "Evelyn's hard work and perseverance, her strength to not be a victim is what brought her here."

My little protégé had graduated NYU with honors, far exceeding my expectations. I saw a lot of myself in her and smiled. A small girl, who rose from disaster and became a fierce woman.

"I didn't think we'd see this moment." The crowd erupted as another name was called. "I really thought... it... that... was the end for my daughter. I'd pictured her waitressing at the local diner and not getting a chance to *live* her life." Her father wiped away a stray tear.

"Here she comes." Al pushed to his feet, his large frame blocking the view of several attendees, none brave enough to say anything.

"Evelyn!" Her father, mother, and I all shouted in unison as her name was called.

Rocco put his hand in his mouth to whistle, but it was Al's deep hollers that had several people turning around. Evelyn faltered in her steps, holding her diploma and staring at us in shock. She looked each person in the face, her awe and happiness filling her eyes with tears. Not only did her parents and I have front row seats with Rocco and Al, but I may or may not have reserved the entire section for every employee of *Energia* Holdings. The room had been throttled by the rising fanfare, the young Evelyn having touched each one of her coworkers with her charm, grace, and intelligence. She deserved nothing but absolute happiness.

Once she'd exited the stage, the faculty halted the ceremony as our entire section left without remorse for the interruption. We'd come to see her, not the rest of the graduates. We made our way outside and the chorus of cheers erupted as Evelyn approached. She was practically glowing as her gown swallowed her small form. She greeted her parents first, then introduced them to each of her coworkers. The buzz in the air was exuberant.

"Miss—" She smiled and laughed at my expression. "Sienna." Evelyn pulled me in for a hug, forcing me to swallow past my emotions. "Thank you," she whispered.

"Not needed." I squeezed her hand and then turned to the group. "As you all know, Evelyn's contract expired once she graduated. I am assuming all of you would like a moment to say goodbye to our beloved intern."

A few faces turned to me in shock and I couldn't even look at Evelyn, afraid her sadness would break me. That was the thing. I'd put her rapist in jail—ensuring he was absolutely miserable while there—

with a promise that she could intern with *Energia*. Nothing else was discussed, even if I did see incredible things in her future.

One glance at Al, and I took note of how he appeared as though he was either going to be sick or murder me.

"No one wants to say goodbye?" Amy, my lead attorney, stepped to my side, addressing the crowd. "Very well. Evelyn, it has been a pleasure to watch you grow and I wish you nothing but the best on your future endeavors."

Evelyn smiled through her tears, maintaining her grace, and embraced us. Al moved towards me, clearly pissed, but I shook my head at him.

I wasn't done.

"Well, if no one else has anything to add before we say goodbye to our *intern.*" And then it clicked, the realization morphing everyone's face. "Evelyn, I'd like to formally offer you a full-time contract to become part of my legal team."

Amy drew the document from her bag, but before she could hand it to the girl, Evelyn screamed a resounding *yes*. "Hey! I raised you better than that!" Amy laughed. "Read the contract before agreeing!"

She was engulfed in more hugs and congratulations as Alexei and I stepped away from the group. Once the excitement calmed down, Al wrapped his large arms around her.

"Didn't see that coming," Alexei muttered, watching Al smile at Evelyn.

"Ditto." I crossed my arms over my chest, planning to make the man's life a living hell until he acknowledged his feelings. He was my best friend after all—that was my job.

"Ready?" Rocco motioned for us to exit, as Al said goodbye once more, before shouting, "Sienna!"

Alexei went to grab my arm as a gun went off in the distance. The attendees on the sidewalk ducked, screaming and running from the threat. But as chaos erupted, Alexei and Rocco disappeared in the masses and I had no idea where the threat was coming from.

"Sienna!"

I turned to run towards Rocco's voice. Then I saw it, my mouth parted, and I screamed for him to get down. Rocco dropped without a second to spare, the bullet just missing its target. "Rocco, are you—" My vision was cut off as something was thrown over my head, thick muscles pinning my arms down and carrying me away.

I screamed and fought, but the man was too large and able to quickly subdue me. I was unceremoniously tossed into a vehicle and the force as it sped away threw me back into my seat. A renewed sense of fight kicked in and I attacked. But a slap across the face had my mind whirling and allowed my captor to overpower me again.

By the time the car came to a stop, I was unsure how I hadn't thrown up yet. Once more, arms were wrapped around me until I was thrown over a shoulder, my bound limbs hanging uselessly at his back. Then I was dropped into a chair with a grunt, and the makeshift blindfold was quickly removed from my face.

Gio's irate expression met me at eye level. "Who touched her?" he asked the man at my back.

"I'll find out and handle it."

Seemingly pleased by that answer, Gio helped me to stand. If I was going to die, I'd do it as Sienna Agostino, CEO and fashion icon. I had never been more pleased that I'd changed into a bright-red Fendi silk Mindi dress. The front had buttons down the center and there was a high slit at my rear. And, of course, the look was paired with diamond-strapped, red-soled stilettos.

"Even more gorgeous than I remember." He motioned around the room. "Welcome home."

"Gio, water…"

He cut me off and ignored my request with a wave of his hand.

"Wh-what? Why?"

"Your beauty is unparallel, Sienna. But that haunting fire deep in those blue eyes makes you radiant." He kissed my hand. "Your years of forced submission have come to an end. *We* will have all the power now." He picked up the large pendant necklace that sat on the swell of my breasts, turning it over and over in his hand.

"And if I don't want it? Then what?" I shook my head, clearing the fog. "I'm tired of everyone making decisions for me."

He sat back in silent contemplation. "Sienna, *that* is why I picked you. You're perfect. We want more than what our families have dictated for us." He leaned forward, his elbows on his knees. "We were meant to lead. We were meant for so much more than what we've been offered, more than New York fucking City."

"You'll give me the world? Everything Lucky's stolen from us?"

His chest puffed out with pride.

"How the hell did you build this empire? And so quickly?"

"I am an entrepreneur. It's a skill."

I pressed him, asking a few more questions, but his answers were riddles.

"Stand."

Before I could comply, he pulled me from my seat and started patting me down. When he glanced up at me, confident I wasn't wearing a wire, I laughed at his audacity. A mob daughter knew better than to snitch.

Plus, where would I hide it in this dress?

"Sorry."

We reclaimed our seats as he spun a tale of deceit, corruption, murder, and abduction. He laid out every part of it for me. It was sickening to watch him smile and happily recollect all the pain and devastation he'd caused without a hint of remorse.

Got you, bitch.

A chill ran down my spine and unease settled into my gut. He wasn't going to just whisk me away and start somewhere new. No. Gio wanted all of it. He wanted the city, and here I was, fixing the crown he placed on my head. I'd made this bed and I was going to lie underneath the fine silk.

"Boss! We got company," someone shouted into the room, and the butterflies in my belly became erratic.

"*Qui non va niente,*" I muttered and Gio laughed.

His grin was malicious and unhinged. "Don't worry, my queen, I'll protect you."

"They're here for me." I twisted against my bindings, finding them loose. "And after all this time, they still don't realize I don't need them to save me."

Gio faltered when gunshots sounded outside.

They'd always underestimated me. Each one of them. I'd planned, plotted, and schemed all along—I was going to conquer the world. I didn't need them to save me. I was far more capable of saving myself.

I was Sienna-fucking-Agostino, and I wouldn't lay on my goddamn back and let someone have their way with me.

CHAPTER 14

APOLLO DELUCA

Fucking Gio.

Everyone said she was taken, but was she really? I scrutinized her behavior, mannerisms, and words on repeat in my head. She was known to make rash decisions but she'd never turn her back on her family.

Would she?

Rocco had eyes on her and the Agostinos were rallying to retrieve her.

A damn fortress lay ahead, situated in an open field. It would take stealth to advance unnoticed. But the closer we got, the less I gave a damn about veiling our approach. The car had barely stopped when I darted out. The house might as well have been painted red, taunting a bull that charged through the open perimeter. I ran with untroubled, solid steps towards the men that begged for their demise.

The perilous fight inside my head finally calmed. The fog settled and I could see clearly. I'd felt like I was unraveling in the deepest bowels of my being. Yet, as I stared at the house in the distance, I was removed from it all. Gun in hand. Calm and steady. They were all dead. I ignored the hail of bullets as I kept moving.

Gunshots erupted in every direction. None of it resonated as my boot went through the front door. Long gone were my pristine suits and designer shoes, opting for tactical gear instead as I intended to rain hell down upon them. I'd end this once and for all. *Il mietitore* kicked in their door, the blade narrowly missing a knife meant for my heart.

Doctors claimed that the human brain switches to "autopilot," enabling you to continue with tasks quickly and accurately without a conscious thought. This meant that our neurons were continuously active, even when we were lost in the moment.

I scoured the living room, then moved into the kitchen and turned down a hallway. I reared back, pain erupting in my chest. Lucky grabbed my arm and dragged me around a corner, tugging my shirt open.

"I told you to fucking wait, goddamn it." He sighed and shook his head. "It's in the vest. You're good."

"Where's Al?" I hissed.

Lucky glanced down the corridor. *"Oh, merda!"* He pointed to where Al lay on his side, unmoving. *"Fanculo questi codardo!"* Lucky signaled, and we both stepped into the hall, pulling the trigger at anything that moved.

"I'm okay," Al grunted when I got to him. "Bastard kicked me in the balls." He wheezed and Lucky chuckled. "Get down!" Al shouted, but it was too late.

The teres minor muscle in my back erupted in pain, the bullet lodged somewhere between that and the teres major. It stung like a bitch but if I watched the blood loss, it wouldn't kill me. I rolled sideways and shot the bastard right between his eyes.

"Fuck!" Sienna's shout pulled us in her direction.

"We need a plan," Lucky said, tugging Al to his feet.

"I have one." I lifted my foot and slammed it through the door. My upper body jolted to the left and I dove behind a bed, scanning the room before I went down.

Sienna was holding a gun to Gio, his realization morphing into pure loathing as he stared into her barrel. Which was pointed at his chest, her face a stone wall. Devoid of emotion.

"Fuck you, Gio. You hate my brother but you're just like him." Her aim was sure and her hand never wavered. "This *empire* you've built disgusts me. All those poor women," she scoffed, snarling in his direction. "I got you now, bitch." She tapped the pendant around her neck.

Gio chuckled humorlessly. "Daddy raised a submissive little whore." He shook his head but leaned forward to whisper, "So. Fucking. Disappointing."

One moment she stood confident; the next she was pinned to his chest, struggling against his hold.

"Look who it is! Her faithful brother and his leashed psychopath," Gio taunted. "Come in, Lucky. Stand up, Apollo."

"Let her go." Lucky stepped into the room, his gun raised and at the ready.

"Why?" Gio looked back and forth between us. "She's *mine*."

The growl that erupted from my chest threatened to shatter the windows. I rushed forward and Gio moved fast to position Sienna between us, the hot end of his barrel at her temple. Halting my attack. He smiled, knowing he had the upper hand.

"Enough games, Gio. What do you want?" Lucky moved to the side as Al stepped in, two more guns raised.

"Her. I want her." He sounded incredulous, annoyed that we *didn't* know. "And everything that is being *handed* to you." He waved his gun around the room.

"Gio, please." Her voice was soft, broken.

His hands were all over her, touching what didn't belong to him. He attempted to stake a claim, but his ownership was a farce, downright entertaining. I was done with all the games, knowing she deserved better. She deserved better than both of us, but between the two, I was the one taking her home.

"I assure you she's leaving with us."

Her eyes went large, filling with a degree of hope and longing, before she quickly masked it with indifference. I took a deep breath, lifted my arm, and fired. The bullet missed its intended spot in his chest cavity, but the spray of blood from his shoulder still appeased a part of my shattered soul. I reached out for Sienna, tugging her behind me as Lucky and Al darted for him, his fleeing form throttling through the window a moment later.

"Sienna!" Mario came running into the room, pulling his daughter from me. Her chin wobbled and I was unsure if the tears were out of remorse or agitation.

"Let's go." I grabbed her arm, and when she fought me, I threw her over my shoulder.

"What the hell, Apollo?" Mario questioned as Sienna asked, "What the fuck?"

She smacked and clawed at my back, her nails digging into the skin. My wounds ached with each step, but I didn't falter as I followed Al and Lucky out the door. Then I set her to her feet, holding her in place by raising her arm awkwardly into the air. "It's clear she cannot be trusted with the enemy. She has a bullseye painted across her back and has made it clear she will run to him. The compound will jeopardize the entire family and the apartment has proven to be a target."

"Screw you. You don't know shit, you fucking asshole." Her words held little power as she fought against my hold. "Let. Go."

I dropped her arm and tugged her directly in front of me. "Secret trips to the jail. Secret phone calls. So. Many. Secrets. Was that call from Gio? Arranging to pick you up?"

"Fuck. You." Her blue eyes turned a deeper shade of navy.

"You already have. Has *he*?" I whispered into her ear, enjoying the way she bucked against me. "You're on a suicide mission and it could've been prevented if you'd behaved."

"He's right, Sienna." Her neck snapped to look at her brother. "Did you think we wouldn't learn about the private visits to see him in jail? The phone calls when he got out? His little gift of roses?"

"I told Daddy! I didn't hide anything!" Her sharp, panting breaths did little to calm her nerves. "Let me go! Christ! Lucky, this isn't my fault."

"He all but gave you a blood oath. Promising he'd come back for you. I won't have you putting Bella at risk." Lucky nodded at me.

"I'm taking her away." I turned on my heel, dragging Sienna along with me while ignoring her cries. "Once we confirm he's out of the city, we'll come back."

When she wouldn't cooperate, I tossed her over my shoulder again. I wasn't going to let anyone touch her. The only person who could tarnish that perfect olive skin was *me.*

She bent her knee and arched her spine, forcing me to tighten my hold. Until a spiked heel was jammed into my shoulder, just above the bullet hole. And I immediately let go, watching as her shoe flew from her hand, and caught her right before she hit the ground.

"Enough!" But, of course, she didn't listen. "I'll call you."

"Fuck you! Let me go!" Sienna demanded, thrashing from side to side. "Someone stop him!" Her cries were ignored as her family all turned their backs on her.

Mario was the only one to step forward, glaring at his daughter for a moment. Then his eyes softened, he kissed her forehead, and he disappeared.

Her fight didn't extinguish, leaving me with no choice. I slammed the lid to the trunk closed on her continuous tirade. Climbing behind the wheel, I waited as the car came to life, but I couldn't put it into gear. The desperation in her pleas grated under my skin, forcing me to consider removing her.

And then the despondency was gone.

"You motherfucker! Let me the fuck out of here!" Her struggle turned antagonistic as she hammered her fists into the roof of the trunk. "I swear to God, Apollo, I am going to kick your ass."

As the car idled, I could hear the undeniable sound of glass breaking. Her kicking continued until the entire taillight was smashed to bits.

"You infuriating little bitch!" I ripped open my door, taking the zip ties out from under the seat, and unlocked the trunk.

I clutched the lid between my hands, attempting to rein in my rage, more than acutely aware of what I needed to do next. I opened it slowly, expecting an attack, not the tears, her delicate body heaving with the motion. I sighed, staring at the sky to appease the chagrin ripping through my system. But as suddenly as the waterworks had appeared, they were gone as she lifted a leg and her knee connected with my face.

My nasal bone and orbital plate took the impact, forcing spasms of pain to erupt behind the eye. I sniffed back the blood trickling down my face while pinning Sienna in place with the one hand, as she fought like a wild cat. *"Piccola puttana!"* I gripped her neck, squeezing tight and ripping her from the trunk. *"Dannazione."*

"Fuck you!" She shrieked so loudly anyone within a two-mile radius would've heard her. *"Non taccarmi, maiale!"*

I pushed her stomach against the side of the car, before twisting her arms behind her back, and zip-tied her wrists together, then did the same to her ankles. She slumped into my hip, the awkward position forcing her to rest against me. Her soft, yet firm body remained glued to me as I held her upright.

Once she was safely redeposited into the trunk, I took a step back and observed her from a distance. Her eyes glowed with need as she watched me remove my shirt. I ripped a small piece off the bottom, securing it into her mouth with a strip of tape, using the rest of the shirt to wipe away the blood from my nose and chin before slamming the lid shut.

I drove for about an hour before the nagging concern of asphyxiation forced me to pull into a gas station. The clerk was a young woman, countrified and intimidated, her eyes large as she watched me wander the store. I approached the counter and realized as I stared at myself in the security monitor that I never replaced my shirt. Her eyes roamed my naked, tattooed chest that had a smattering of blood across it. I tossed her a hundred-dollar bill and her hands shook as she tried counting out the change.

I stepped outside and popped my scalene muscles—the small grouping in the neck eased movement, and proper stretching relaxed the spine, allowing your body to prepare itself for an attack.

And then… I opened the trunk.

Thankfully, Sienna was calm as I helped her out and sat her on the bumper. I ripped the tape from her mouth to be met with a combination of English and Italian expletives. The harsh language was meant to be a defense mechanism, considered taboo, made others uncomfortable. So when Sienna was being controlled, it was her tactic to dictate others' emotions.

"Shut. Up."

She stalled. I was losing control and could feel the red haze of indignation settling over my consciousness. If she weren't careful, *that side* that I'd kept from her would devour her whole. She thought she'd seen me at my worst, cleaning up the remnants of my stifling despair that had ended lives. But it had never been directed *at her*.

This time, I placed the tape on her mouth and laid her on the back seat, forgoing the trunk. But instead of being indebted to my kindness, she offered me incessant whining as the car traversed the broken gravel that led to a small cabin in the woods. It was the sort of solitude that ensured the little princess didn't do anything stupid. I pulled her free and tossed her over my shoulder, carrying her inside before slamming the door closed behind us. I cut her hands loose and she slammed into the wall, scrambling to get away from me while clawing at the tape on her mouth.

And then she was on me.

"How could you?" Her small fists began hammering against the meat of my chest.

"You wanted a monster, you got him, Sienna." I forced her against the closest solid surface and shot my fist through the sheetrock. "You just had to push me!" I punched the wall again, feeling the frame shake under my force. Our fronts were perfectly aligned as her breasts melded against me. I could feel the charge racing to the surface, the *need* only she brought out in me. My dick was stirring to life and I needed to punish her. I salivated at the prospect of slamming into her, throttling her entire system as I staked ownership. "Who did you choose, Sienna? Gio or Romano?" My tone elicited goose bumps across her exposed skin. "Or did you want to fuck them first, then decide?"

Her head hit the wall, her breath ragged and her pain palpable. She put her hands on my chest and pushed. The beast rattled the door of his cage. He was unable to step away, enjoying her discomfort. I had every intention of wrapping my hands around her delicate throat, and when she begged me to stop, I'd silence her with my dick. The fog ever-present in the recesses of my brain surged forward, urging me to end her. It kept whispering in my ear.

"She's the reason for the rage, your problems." If she were gone, removed from my life, I could think clearly again.

Your body produced physical and psychological responses, the dependence became addictive, and you yearned to fuck your partner. Love was simply neurochemicals that flooded your brain to the specific parts that are associated with pleasure—a rewarding euphoria.

Sienna was lost in the oxytocin that was running full speed ahead. She was a glutton for punishment and I was just the sick motherfucker to give it to her. I'd destroy every chemical associated with her pleasure and incite pain—I'd fucking break her.

My hand gripped her neck, pulling her face forward until it was a breath from mine. "You seem to forget, Sienna... You licked your virgin blood clean from my dick. *You* decided to hand yourself to me on a platter of broken dreams you knew would never come to fruition. You have no one to blame but yourself."

She bucked and swayed, trying to push me away. Her distance from me would give her the strength to go back to her practiced indifference, a misplaced belief that her emotional fluctuations were dependent on my behavior. Her hand lifted but I caught it a second away from my face and slammed it above her head. Clicking my tongue at her, I pressed my lips to hers, her growled protests turning to moans as she opened for me. The moment was brief before her fire reignited and her teeth clamped down on my bottom lip, metal and poison filling our kiss. It stung but my blood cells immediately charged to the area and began their process of sealing the wound. Much like how Sienna had just sealed her fate.

"Please... let me go," she whispered but didn't push back against me.

"Know this, Sienna. No other man will touch you. I will fucking maim him. Right. In front of. You." I bit her throat, grinding my erection into her and earning a delicious moan. "And then I'll fuck you in their blood, let your pores devour their lifeforce as it depletes from their souls. So you'll forever remember that it was you who sent them to hell."

"Fuck me." The command was barely above a whisper but her cry for more was sensuous. "Do it. Fuck me, Apollo."

I turned and dropped us to the bed, enjoying how her tight body bounced against the mattress. Her dark hair was sprawled around her like a broken angel, haunting and so fucking beautiful. She was a dark and murderous woman with a celestial soul that threatened to ruin her from the inside out. She wouldn't survive her demons, and if by some miracle she did, then mine would destroy us both.

I ripped her shirt down the center, my stomach tightening at the thought of someone else touching her. I pulled my knife from my pocket, shredding her pants and aggressively ripping them from her body. I removed my shirt and unclipped my belt, my need to fuck her clouding my vision. Then I pinned both of her arms above her head and positioned my torso to secure hers to the mattress. My knife lifted as if on its own accord before lowering its edge to the brachiocephalic muscle in her neck. The slightest of movement and she'd bleed out on the white sheets.

"Did they fuck you?" The blade trailed down her subclavian vein and across her breasts, stopping above the pulmonary artery in the left ventricle. "Tell me, Sienna. Does your heart bleed for them?"

"No. No one has touched me. Only you." Her entire body stiffened, anticipating what was to come.

"Then keep it that way." My mouth crashed to hers and I let my darkness loose.

"Apollo…" A throaty whisper called out to the beast.

The temperature in the room seemed to drop twenty degrees. "I can't touch you… yet all I want to do is rip you open, just to watch you bleed. The thought of shredding your carotid, the blood flaring with your pulse, the vision makes my dick hard." I ground myself against her. "Are you wet? Are you as turned on at the thought of your death as I am?"

"No," she moaned, her head shaking from side to side.

"Liar," I whispered into her ear. "I can smell it. Remember, I was your first. I'm the one in control of the euphoria your body demands."

"Shut up." She twisted, screaming as she bucked against me.

I smiled, knowing I'd pushed her over the edge, her control shattering. Gone was the weak little girl nipping at my heels. When I got closer, my mouth hovering above hers, she didn't hesitate. She latched on to it with her teeth and tore, the metallic flavor erupting in my mouth. I could feel it running down my jaw to my neck.

If she wanted my blood, that was fine, but she owed me hers in return.

"I hate you." She shoved harder, the tacky red substance coating her lips and teeth.

"It's a proven fact that hate sex delivers the most pleasure, so I hope you loathe me, Sienna." I grinned before adding, "The medial prefrontal cortex regulates decision-making, triggers a reaction when you see someone you are physically attracted to."

She struck out against me before rolling to her side and climbing across the bed. She shrieked as I pulled her back by her ankle, her leg kicking out and meeting air, my movements agile and deadly as I countered each strike.

"The dorsomedial prefrontal cortex lights up whenever you're near, sends impulses that allow my blood to flow, and creates pressure in the corpora cavernosa, making my dick hard. For you."

She scratched and fought against me.

"Fight harder."

One moment I felt her pushing me away, the next she clawed for me to get closer. I stopped above her, my lip still bleeding and my neck littered with scratches.

"Fuck me," she commanded again, throwing her head back as I filled her with one hard thrust of my hips. "Shit!"

I didn't relent. My pace only quickened as the painful truth dissolved between us. Slowly, my soul lightened, pulling back from its internal disruption of agony. I licked a tear from under her eye and she moaned as I thrusted harder, my breath coming out in short pants. My muscles tensed as the strongest orgasm settled into the distance and I ran full steam towards it.

She scratched, moaned, and begged as I ripped orgasm after orgasm from her body. I kept up a relentless pace, surging all my agitation into each thrust. Punishing her. Pleasuring her was my way of showing her how much I cared. It was my version of giving her something back after all I'd taken.

I told her small truths, but the most deceptive lies were the ones she created in her head. She blamed me for the brutal honesty of what I wasn't capable of. She despised the fact that the truth wasn't what she wanted—something she couldn't control. I was her protector, but I wasn't sure if it was enough.

For either of us.

She curled up on her side, putting as much space between us as physically possible. The distance didn't matter. This push and pull was relentless. And I'd come to the realization that this only ended one way.

With one of us dead.

I left her in bed, her toned ass peeking out from under the covers as she lay on her stomach. My dick hardened at the promise of being buried inside her one more time. Instead, I slid into my pants and closed the door quietly behind me. I needed to make a call to confirm it was safe to come back.

"Where is she?" Alexei answered on the first ring. Once I told him she was fine, he quickly turned the conversation on its heel.

"Let me correct you. One, her *passion* is merely lust, a chemical buildup in the brain. Two, her irrational anger had her turning her back on her own family, branding herself a traitor."

"That's what you think?" Her pained voice sounded behind me. "That I'm so far gone that I'd allow my anger towards my *family* to make me a traitor?"

I stood up to look at her, admiring her in my black shirt. "A traitor is a noun. A person who betrays another." The silence stretched between us. "You betrayed the family for a crooked crown granted to you by our enemy. It's a factually based assessment, Sienna."

"Take me home," she demanded, turning before twirling back around and yelling, "Gio was released because John was protecting Persephone. I have everything they need to take him down." She tapped her necklace and pivoted on her heel, disappearing inside the cabin.

"You idiot," Alexei muttered. "The FBI's too close. She didn't want to see any of you behind bars, so she set him up. She recorded his fucking confession, jackass." He hung up on me.

Fuck, how had I gotten that wrong?

The car ride was filled with an ominous silence but also riddled with a sexual persistence that forced me to steal glances of her. Her quietude was disconcerting and, without words, I could already tell her mind was actualizing a plan—one that would no doubt end with chaos.

"I'm not a traitor." She was staring out the window as she spoke. "Persephone wouldn't have made it through a trial. I did what I had to do." She tapped her pendant again, stroking the chain with nimble fingers.

She'd set him up. When we charged into the room, she'd already been holding him at gunpoint. She played him at his own game and came out the winner.

This woman. She was both heaven and hell, effectuating a cataclysmic ending, and my only solace was the promise of her trembling beneath me. I wanted another taste, craved it. We pulled onto the highway, heading back to the city, but my thoughts were pillaged by images of her naked and moaning beneath me. My breath quickened, needing her to look at me. I wanted one of her hidden smiles. The most simplistic glance before I drove her wild and ravaged her tight body. I wanted her to moan my name and accept the cruelty I needed to enact on every inch of her skin.

"Pull over."

I glanced up, realizing she'd been staring at me.

"And fuck me."

I gripped the wheel tighter, threatening to rip it from the dashboard, as my mind was dislodged into a tailspin.

"Apollo." It was whispered, a plea. "Apollo!" she screamed.

"Shit!" I snapped out of it, jerking the wheel to avoid a truck merging onto the highway. Once the car was righted, I looked at her again. She was glaring at me, her whispered moans a figment of my imagination. These strange recurring episodes were telltale signs of a disorder. Maladaptive daydreaming. In layman's terms, intense moments where a subject became highly distracted and would stop engaging with reality. They became hyperfocused on whatever was in their mind, forging out their physical presence. It was a psychiatric condition often triggered by real-life events.

For example, Gio-fucking-Moretti. Another, Sienna-fucking-Agostino.

His exit from prison was due to plausible deniability. He was laying waste on the Agostino family, simply because he wanted things that didn't belong to him. Like Sienna.

"What?" Sienna's question forced my attention to her. "What's *yours*?"

"I didn't say anything." I stared back at the road, my heart rate increasing.

"You haven't shut up the entire ride home. You've been mumbling for the last hour." She crossed her arms over her chest, drawing my attention to how the material of her shirt—my shirt—pulled tight with the action.

"I didn't say anything," I repeated, my nose twitching as I fought to maintain sight of the road.

"Did you have a problem sharing toys as a kid? *Mine. Mine. Mine. Mine,*" she mocked, her snarky tone drawing the dark presence within me to the surface.

"Sienna. Stop." I barely recognized my own voice, my hands shaking as I clenched the wheel.

"*Sienna. Stop.*" She continued her parroted indignation. "*Mine. Mine. Mine.* God, you're an asshole."

A chill settled inside the car, my hands shaking and my mind racing as I fought with myself to leave her unscathed. She was dancing with fatality, unimmune to the savage depravity that lurked in my soul and seeped free from my pores.

I already told her once. If she wanted him, she got him.

CHAPTER 15

SIENNA AGOSTINO

He had officially lost it. He'd spent the last hour disconnected from reality as he rambled incoherently. I only got small pieces, but those tiny parts killed me a little more. His need for me was there but it was never going to willingly reach the surface.

"Need help with that?" I stared at his dick, hard and pressing against his pants.

"Sienna."

Was that a warning or a request?

"Just an offer." I glanced out the window. "You do owe me for locking me in the fucking trunk."

"Sienna." *That* was irritation.

"I'm hungry."

His neck twitched and I laughed.

"Food, Apollo. I need food."

"When we get closer to home." He was watching all the mirrors as if someone besides him had a clue as to where the hell we were.

"I. Need. Food."

His neck twisted in my direction, his lip snarling. Apollo was gone. I'd pushed him to his limit plenty of times before, but this was different. When this band snapped, it was going to open a portal into a dimension I hadn't seen before. But I had a death wish, so I pushed on.

"And. Dick." I stifled my laughter. I had a hell of a lot better comebacks than that, but I couldn't help myself. With absolutely no qualms, I pushed to see if I could survive all parts of him. Another comment was ready when he slammed on the breaks, my seat belt digging into each of my pressure points.

He swerved to the right and the car flew onto the shoulder, the tires skidding across rocks. I screamed until it came to a stop just before a grove of trees. He ripped his seat belt off, flying around the hood of the car. His look told me I was fucked and I couldn't tell my hands to move fast enough. My door opened, practically ripped from its hinges, and the seat belt held me in place when he tried tugging me out. I heard the click and saw the glint of silver right before the belt was shredded and I was wrenched out by my arm. His grip on my bicep was impenetrable as he pulled me into the trees. My heart was lodged in my throat and I suddenly resorted to begging. I just didn't know exactly what it was I was begging for. God knew I'd pushed him too far. I knew it was coming, but I'd done it anyway, taunting *il meititore* to come and play.

Instant. Regret.

I glanced around and things slowed, everything falling around me. The trees turned red, my blood dripping towards the ground and turning to ash before floating in the air. I wanted him to show me the fire, to let me feel the burn and spiral into the tunnel of never-ending sorrow and pain. Rose petals mixed with the ash before floating towards the sky, and drops of blood glittered in the glimpses of sun, making their way through the drifting embers.

I tripped, but his tight hold forced me to stumble beside him. He didn't speak, dragging me farther and farther into the unknown of the smoldering forest. Then the blood turned to flames, the fire burning my skin as someone whispered *sinner*. The voice sent a chill down my spine.

His face was devoid of anything, as he stared at the sky like he was pleading with something in silence. He wasn't saying a word, but he might as well have been screaming at me. This was it. Even if he didn't kill me, this was my ending. Our ending.

Could it be the ending if we never really had a beginning?

He was beyond reproach, so damaged I didn't recognize him anymore. His demons were catching up to him and I was beckoning them forward. I was only adding to the monstrosity inside his soul.

When he looked at me, my gut clenched and tears immediately dripped over the edge. He showed me his pain, his eyes filling with something beyond tender and filled with defeat.

Don't let me go.

I couldn't say the words out loud. But I knew this is what it was. He was saying goodbye. Nothing would be the same. One of us would die if we kept this up and all it was doing was destroying us both.

I nodded in understanding, wiping my eyes free of my sorrow and approaching him slowly. He stepped into my embrace and held me to his chest. His body was twice as wide, his fists able to kill me with one blow. Yet my death would be at the weakness he was displaying, his shaking plea to let him go. And I would. I would tell him goodbye just to save him. To save us. His thick arms encased me and I held on for dear life.

"I'm sorry," I whispered, taking his face between the palms of my hands.

"Sienna..."

I silenced him with my mouth, savoring his taste as I said my wordless goodbye. He lifted me with ease, my legs wrapping around his torso on their own accord. He dropped to his knees, the scent of earth drifting closer as my back met the cold leaves. I tugged his lips to mine, devouring his harsh kiss and moaning into his mouth. Pulling back for a moment, he stared at me with the same lost look. Then he dropped to his elbows on top of me, sweeping a trail of kisses from my ear to my breasts.

He took me, slow and sweet, in the middle of the woods that seemed more fitting for my burial than his passion. I guess, in a sense, I was burying my heart beneath the cold earth. I couldn't stop the tears that flowed, crying harder when he kissed them away.

I was a vessel of emotions—pleasure and pain—with no guidance as they took control. I cried harder and hated every second of it but loved the buzz that was left in its wake. His hands were all over me, memorizing each curve. His kisses touching every sensitive part of my body until I couldn't take it anymore and crashed. I tipped over the brink of sanity as my mind gave up fighting.

I knew that falling out of love was going to be the hardest thing I'd ever have to do. I steeled my spine, my stiffened body forcing him off me. He helped me to my feet and we cleaned ourselves off as everything inside me wanted to scream.

Everything that we had was gone… There was no gravity tethering us together anymore.

"How do we get back to the car?"

He looked over his shoulder, the tenderness gone. His chest was heaving while the molten lava was dripping the honey pools into a violent storm. He laughed, catching me off guard as anger replaced the lofty sound. I silently followed him out of the clearing as his mumbling returned, mixing with pockets of delirium.

"Motherfucker!" he belted out suddenly, turning to the nearest tree and imbedding his fist into it over and over.

"Stop!" I *knew* I should take caution. "Apollo, stop it!" But I didn't.

My scream caught his attention, his entire body twisting into an unrecognizable hellhound that was charging at me. I couldn't tell my legs to run before he was on me. I jumped backwards, landing on my ass, as he loomed above me. This was the face hundreds of men saw prior to their brutal murder—a part of himself he kept hidden from me.

And now I understood why.

My hands shook as I kept them raised, too scared to touch him as he hovered over my face. His lip raised in a dancing snarl, his jaw clattering under the pressure and his eyebrow raised in challenge.

I was goddamn petrified. For once in my life, I couldn't say *he wouldn't hurt me*. I was near certain he needed to hurt me, to cross that line he knew there was no coming back from.

"Pl-please." Sienna Agostino was dead and buried. In her place was a scared little girl who had gotten in way over her head. I'd begged for this, for him to lose control. And he finally gave it to me.

I'd never regretted anything more in my life.

And then he was gone. I was suffocating. I was a tortured soul, unable to be fixed, and everyone just needed to let me go. He slowly started to disappear into the trees, but I couldn't tell myself to go after him. Bears. Bears sounded like something I could deal with more than him. To be caught in a metal cage with him like this, no thank you. I waited a few minutes, allowing myself to calm down before brushing off the dirt from my ass and following in his wake.

I took a few deep, calming breaths and got my head on straight. I just needed to get back to the city and then this was over. I was going to start on my own, maybe take Alexei or Romano up on their offers. Disappear into a new life, one far less complicated than the one I'd been given at birth.

"Motherfucker!" he roared in the close distance.

Only… he wasn't alone. I heard more voices cursing, feet shuffling, and what sounded like a fight at the street's edge. I charged through the clearing of trees, watching three men circle Apollo, who was heaving like a rabid beast. A fourth man was at the driver's side door, trying to jimmy it open.

Lovely. A carjacking on top of an already shitty day.

"Lookie what we got here, boys." One of the dead men laughed, staring at me. "So pretty."

They fucked with the wrong car, the wrong passengers. Their mistake was going to be their death. Apollo glanced at me before rolling his shoulders and returning his attention to the men.

"Come here, honey. We'll give you a ride home." The one idiot reached out a hand, turning his back on Apollo—a fatal mistake.

"Don't touch her." Apollo grabbed him by the scruff of his neck, throwing him to the side like he weighed nothing. "Sienna." He pointed to the spot next to him and I moved to follow his command.

The guy breaking into the car managed to get the door open, the screaming alarm barely noticeable over my hammering heart. He stepped forward, approaching his three friends as they regarded him.

"Not so fast." One reached out, tugging my back to his front and placing a knife to my throat. "This could've been easy if you would have just let us take the car. Now I'm gonna hurt her... and make you watch."

"What did you just say? Say it louder," I told the idiot holding me. "You just signed your own death certificate. *Riposare in pace.*"

"No, honey. Your boyfriend's dead, and you'll wish you were." He laughed, sniffing my hair.

"Hey," I whispered so he'd bring his ear closer. "He's not my boyfriend. He's the fucking reaper." I pulled my head forward, then back, crashing it into his.

The sickening crunch of his nose echoed with his bellowing agony. I rammed my elbow into his side and charged forward, except I tripped, landing painfully on my side behind Apollo. I rolled over, only able to sit with my jaw slacked, and watched the horror movie unfold in slow motion. Apollo didn't just kill them; he maimed them.

Limbs were broken, the flesh on the inside hanging out. He wedged his fingers into another's eyeballs before turning their own knife on them—gutting them from throat to groin. There was so much blood, terrifying screams, and mutilated body parts. I felt my stomach turn before I twisted and released the contents on the pavement. Apollo was a raging animal. I half expected to see him chewing on their bones.

He stopped for a moment, ripping off his blood-stained shirt and throwing it to the ground. It made no difference; his chest was soaked with their blood and entrails. He watched me in silence, his chest heaving as I wiped the spit from my chin. He took one step closer, but I crawled backwards, unsure if he would hurt me too.

"Freeze!"

I turned towards the sound. Two highway patrol cops stared in shock, looking between the dismembered corpses, Apollo, and me. They were barking commands at him to raise his hands and drop to his knees, but he didn't move. The twitch in his shoulder told me he was hyperfocused on me, as I pushed to my feet and forced my palms up towards the sky.

"Ma'am, are you all right?" One officer motioned for me to come to him. "I said freeze!" he shouted at Apollo when he started moving.

"Stop right there or I'll shoot!" the other screamed, but his terror made him hesitate. For just a moment. But it was long enough for Apollo to tackle him, throwing him into his partner. All three of them clattered to the ground. Mace was sprayed, commands were barked, and Apollo just kept grappling. He was going to kill one of them if not both, so I had to do something.

He had the officers on their backs, one on top of the other as he held them in place, attacking with his meaty fists. I saw a large branch to the side and moved towards it before quietly stepping up behind him. It took two strong swings against the back of his head to have him stumbling enough that they were able to take control. They got him onto his stomach with is hands cuffed behind his back before he snapped out of it.

"Apollo, enough." I stood in front of him, hands raised in surrender, to keep him calm.

"Ma'am." One of the cops gripped my arm, tugging me behind him.

Big mistake.

Cuffs be damned, Apollo charged at him, ignoring the taser that was pinned in his back. They fought with him for a bit before I picked up the branch once more, this time standing in front of him so he could see me.

"Want another?" I asked, my words finally giving him pause. He stood tall, one of the cops dangling from him with a hand around his neck. "Get in the car. I will call Lucky."

When he turned towards the SUV, the cop dropped from his back, flopping to the concrete in a panting, bleeding mess. I stopped Apollo long enough to take the car keys from his pocket. He turned sideways to squeeze his large body into the tight confines. I placed a chaste kiss to his head and shut the door.

"Quite an interesting sight."

I stalled to stare at the newcomer. Romano was leaning against my door while Romeo chatted with one of the still-conscious officers.

"Wh-what are you doing here?"

His scar danced as he clenched his teeth, taking in the scene before him. "Chivalry isn't dead, evidently." He tugged on his cufflinks. "Your chariot." He motioned me towards his idling car, and without a second thought, I complied.

I climbed into the vehicle, wanting nothing more than to escape. I didn't look twice at the battered bodies on the ground as we peeled out from the shoulder. I called my brother and he answered on the second ring, questioning my whereabouts.

"You need to call an attorney," I interrupted him. "This is going to cost you big time, my darling brother." I ignored my shaking hands, panting as the adrenaline started to fade and exhaustion took over.

"Where are you? What did he do?" He started shouting for my father to call the attorney.

I relayed the gruesome scene to him, explaining all that I'd witnessed and the issues Apollo was going to have with the police. I skipped the part about our once-tender goodbye in the woods. "I'm half an hour from the compound. Lucky, I..."

"Sienna, get home. We got you." He was yelling more in the background. "Do you want to stay on the phone with me?" His voice softened.

I pushed myself into the seat, away from Romano and Romeo in the front. "He... he tore them to shreds, Lucky." I swallowed roughly, the images forever burned into my brain, while giving my brother a graphic play-by-play with each explicit detail. "He's officially lost it. Fuck, it was so bad. I won't fight anymore. I-I... We... Lucky, I'm going to leave the city."

Romano took the phone from me. "I've got her." He didn't speak for a moment, just listened to my brother before agreeing and hanging up.

"What were you doing up this way?"

Romano glanced at Romeo, having a silent conversation before answering. "Your father called and asked for support." He said it so simply, as if he hadn't just rushed in to save me.

"Oh."

He coughed out a chuckle, laughing at my expense. "Would you care to elaborate on your plans to leave the city?"

I didn't know how to answer him. So, instead, I stared out the window as we rushed back home. I had so many things I wanted to say, had so many thoughts swirling in my head. As I stared at my distorted reflection in the tinted glass, I wished I had a pair of scissors. I'd cut off all the parts that he'd touched, destroy the flesh like he'd done my heart.

"I'm forced to be the lead character of their play, conforming to their needs. An award-winning actress, playing the role they chose. But if they open their eyes to the truth, my lies would destroy them." I ran my pointer finger across the window, painting an unknown image as my voice dropped to a whisper, "Instead I let them destroy me."

"You crave a feeling of belonging, but you don't fit into their puzzle." He stared out the windshield. "So, again, I ask *what are your plans?*"

I told him I couldn't answer—that it was a mystery even to me. As much as he didn't deserve my continued loyalty, I'd make sure Apollo was freed. The silence was all that remained the rest of the ride, until we pulled down the long drive.

"Will you tell me?" Romano stopped me from leaving. "When you know."

I nodded and closed the door. As I made my way to the front of the house, I saw my entire family on the steps waiting for me. The moment of serenity was ruined when I recalled all the wrongs they'd enacted against me.

"I need every detail." A female voice came from behind my father, a woman in a power suit stepping around him.

"Please, this way." Marco appeared out of nowhere and guided the young beauty into the house.

"Christ," Al muttered, as Bella added, "We don't need this, Marco."

"Let's get this over with," I urged everyone forward.

"Oh, God..." Bella gasped, causing everyone to turn in her direction. Her face paled as she stared back and forth between me and my mother. She clapped a hand across her mouth and charged past Lucky, shoving Al as she barreled into the bathroom. The door didn't even close before we all heard her gagging and emptying her stomach into the bowl.

"Maybe a shower first, dear," my mother admonished—only then did we notice the blood on my shirt... and now on hers.

Ignoring her request, I entered my father's office and listened to the attorney weave a story for me to repeat. She spun some crazy tale of wild animals, heroic Apollo saving the damsel—coincidentally me—while coming to the aid of the two officers. She stated from the images I'd described, an animal attack sounded accurate. I had no clue how this was going to work, but her confidence made me believe her.

Lucky and Al disappeared behind the attorney as she left, bound for the police department. I flopped into the chair in the center of my father's office.

"Lucky said you want to leave." My father claimed the seat beside me.

"It's for the best." I smiled, patting his leg and refusing to elaborate. "I have several things to handle first, then I will make *my* own plan."

"And who is included in that plan?" Romano stood in the foyer.

There he was, the man I thought could save me from myself—from my family. Only now did I realize that he was the same type of man I was trying to avoid, just from a different city. I wanted out, away from all these mafia games. His dark eyes turned almost black, as if he could read my thoughts.

"Get dressed. I want to take you out." Romano left little room for argument, but even as I stared at him in suspense, my fight dwindled. "Your father gave his *blessing*."

What a curious word. And even more curious... was the fact that I was too tired to fight, so I agreed.

My father was unusually quiet, his eyes flicking between us. The man I adored, the man that slayed the monsters under my bed, was long gone. His two daughters had been destroyed—one leaving, the other still missing. The realization settled heavily on my shoulders as I noticed just how much he'd aged.

My hair was mostly dry as I ran a brush through it and piled the locks into a high ponytail, adding a slight curl to the ends. I kept my makeup natural with a light blush and winged liner. I added several thousands in diamonds to my ears and neck before stepping into my *Oscar de la Renta Magnolia Guipure* lace dress. I then added my bright-red *Louboutin* pumps to add a pop of color. One last glance in the mirror, and I hated the reflection silently judging me.

"Mirror, mirror on the wall… tell me I'm the perfect queen." I ran a palm across the image staring back at me before heading out.

"I win that bet, Romeo." Romano stepped closer to the bottom of the stairs, his hand out to help me into the foyer. "He said I'd picked the wrong venue because this time of night you'd be anything less than stellar."

I smiled as he whisked me out of the house, Romeo holding my door open for me. The sound of Frank Sinatra crooning in the background was the only noise the entire ride. We drove just outside the city to an opulent restaurant I'd never been to before.

We stepped inside and the dining room was filled with people, all stopping to stare. They watched in silence, too frightened to speak as we were ushered into a private section. The room was a wide-open space with a single table, two chairs, and long-stem roses placed in the center. It was only illuminated by candles, the light from the outside diminished as Romeo closed us inside. The chatter and slight music from the other room was muted, a calming silence settling between us. Afraid of having nothing to say, I was saved by two waiters who quickly filled our wine glasses.

The conversation was light and friendly, normal and enjoyable. We laughed about the most asinine things. Once again, I was taken aback by how easy it was between us. He seemed interested in continuously getting to know me and for a brief second, I allowed myself to enjoy the moment.

Until he ruined it.

"You seem particularly close to your father."

I nodded, my hackles rising. I knew what was coming next.

"What secrets does the illusive Mario Agostino keep from his favorite daughter?"

It wasn't necessarily the question that irked me; it was the tone and serious expression that accompanied it. I remained quiet, while the anticipation of which way this would go seemed to clog my throat. I was officially skeptical of the man in front of me.

A man with many faces.

"The skeletons in his closet are breaking free, Sienna. Who else will pay for his sins?" Romano's finger lightly traced the rim of his glass.

I was no longer interested in where the night could lead us. I tossed my own wine glass back, swallowing the contents in one gulp before dropping my napkin on my plate. The scar on his chiseled face suddenly mocked me.

My father had trusted him enough to come and get me when I needed rescuing. Romano had seemed to be in agreement with whatever matter they were drawing up between them. Yet, here and now, this individual before me seemed ready for a fight with the head of New York.

"What's the matter, Sienna? Daddy got your tongue?" He looked at his watch.

"I think it's time you took me home." I pulled back my chair the same moment Romeo stepped into the room, his kind face suddenly closed off.

"Have you ever wondered if *Daddy* wasn't telling you everything?" Romano smiled as my attention snapped to him. "Mario has lost control of his city and is handing a flaming pile of shit to your brother. And then there is Octavia."

"Do not. Talk about her," I warned, my palms itching as I clenched them together.

"Does anyone in your family? To me, it seems she's off-topic and no one is wondering why she doesn't want to come home." He slowly rose from the table, taking another sip of wine. "Funny how your *weakest link* was able to escape. Don't you think?

"I'll get my own ride home." I reached into my clutch for my phone, his calloused grip stopping me.

"Now, now. I didn't mean to upset you." He motioned towards the door. "I protect *things* in my care and promised your father I'd get you home in one *piece*."

I hid the shiver that took over my other senses.

Once again, someone looked at me as a possession.

I didn't wait for security as I walked through the dining room. My head held high, even if my insides were screaming. What the hell just happened? It almost seemed like a threat, but in the same breath… like he was trying to tell me something about my sister.

How did he know she didn't want to come home?

"Your father told me."

I jumped, realizing I'd asked it aloud.

"Your father needs more help than he's telling you."

"What aren't *you* telling me, Romano?" The car came to a stop in front of the compound several minutes later, security lining the front of the house. "What was the point of this dinner?"

"I enjoyed the company." He got out and walked around to my door. "Until next time." He kissed my hand before climbing back into the car and I watched it pull down the drive.

As if in slow motion, I turned on my heel with my clutch in my hands and floated into the house. Security opened the door and I drifted inside, ignoring everyone as I continued up the stairs to my room. I closed the door lightly and went through the motions of getting ready for bed.

Romano wasn't at all what he appeared. I kept replaying the conversation over and over, coming up with more questions than when I'd started.

What the hell was up Romano's sleeve?

Tonight was the last straw. The single thread that broke me and made my plans transparent. My family wanted me gone? Well, they'd won. I'd finish what I needed and then I'd disappear.

I had a confession to make. *Nobody owned me.* And damn if that realization didn't feel good.

CHAPTER 16

SIENNA AGOSTINO

It was funny how, at first, my family had all but forced me to leave. But now that I was planning to go on my own accord, they feigned sadness. As if they assumed they could dictate the specifics.

The dinner a few weeks ago was the last time I'd talked to Romano. Whenever my father asked, I changed the subject. I had nothing to say.

What could I tell him? He asked me a bunch of prying questions about you and the family? That you should start a war off a gut feeling?

Alexei and I had come up with the plan. We'd squared away most of the pending deals and prepared my team to handle the rest. I had one last client I was going to meet for dinner before it solidified everything on our to-do list. The new client wanted to sell a patent for a state-of-the-art security system he'd created. I was going to meet with him this evening, then tomorrow Alexei and I were gone. My family knew I had plans, but they didn't know the details. It wasn't their place to worry about me anymore. I'd hired a COO to run *Energia* and had a secured channel they could use to contact me. But that was it. I wanted to be a ghost as we worked to bring Octavia home.

I'd done my part. Apollo was released with time served, after my heartfelt testimony deeming him a hero. Bella told me the first thing Apollo did when he got out was search for me. But I'd been hiding at Nikolai's compound in New Jersey. Alexei's uncle was back in Russia, handling *Bratva* business, and allowed me refuge.

I only spoke to Bella, who kept me apprised of Apollo's continued unraveling. It was so hard to breathe. I needed him like I needed air, but the pain of our separation was going to be my cure. He went through bouts of anger that were pointed at everyone but himself. If it wasn't at me, it was my family for *hiding* me. My father and brother would eventually get him back under control and he could return to their side. And I would get some peace. Maybe even find a new Apollo—a less toxic version—to settle down with.

Now that was comical. Goddamn sad *but* comical.

"Where are we?" I asked my driver. I was so lost in my own misery that I hadn't noticed we were on the side of the road. It was raining, an absolutely miserable night that matched my miserable mood. I couldn't make out much besides the trees to our right and the dreary, darkened clouds looming above.

"Where are we?" I asked my driver. I was so lost in my own misery that I hadn't noticed we were on the side of the road. It was raining, an absolutely miserable night that matched my miserable mood. I couldn't make out much besides the trees to our right and the dreary sky looming above us.

I was forever cloaked by the dark cloud that followed me.

Usually that thought was metaphorical, but now it was physical as the car was pelted by a sudden flood of torrential raindrops.

"Sorry, miss, engine problems." My driver slid out of the car before I could respond. The hood raised and blocked my view of the road ahead of us. Pulling out my cell phone, I started checking emails before an odd noise caught my attention. Dread settled into my gut, but I swallowed back my nerves and opened the door, stepping out into the storm. In more ways than one…

"Everything okay?" I shouted as I approached the front of the car.

"Sienna." My name was called out from behind me.

Haunted. Distant. And *fucking* angry.

"W-what're you doing here?" I hated the weakness in my voice but the animosity in *his* rattled me.

"I've come for you. Isn't that what you wanted?" He took a step forward and I took two back, calling for the driver. "He's dead." The words came without remorse. "He was going to hurt you. I saved you, Sienna. Just like in one of your fairy tales." He was mocking me, his vacant eyes burning with cruelty.

"What do you want from me?" I rushed forward. Fuck self-preservation. I always knew my temper would be the death of me. "Tell me!" I slammed my fists into his chest, my pain and guilt driving each blow.

"I find it absolutely insulting that you haven't thanked me yet."

My heart was lodged in my throat as he pulled me closer. "No." I tried to push him back but all I could do was continue to flail my arms. He ignored me, grabbing both of my hands in one of his and slamming my body against the car. He pinned me in place, his much larger torso rubbing into mine. I could feel his arousal against my stomach and dread cemented my limbs, stalling my fight as if I were somehow locked in his palpable animosity.

"Fine. I'll *make* you thankful." He wrapped his free hand around my throat and tugged me forward. His muscles flexed and the tattoos on his arm seemed to dance with the movement. Mocking me.

I latched on to his wrist, scratching his skin as he opened the back door and threw me inside the car. When my pencil skirt hindered my legs from widening, he shredded it down the center and stepped between them. His fingertips roamed from my thighs, up to my panties, and rubbed me through the fine silk. He hummed his appreciation before traveling north, groping my breasts and pinching my nipples through the material of my shirt.

I managed to wrap both hands around his wrist and tug. Then, using all the force I could muster, I bent it backwards. He reached out on instinct, slamming his meaty fist into my cheekbone. My brain bounced around my skull for a second before my nails found his face, embedding into the flesh until I could feel the trickle of blood.

"I fucking hate you for what you've done!" I screamed, kicking out at him. He was temporarily taken aback, and I sought my moment to attack with everything I had. He fell out of the car and I climbed across the center console, trying to get into the driver's seat. Before I could, he grabbed my ankle and jerked. My face slammed into the gear shaft and blood erupted from my nose.

"You know you want this. I saw it in your eyes when you came to visit me. You wanted me to use this body, so there would never be anyone else after I was done with you." He kept pulling me.

I tried to catch myself as my stomach slid off the seat and my shoulder took the impact as I plummeted onto the concrete. "No, please. Don't do this."

He dumped my body into the overgrown grass and ripped off his suit jacket, dropping it beside me before reaching for his zipper. His hand was heavy against the center of my chest, pinning me down and making it hard to breathe while the rain coated my face and soaked my remaining clothing, chilling me to my bones.

"Please don't," I begged in a half whisper as I felt him tug my panties to the side and settle his erection at my entrance.

"That's it, baby." He licked along my jawline. "Give me those filthy lies. Pretend you don't want this."

My brain was foggy, my fight dwindled, and the blood in my veins stalled as he slammed into me. This was it. This was the moment I died. It didn't matter if I physically survived his assault. Because, either way, Sienna Agostino was dead. He pulled back and slammed into me harder, the wet grass slicking my spine and gliding me through the mud.

I turned my head, unable to look at the traitorous bastard so keen on destroying me. I prided myself on the fact that I was strong. That I'd overcome the stereotypes of being born a woman in the mafia. Then shattered my image by believing it somehow made me worthy of love, a ridiculous ideology that women were given at a young age.

And, in the end, it ruined me.

He was so large I couldn't see past his body, unable to beg the stars for reprieve. But God must have turned his back on me long ago. It was the only explanation I had in this moment. There was a time when

I believed people were given trials and tribulations in order to teach them a lesson. A message sent from a higher power to tell us something. There were instances where it took a while to understand while others seemed to slap you in the face without much thought. I needed God to tell me what this was supposed to mean. What lesson I was meant to learn. Instead, it was the devil who heard my please and showed me the way out.

And I understood. I saw it.

The handle sticking out from under his discarded jacket. Just within reach. I looked up and his eyes were filled with lust, devoid of the man who'd once protected me. There was no redemption after this. Not for him and not for me. I was done with my heart getting broken again and again. My body was overwhelmed with agony as he pounded into me. Harder and harder with each thrust.

My chest ached but I knew I had to do it. My arm stretched forward, my fingers digging into the mud until I felt the cool, hard metal. It was slippery in my grip, but I managed to pull it closer. He dropped onto his elbows, his face inches from mine as he panted against me. "You fucking love it. You love everything I do to you." His breaths became faster, harsher.

"Lies. It's all goddamn lies."

He stopped thrusting for a moment to stare down at me in shock.

"You may think you've *ruined* me. But I'll fucking end you." I raised my arm.

"You don't have the balls…" He stopped when I pressed the barrel to his temple. My heart was beating out of my chest, and for a moment, I thought he was right. I thought… *I can't.* I can't do this to *him*—but this man didn't deserve anything from me. Nothing but hatred.

"Your tiny balls smacking against my ass are nothing compared to the ones in my designer panties." It was raining harder now. "Fuck. You." And I pulled the trigger.

His blood sprayed in the air, mixing with the rain and pouring down over me like a hailstorm of carnage and brain matter. I could taste it in my mouth and was overcome by the sudden urge to dry heave. His large body dropped onto mine, and an agonized cry expelled from somewhere so deep within me that my throat burned as I extinguished it. All the pain, anger, sadness, and guilt transformed the scream into a crescendo of despair.

I did it. I fucking killed him. I didn't know what I expected to feel after pulling the trigger, but this wasn't it. I was numb. A huge part of me died along with him, and there was no coming back from it.

"Look what you made me *fucking* do!" I hissed into the air, the numbness fading as a fresh wave of guilt tore at the shattered remnants of my heart. I needed to leave. To go far away. From my family and their city before it was too late. There was already nothing good left of me and seeing *their* hatred would only make *me* hate myself worse. I knew if I stayed, I'd never survive.

Not after what I'd done.

Headlights pulled up behind the car and heavy footfalls echoed in the distance. Charging towards me. "Sienna!" my brother shouted as I struggled to shift the body off me. "Sienna! Fuck! What did you do? How could... Sienna!" he grunted my name. Bella sounded from behind us, and the realization had me choking on air. "No! Bella, baby, stay back!" Lucky helped roll the dead weight to the side, pulling me to my feet and wrapping his suit jacket around me.

"No..." Bella whispered, and my gaze snapped to hers. The look she gave me added to the torment I'd already inflicted on myself. There would be no reparations for our relationship. I'd ruined my family. "What did you do?" Tears filled her mismatched eyes as she tried charging forward, but my brother pulled her into his arms, holding her tight as she broke.

"I can't believe you fucking did this." Lucky sounded distant, a radio static filled my head, and I barely felt the harsh bite of the pavement as my body slammed into it.

It wasn't all that long ago that I had begged this man to give me everything I wanted, everything I thought I deserved. I thought he'd be my savior in a world built by men and against women. I wanted to be the queen on the arm of the mad king. Instead, he broke me beyond repair—something I thought I already was, but quickly realized I wasn't. Not even close.

Until now.

I rolled onto my side, pulling my knees to my chest, and stared at his motionless body. I did it. I killed him. I thought I'd feel better. But his lifeless eyes stared back at me, forever cemented in my brain. Left to haunt me.

They were the last thing I saw before everything went black. That one thought playing over and over in my mind.

I killed him. I killed... Gio Moretti.

"Where is she?" Apollo exited the second car and charged forward. "Sienna!"

I swayed on the spot. Just hearing his voice had me wanting to break my promises of leaving. But one glance at Bella crying over her brother's lifeless corpse, and I knew I had to go. I felt like I was having an out-of-body experience, seeing all of this from a million miles above. I'd killed before, but never someone I'd known so *personally*.

"Are you okay?" Apollo asked, holding me at arm's length. "No…" That one word was spoken so harshly as he stared at my legs.

I looked down and realized what he was focused on. Bella and Lucky followed his line of sight, looking at my shredded skirt and bleeding thighs. I tried covering myself, clinging to my brother's jacket, but Apollo ripped it from me. I glanced at Lucky, who was glaring at Gio's body in disgust.

"Did…" Apollo coughed. "Did he…?"

My head dropped and I gave the smallest nod.

Bella was caressing her belly as her tears turned angry. She stared at me, her eyes a picture of pity and sadness. I didn't want it.

This too shall pass, I thought. *Eventually…*

"It's going to be okay." Apollo wrapped his arms around me, hugging me tight. "I've got you."

As much as I didn't want to, I pushed out of his hold. My body began trembling as realization settled in, the adrenaline fully depleted. I heard voices but they sounded distant, a radio static filling my head. I barely felt the pavement as my body slammed forward.

"Not until her attorney is present." Apollo's tone stirred me from a miserable sleep. "She won't waive her right to counsel, John."

"Wh-at? Where am I?" I covered my eyes with my hands, the bright light assaulting my already-pounding head.

"The hospital," Alexei said, suddenly at my side and shutting off the overhead light.

"I need a statement." It was John, the FBI agent.

"Later."

I hated how I wanted to seek shelter in Apollo's embrace as he controlled the room.

"Miss Agostino, I need a few moments—"

John was cut off by Alexei rushing around the bed. The three of them started shoving each other and arguing before a horde of security and nurses stormed inside. I closed my eyes, swallowing past the nausea that had settled in my belly.

"Enough." My father pushed through the door, looking between the three of them before clearing the room. "Don't scare me like that again," he said, once everyone was out of earshot.

"Sorry." I had no idea why I was apologizing. It was my name and the allegiance to my family that had gotten me…

Oh…

I stared at my father as tears filled my eyes and more nausea coated my stomach, threatening to haul out of my throat.

Gio… He… I… I was…

I couldn't even think the word. Four letters had never held so much power over me before.

"Sienna, don't cry. Please." The pain in my father's voice was messing with my spastic emotions and I couldn't handle it. "I'm sorry for everything. I swear I won't fail this family anymore."

His sincerity gave me pause. I blinked past the tears to take in the shattered man before me. My father was gone and a shell of the powerful man was left in his wake. All his past sins had come to haunt him, wreaking terror on his children, wearing on his shoulders, and embedding shrapnel into his soul.

"I promise. I am going to get down on my knees and make peace with God. I will move heaven and hell to right all my wrongs for you and Octavia."

"We don't need your prayers to save our souls. Just find her." I gripped his hand.

"Sienna, I need you to go to Philly." My jaw dropped as he continued to urge, "I mean it, Sienna. Leave. Pick Romano."

"What the hell does Romano have to do with this?" I winced, shifting in the bed as my abdomen pinched with pain.

He glanced at my hand on my stomach, the truth coming to the surface. "Did… Did Gio?" He couldn't speak the words either, yet he expected me to show strength by admitting the truth.

"The wicked won't ever rest, not with the taste of blood still lingering on their lips. There's nothing sweeter…"

And now I sounded like Apollo, with my pretty words and hidden meanings.

"Sienna, Romano is a good man. Leave New York and live a life where you can be happy."

I stared into the eyes that matched my own, except his were devoid of everything.

"I've been brokering a deal for your protection." Life. Extinguished.

"Let's not pretend like this isn't the end." Sienna Agostino was gone and someone more powerful would rise in her place. "Another city. Another made man. Another travesty against me. Let me go, Daddy."

"Romano will take—" He started but I cut him off.

"It's my choice!" I hadn't realized I was shouting until my brother stormed into the room, watching us both closely.

"Sienna, calm down," Lucky chastised me, and his blatant disrespect did me in.

"Calm down? You… You want me to calm down?" I licked my lips, enjoying how their expressions twisted with shock. "*Your* brother-in-law raped me and you want me to calm down?" I laughed harder.

"We're a family, Sienna. We will get through this together." Lucky lifted his palms, approaching me like I was a wounded animal.

"Octavia is missing and doesn't want to come home. Gio. Gio hurt me. And you think *we'll* get through this *together*?" I laughed until I was gasping for air, drawing the attention of a group of nurses. "I vote we set fire to this family tree because we're all fucked."

The doctor pushed into the room, with several nurses, and ushered my family out. One of the nurses came to my side, whispering that someone needed to speak with me alone—a young woman. I was scared she meant Bella, but I swallowed back my panic and nodded.

Once the hallway was clear, the door opened, and a blonde pixie stepped inside. "Hi." Persephone smiled and I was in awe of what I saw.

She was beautiful. No one could deny that. But gone was the wild, vacant eyes and crazy mannerisms. She was calm, seemingly at peace. She'd been locked away to heal, but I didn't anticipate this level of tranquility. She smiled down at me like she could read my thoughts before reaching for my chart.

"Why would they have you on so many antibiotics..." She dropped the paperwork, her mouth open but nothing coming out.

"Yeah," I muttered, my chin quivering as I attempted to school my features.

"Don't. Don't you fucking dare," she scolded. "This is on *him*. You do not feel sorry for yourself."

It took a moment for me to calm down and listen to what she was saying. She didn't give me the details but the shared experience seemed to bond us. When I looked into her clear-blue eyes, I saw the truth. I would survive this.

"You look good," I said honestly.

"Thanks. Mental health is a bitch when you aren't taking care of it," she scoffed. "I wanted to tell you that you don't have to worry about being charged. John is protecting you. Your name won't be tied to *his* anymore, not even in death."

"Thanks."

She squeezed my hand. "No, thank you, Sienna. You took away all the things that went bump in the night for me." Her sad smile nearly broke me. "Just wish I'd gotten to him before he *touched* you."

"I'm sorry too. I should've ended the game earlier."

She shook her head at me, wiping away a tear. "Listen. I think I know where your sister is. Innocents don't deserve to be hurt in someone else's game. Once I know who we are dealing with for sure, I'll tell your brother."

"Tell me first," I spit out quickly. "I'm leaving. Disappearing. But when you find her, I'll bring in reinforcements."

She nodded after a moment before asking, "How is Apollo?"

As if he could hear us, he stood on the other side of the glass, his spine straightening just as Dom Moretti walked up. I took a deep breath, causing Persephone to glance over her shoulder.

"Don't worry. He's happy he's gone. We each have our own scars from Gio Moretti, his brother included."

Dom gave her a panty-dropping grin, beckoning her to his side. Apollo was staring at me, ignoring everyone else in the room. I had an image of the old Apollo, the one who was clothed in an expensive suit and watched me with a feral, yet calm intensity. After everything, our two biggest moments were born from our biggest setbacks—his swim in the Hudson and my rape.

The doctor walked in again, and Persephone smiled and patted my hand. "Once I confirm the details, I'll give you first dibs."

I continued to stare at Apollo on the other side of the glass, the only thing separating us. The bile rising in my throat belonged to him. I was so tired of being here. My whole life I'd been held back by irrational love and a false perception of *what if.*

I hated him.

Something caught my attention and I turned back to the doctor. "I'm sorry. What did you say?"

I was tired. Spent. Exhausted.

I didn't think this night could get any worse. Life seemed to have a way of fucking me, but it couldn't get me off. The doctor loomed over me for a few more minutes before I pretended to fall asleep while ignoring Apollo wandering to my side. I had nothing to say and didn't want to hear his bullshit.

It was too late and too many things had broken us. The decision had already been made for me to go, but now it was cemented in place. No one could protect me from him… only me.

And that meant leaving. As soon as the doctors released me, I was escaping this hell and following my exit plan.

Disappearing.

CHAPTER 17
ROMANO BIANCHI

W*here the fuck is she? She's ruining everything.*

CHAPTER 18

APOLLO DELUCA

"Will the defendant please rise," someone commanded but I barely registered their words as I followed the motions. "In the light of Miss Agostino's testimony, the prosecutor has dropped all charges." The judges gavel pounded the counter, the sound reverberating in my mind.

My attorney turned to look at me. "Honestly, I was betting 60/40 you were leaving here with a set of permanent bracelets." Her amusement was at my expense.

"Great." I flexed as they removed my cuffs.

"You realize it was all Sienna, right?" The sound of her name on my attorney's lips forced me to glare in her direction. "Even after whatever you did to her, that girl is still loyal." She turned on her heel and strutted away.

Loyal. Sienna was loyal to a fault.

"She's right, you know." Bella caught my attention as we stood in front of the courthouse. "Sienna is loyal. To you. To this family. Sound familiar?"

There was that word again.

Loyalty: noun. The state or quality of being loyal; faithfulness to *commitment or obligations. An example or instance of faithfulness, adherence or the like.*

I had plenty of time to think while I was locked away and made a few neuropathic connections. Studies had implicated that the striatum, an area in the brain known for calculating anticipated rewards, was directly associated with loyalty and faithfulness. Sienna likely experienced increased activity in the striatum, proving loyalty was associated with benefits of greater emotional attachment.

I'd always assumed she had a vicarious limbic structure that was overwhelmed when it came to behavioral and emotional outbursts. The limbic system was located deep within the brain, interconnected structures that controlled one's emotional state.

But when you took everything into consideration, it all came down to the same variable.

"Her loyalty is a shield. It shows you she will do anything for you, no matter what it does to her," Bella continued. "You hide behind loyalty much the same, except it closes you off to believing you can't be anything else."

Fuck.

"She'll probably gift that loyalty to someone else. Someone who appreciates it."

My neck snapped in her direction. The thought of someone else touching Sienna made me murderous.

"She isn't going to come back," Bella added with a shake of her head.

"Yes, she is. Even if I have to drag her back by her fucking hair."

I cracked my knuckles, ignoring Bella's muttered, "Finally," as I left the courtroom behind me, in search of a certain mafia princess.

Sienna had disappeared. Her normal pattern of behavior would have her returning once she composed herself. Her absence spoke volumes to the discord that continued to plague this family.

Sienna turning Gio's own gun on him set in motion an uncontrolled cataclysm. Enemies were materializing out of thin air, looking for their pound of flesh. We'd learned Gio had legally bound, open contracts with hitmen—who'd been prepaid to avenge his death.

And I continued to work diligently to ensure Sienna's name was kept out of the mix. The underworld was guessing, at best, that the Agostino offspring were involved, while I was lining up one body after another, keeping my promise to protect this family.

Especially her.

Gio had taken what didn't belong to him. Had taken what *belonged* to me. And I wanted… no, I *needed* her back.

"Where have you been?" Mario stopped me.

I held my breath, using my newest coping mechanism to stifle my uncontrollable rage. I counted in my head as I pressed my thumb to each finger before responding. He knew the answer, but harbored such animosity in the wake of so much destruction that he needed to hear it for himself.

I didn't suffer from the fake ideology that I was, socially acceptable or otherwise, *okay* by any definition of the word. I'd closed myself off after the trial, dumbfounded by the repetitive reel in my head of Sienna's loyalty throughout the years. In her absence, the need to speak to her was chronically debilitating as every attempt to find her turned up empty.

Mine. I would protect mine.

"Did you handle them?" His question only infuriated me further, but I swallowed it back and nodded. "Good. On to the next."

Sienna is next, I thought to myself, because I *would* find her. And soon.

His silent dismissal wasn't going to work this time. I'd replaced my entire Brioni collection, rebuilt my apartment in the city, and bought another piece of land near the compound. I was focusing on building a life outside of the mayhem I imposed.

Do not allow these facts to muddle your perception of me. I still did whatever was needed to protect this family.

I needed her return to confirm my hypothesis. It was a logical assessment, the belief that we shared the same sense of duty above all else, but I had to see Sienna to put the puzzle back together. I'd come to the realization her loyalty matched my own. And with that loyalty came ownership.

She belonged to me and I'd kill anyone that came for her.

I climbed into my newest toy, my Lamborghini Veneno Roadster. It cost me almost five million by the time I added a few bonus features. Prior to this, I cared little for the formidable amount of money in my bank account. I wanted things for myself now.

And I wanted her.

"Fuck!" I hissed while narrowly avoiding Al, who was charging towards me from the side yard. "You motherfucker!" I pulled the car to a stop and stepped out, checking the front tire well, which had slipped into the rock embankment.

"Apollo! Those are my hydrangeas!" Isabella Agostino shouted from the stables.

"He made me do it!" It wasn't one of my finer moments, but it was a factually based declaration.

Isabella trotted over on one of her horses, hopping down gracefully and tying her thoroughbred to the fence. She waved for me to reverse my car and before I even stepped out again, I could see her displeasure. Al and I stood side by side, like a pair of petulant children about to be scolded.

"This is the first season I've gotten these damn things to bloom and then here you two come along!" She picked up a snapped blossom. "You! They! Ugh, forget it." Her chin wobbled and my jaw clenched. She yelled out a few choice statements about her inability to *keep nice things intact* before hopping on her horse and taking off across the field. I retrieved my phone from my pocket and looked at Al.

"It's a damn bush," he scoffed, earning himself a palm to the back of the head.

"It's a lot more than that, *asino.*" I called Mario, relaying the message and directing him to Isabella.

I inspected my car once more, turning at the sounds of fast-trotting hooves. Mario raced out of the stables, heading in the same direction his wife had fled. The family was falling apart, and Mario was taking all of it on himself. He'd chosen this life for them and everyone was paying for his mistakes. But he wouldn't let any of us help him through it.

"Was there a reason for your asinine display, other than a death wish?" I inquired, picking a stray piece of nothing off my suit.

"Sienna's apartment alarm was going off." Al's chest heaved as I turned for my car and we sped down the driveway.

We were born, we lived and then we died. To some, it was a daunting truth they preferred to ignore. But when the sun rose on each new day and you awakened to realize you survived again, life was good. If the sunset didn't set you aflame, it was the devil knocking on your door who would drag you to hell.

"You really don't know where she is, do you?" I asked while aggressively honking my horn at a cab.

"I don't." His anger spoke of his truth. "I don't think anyone knows where she is, just that she's okay."

"Unacceptable," some bastard hissed in our direction, and I scoffed at the cab's passenger presently rolling down his window to shout at us. "Talking to you, ya fucking idiot!" He threw spare change at my windshield, the offending copper pinging off my tinted glass.

"*Che cazzo.*" Al chuckled. "No, Apollo!" He reached for my arm, but it was too late.

As I stepped from the car, I shook out my jacket, showing my Glock safely tucked under my midnight-blue Brioni suit. I bent down and picked up one of the pennies from the ground, tossing it into the air and catching it.

"You dropped this." I pinched the dirty copper between my thumb and pointer finger, reaching just past the bastard's window. "Take it."

"Man, I'm s-sorry." He slumped farther back in his seat, trapped like a rat in a small cage.

"I said. Take. It." Then, moving quickly and with deadly precision, I latched my hand on to his jaw and tugged him forward. His mouth opened in shock, and I jammed the penny inside, clamping it closed. He sat immobile, watching me, unsure what was next. "Swallow."

Before I could force the command, Al was at my back, muscling me into my car. "You good?" He slid in beside me and I nodded. "I know you've worked hard to collect yourself. But, shit, did I miss that part of you." His amusement only heightened my serenity.

"If there truly is a god, he made me a sinner and I'm content with who I am." I couldn't hold back the grin ticking the sides of my lips.

"And, fuck, if I haven't missed it."

As much as I didn't want to admit it, *I* missed this back and forth too. I was in control and there was no going back now. I had a lot of wrongs to right and this visit was just the first of many. A part of me was missing in her absence. Something dark and sinister always consumed me but she was the final piece of the puzzle I needed to feel whole.

Tasks like this were what kept my mind busy. Approaching Sienna's apartment, Al and I motioned to each other before breaching it. Slowly, the door slid ajar and I held my position and waited. As expected, they began firing through the opening, quickly depleting what I was sure was their limited arsenal. After a moment of silence, one of the fuckers stepped closer to peek around the corner.

"Hello." I smiled, while his look of dread and the smell of defecation had that smile widening into a full-on grin. It took less than a minute to subdue the intruder and his cohort, both unable to stand their ground.

"I'm not telling you shit!"

I narrowly missed the wad of spit descending towards my Alessandro Galet Scritto Leather Oxfords. Al chuckled, looming over the prone form behind me. I drew my foot back and my three-thousand-dollar loafer broke his tooth, forcing his neck to crack to one side. His incoherent mumbling was a consonance of pride that built within me.

I was back. A rejuvenated version of myself at least.

I unbuttoned my blazer and placed it on a chair, rolling my sleeves to my elbows. I glanced at the counter, faltering as the iridescent metal glinted under the light. A gift I'd given Sienna. "A memento, how fitting." I gripped the cool steel in my hand, enjoying the snap and the glint of the sharpened edge. "The parotid duct is what releases your saliva and I can very easily get to it with one solid swoop of this blade." I waved the knife around for effect.

"N-no... I-I won't-t t-ta—" he stammered.

"Your increased heart rate, erratic breathing, and the sudden rush of epinephrine and adrenalin from your amygdala is inducing that stutter. I suggest we counteract your body's natural response to fear." Slowly, I took in a breath through my nose and exhaled out my mouth. "Here." With a flick of my wrist, the seven-inch serrated knife embedded his hand into the wall. There was a crescendo of screams that made my nerves settle and a visceral calm float around me.

"Looks sharp," Al taunted, the man beneath him moaning.

"Doesn't take much pressure to slice through the risorius and buccinator muscles in the cheek. Then you'll never be able to spit again." Another kick to his face stained my leather shoes red. "A future of drooling and groaning, unable to communicate." I pinched the muscles in question between my fingers, straddling him when I saw the puddle he produced. "There, there." I went to pat his head, stopping at the excessive release of sweat from his eccrine glands. "Who sent you?"

"I-I can't." His shrill voice was like nails on a chalkboard.

"*Can't* insinuates you're unable. You are, in fact, able. Just unwilling. However, I can change that. And I do promise you won't like it." When he didn't answer, I sat back on my haunches. "As you wish."

I stepped to his partner, who was still sprawled beneath Al, the bastard's eyes wide with fear. It was so sad really. They were nobodies, hired for a simple snatch and grab. They wore cheap suits and used too much hair gel. They were attempting to work their way up in an organization that didn't prepare them accordingly.

I lifted my gun, the sound echoing across the marble floors as the bullet tore a hole through his partner's head.

"Are you ready?" I ripped my knife from his hand, dropping to his level as he blabbered with a mixture of snot and tears. "Now, tell me."

"It-it… doesn't matter! I'm already dead!" His good hand was too slow as he struggled to draw his Glock from his back.

"Do it," I challenged, wanting him to have the courage to be a man once in his miserable excuse for a life.

Instead, he raised it in one shaky swoop, pressing the barrel to his throat. But his angle and the bullet trajectory were all wrong as he pulled the trigger. The projectile tore through the omohyoid muscle in his neck, his jugular detaching as he slowly bled out. I watched with a detached fascination as the life drained from his eyes until his body stopped twitching.

"I'll be damned…"

I turned to Al, my eyes dropping to the wallet in his hand.

"He's from Philly."

I stared at Al in confusion, his expression mirroring my own. Either this was a threat against us or an attempt to steal Sienna for himself. Each possibility was just as likely and would be Romano's undoing.

I stepped to the window and stared out at the city that I called home. The calamity of the mafia was hidden amongst the common people who littered the sidewalks. We were a prosperous organization that did what it had to, to earn a profit and protect the streets that belonged to us. Now we had a new threat.

Romano Bianchi wanted to take what didn't belong to him. But he'd never live to tell the tale.

CHAPTER 19
SIENNA AGOSTINO

Someone help me! Please! I didn't want to do it, but he'd never stop! I knew if I didn't kill him, he'd hunt me down until he took everything from me.

Didn't he already do that?

My knees sank into the mud as the rain poured onto my back, my head, and my hands as I listened to Bella's agonized wails. I'd killed her brother, but not before he destroyed several parts of me.

I took a chance and looked around at the people closest to me. My brother stared at the body with a sort of detachment while holding his wife. Apollo seemed unbothered, if not annoyed, knowing this was his mess to clean up. He ran a tender hand down Bella's back, ignoring me as I clutched my stomach. As the endorphins from the attack started to wear off, the pain between my legs was becoming unbearable. I did my best to block it out as I climbed to my feet and gripped the jacket draped across my shoulders.

"Bella," I tried, but she turned into Lucky's embrace.

"Sienna, please." My brother eyed me with concern, but I could tell it was for his wife. Not me.

I was hunched forward, an arm bracing my lower stomach as I fought the looming nausea. I didn't want Gio dead, but didn't they see

168

that it had to be done? They played so many games, for so long, with so many people; where as I had made the correct decision for myself, but could feel their animosity slapping me in the face.

"Did you tell him no?" Apollo's question forced me to look at him. "If we didn't show up, would you have killed him? Or would you have ruled at his side?"

I didn't think. I didn't feel. I just reacted. I lifted my palm and slapped him across the face with everything I had. "How dare you?" My scream bounced around us. "You all did this to me! Because of you, each and every single one of you, I'll never be the same!"

"Fuck." I sat straight up in my bed, staring at the new space I called home in confusion. "Still?" I questioned as I threw the blanket off. The nightmares came randomly, even after all these months.

Going on years…

Their looks of pity, sometimes hate, haunted my subconsciousness and I couldn't seem to shake them. My mind was conjuring conversations with Apollo that hadn't even happened.

I felt like a zombie wandering down the stairs in search of coffee. It was a sad confession that my body was feeling the effects from the sleepless nights and debilitating dreams. I was either highly caffeinated or in a coma. There was no between.

"Did you sleep at all last night?"

I barely acknowledged Alexei, my eyes glued to the coffee maker.

"Sienna, this isn't healthy."

"You're not healthy." I ignored his muttered reply about me being *childish* and added, "I've secured another contract."

"I thought the whole point of getting away was to leave your family *and* work behind." He sipped his own mug, watching me over the brim. "It's been months and yet you're working even harder *now.* Why?"

I refused to voice the answer because it was embarrassing. I'd had time away from *him* to heal myself in more practical ways. But now, I had a whole new reason for living. I should've taken caution when it came to my heart. I wasn't strong enough then, but I am now. I've turned into something my family wouldn't like, but the heartless part of me didn't care. Only one thing kept me going anymore, and I'd cherish it until the day I died.

I didn't need the money. I needed the distraction that work allowed me. It had been a while since Alexei and I fled from the hospital. My records were erased, as if I had never been there. I needed the anonymity to heal myself after the mental and physical trauma that Gio inflicted on me. However, those monsters would never go away. And I could never go home. If I did, they'd all hate me for what I'd done. It didn't matter that it was right, that I'd done it for myself, for my future. They'd hate me all the same. Even worse, I knew if I went home, the look he'd give me would break everything I'd worked so hard to rebuild.

"Want to go for a walk?" Alexei asked, knowing what my answer would be.

Just feeling the sun on my face and the peace our simple country life afforded me was a slice of heaven. I thought I wanted to rule New York, but after having a taste of this, I'd come to love the serenity the open space gave me. I could laugh, smile, and feel free for the first time in… ever. Alexei had helped me achieve it, and for that, I'd be forever grateful. But I knew I'd eventually have to go back. To face the people I loved and accept their hatred.

Our days at the cottage—and by cottage, I mean four thousand square feet of modernized living space, overlooking a private lake, with no neighbors for miles—were simple. We took walks, I worked endlessly to continue my empire, and Alexei cooked. It was something he picked up because he was tired of driving forty-five minutes for subpar meals that were loaded with fat.

At first, I struggled with the emotional side of things. My hormones were on overdrive and the more distance I'd put between me and my family, the worse it got. I'd drowned myself every day in my work and that was what kept me sane… my work and moments like this.

"Do you think he will hate me more than I hate myself?" I asked as we sat down on the edge of the dock.

"Do you really hate yourself? Or do you hate that he isn't part of your happiness?" Alexei gestured a hand over the water. "That he isn't here to experience this with you."

"Both." I answered truthfully, tilting my head back to feel the sun. "I've given all of them so much of myself, never putting my own needs before theirs." He nodded and seemed at a loss, so I continued, "They may not understand my reasoning, but it's what was best for me. For us."

"My uncle saw him recently. Said he is more himself, in control again."

The damn butterflies never got the message to leave. "How would he know that?"

He opened his mouth to reply when we both heard the sound of an approaching vehicle. "Fuck, get inside. Quickly." Alexei charged for the side of the house while I darted up the secluded path to the back door. I felt like a million pounds were holding me down as I fled up the stairs, darting to one of the various spots where I'd hidden guns. No one would force me to leave.

"Lock it down," I shouted at the maid. I shoved the Glock into the waistband of my pants and darted back outside. I trailed the shadows around the house, my back sliding across its exterior as I listened to the short, even steps of someone approaching from around the corner.

"Fuck!" a masculine voice hissed out as my hand connected with his throat. He moved fast, grabbing my arm and attempting to twist it behind my back. I shrugged him loose as he swung an elbow, but unable to avoid it, I clenched my teeth as it connected with my cheekbone.

Pain exploded behind my eyes—effectively knocking the wind out of me—but I kept moving my feet, ducking, and swaying to avoid having my arms pinned down. He grunted and cursed as we danced. I fed off the pain I inflicted on him, my own injuries stinging just a little bit less with each blow I delivered.

"Motherfucker." The man dropped as someone tackled him against the house and he landed like a ton of bricks.

What do you get when a mob boss, five armed men, and a gorgeous blonde head out into the middle of the woods? Vengeance.

"I found her," Persephone called out. "Are you okay?"

I swallowed back the pain rising in my throat. "In not so many words, yes." I couldn't help the grip I maintained on the Glock as they approached.

Dom Moretti eyed me as if I were a ticking time bomb, his hold on Persephone soft—yet it served as a clear, unspoken warning as well.

You killed my brother.

Did he want revenge? I felt like I could trust Persephone; she'd kept her promise to me. But could I trust the rest of them?

"Please don't draw that gun from your back," Dom stated, causing his men to tense, their fingers itching to grip their own weapons. "We mean you no harm."

"I'm sorry…" I started to say, but he stopped me.

"I'm not. My brother was an absolute piece of shit and you did all of humanity a favor by killing him." I could tell he meant every word. "We've all been at the receiving end of his cruelty." Dom unfastened two more buttons on his white shirt, showing me a large scar that seemed to run along his chest. It was somewhat faded but still grotesque.

I motioned everyone inside.

"How are you… really?" Persephone stepped out of his grasp, her soft hands rubbing my arm.

"I'm okay." I nodded. For everything he'd taken from me, I'd become ten times stronger. I had to be. Just as I was about to speak, a noise from upstairs pulled everyone's attention. Persephone glanced at me, her lips curling into a grin, before she coughed back a giggle.

"Good for you." She smiled. "Some of us can rebuild ourselves on our own, like you."

"And you," I said, but she looked at Dom with a coy smile.

"No. I needed help. Now, shall we?" She motioned towards the dining room table.

By the end of our brief exchange, I still had more questions than answers. But I did learn a few things. Persephone would negotiate Octavia's release to me. But, to be safe, we needed to call in outside reinforcements.

"You're sure about this?" Alexei asked for what felt like the hundredth time since we got in the car.

"Stop trying to talk me out of it." I was giving up my peace for my sister. The only one of us who deserved to be saved. I'd savored my freedom these past several months, but as we approached the city, my heart lodged itself in my throat, choking me. Every nerve ending in my body knew going back was a bad idea, but I would do anything for my sister.

Even this one last act of self-sacrifice.

"We'll get Octavia and then you can leave. You don't need to confess..."

I cut him off and steeled my spine, knowing every ball was in my court. "It's my decision. It'll be fine." I pulled the visor down to stare at my reflection in the mirror.

"Who are you trying to convince? Me or yourself?" Alexei's words hung heavy in the air.

In a game of cards, you had no one but yourself on your side. The dealer would bet on the house, the house didn't want to lose, and the man next to you was out for cold, hard cash. Yours, theirs, it didn't matter. I might have had Alexei in my corner, as he corralled the Russian *Bratva* to meet us at my family's compound, but I had to protect myself from *il famiglia*.

They—he—might just want to kill me. Once the knife in my grip shredded through my veins, the deceit I'd been harboring would change everything.

I walked into the compound with my head held high and ignored the unease churning in my stomach.

"Back up." Dom pushed Apollo aside before inserting himself between the object of his contention and Persephone.

I couldn't even look at *him*. Alexei stepped to my right, intentionally shielding me. It worked both ways. I was blocked from Apollo's view and he was blocked from mine.

Could I do this?

I swallowed roughly as the entire group settled into my father's office.

"I entered this game seeking revenge. Not to stand by and watch more innocents get hurt." Persephone's words had the entire room tensing.

"Where is my daughter?" my father ground out, his arms engulfing my mother as they both awaited the answer.

"We had nothing to do with this. With Octavia," Dom added. "I want to make that clear."

"Who has her?" Apollo urged, his patience clearly waning.

Persephone turned in his direction, and her expression lit up as she eyed my shadow lurking in the doorway. "You should be more concerned with who has the plan to get her back."

Dom laughed under his breath. But before anyone could respond, I stormed across the threshold with Alexei at my heels and a small Russian army at my back. I could tell my family wanted to ask a million questions, but they all faltered when Nikolai walked into the room.

"We're brokering a deal, Mario," Persephone explained cryptically.

I could *feel* his approach. He moved subtly, but I could sense it like an open flame against my skin. His growl told me he saw the bruise on my face and the sound sent chills down my spine, even as my father's tone left little room for argument. He commanded Apollo to back down. He'd just gotten me home and the sincerity in his voice showed me how heavily my disappearance had weighed on my family.

"*Who* fucking touched *you?*" Apollo pressed me for answers, despite the men attempting to drag him out of the room. I swallowed past the pain in my hollow heart. "Was it you, *fica russa?*"

I didn't have to look to know the insult was directed at Alexei. "*Dio dammi la forza,*" I prayed for a moment, closing my eyes to regain my composure as Apollo was finally escorted outside.

Persephone was working to negotiate a meeting spot. Once that was determined and we confirmed a date and time, I was the point person. I was supposed to bring Octavia home and avoid all-out war. They thought I'd be the calm in the anticipated storm, but I planned to teach them a lesson for hurting my sister.

Once we'd updated my family, I pivoted on my heel and marched out of the room as quickly as I'd entered. Marco stood to the side of the house smoking a cigarette. I could smell the alcohol on his breath at a distance. Several Russians in suits circled an idling SUV, their conversation ending the moment we approached.

When the rear car door opened, I watched my brother's jaw drop, his cigarette falling from his lips and hitting the ground. "Well, fuck me…" Marco muttered the moment his eyes landed on the girl presently stepping onto the gravel path.

"Come, *malyska.*" Nikolai made his presence known and his men parted like the Red Sea. "Mario invited us to stay while everything is being settled. We'll go retrieve our belongings from the hotel now."

I nodded and smiled at Alexei's sister. "*Do svidaniya,*" she said as she promptly followed her uncle.

Uh-oh…

My brother's face gave nothing away, but something told me the gorgeous Russian doll had his full attention. Before I could ask him about it, Marco turned on his heel and hightailed it inside, leaving me alone with the man who still haunted my dreams… and starred in my nightmares.

"You look good." His voice at my back sent goosebumps down my spine.

"Eat your heart out." I tried to hide my body's natural reaction to his presence but knew that I'd failed.

"I'll save that for the monster I left in the woods."

I spun so quickly I had to catch myself from snapping a heel. "He already ate mine."

"And it was delicious." Apollo pulled me close, inhaling my scent as if he didn't recognize me. "Tell me who touched you."

"Don't think for one second that my return has *anything* to do with *you.*" I thought I was maintaining my composure, holding my own against the beast in my midst, but his crazed smirk told me I needed to run. "Have a good night," I threw over my shoulder.

He called out my name, and something in his voice gave me pause. I stared at the darkened sky before slowly turning to him, my expression giving nothing away.

"There's a darkness inside me but it's also what draws you to me." He stepped closer.

And I swallowed back the weakness threatening to overtake all rationality. Instead of crumbling, I held on to my anger. "The fuck does that mean?" I rolled my eyes. "Stop talking in fucking riddles. I used to think it was attractive. Now it's just exhausting."

"It means…" His jaw clenched as he gestured between us. "This. Us. We're toxic."

"Okay? And?" My walls immediately began to rise.

"Toxic or not, you're mine. I need this." He took another step forward. "Crave this." He ran a finger down my throat, to my breasts, before pulling me in for a kiss—one that whispered his deepest, darkest sins.

I moaned into his mouth, feeling his arousal against my stomach. I wanted him to drop to his knees. To thank God or praise the devil for my return. And while that fantasy was not in any conceivable future for us, I *would* watch him fall… with a perfectly timed blow to his balls.

"You lost your privilege of taking without asking." I spat on his hunched form, much like he'd done when he called me a whore. "Don't make it a habit." Then I sauntered inside the compound with my head held high.

"I deserved that," he grunted in reply. "Fuck."

"Trust me, I deserve worse," I said to myself.

Hello. My name is Sienna Agostino, and although I'd lost a valuable part of myself to a man who didn't deserve it, I was back. My strength was an integral part of the story I was weaving. I wanted Apollo Deluca to fall at my feet of his own accord, and if he chose not to, then I'd make him regret it.

"Good to see you." Lucky pulled me in for a hug the moment I stepped inside. "Are you staying here tonight?"

"Sienna…" Bella's soft voice drew my attention to the stairs. My beautiful sister-in-law stood before us like a goddess wrapped in a white silk gown. She looked demure, yet radiant with a new glow to her skin. But I couldn't help but laugh at the oversized baby hanging from her arms. "Come meet your nephew. Nico." She continued down the stairs, and Lucky immediately rushed to her side.

"*This*. Came out of you." I gestured to the infant, the rest of the family laughed, and I finally felt at ease.

For as tiny as Bella was, especially when compared to my brother, she was dwarfed by their oversized son. He was big for his age, with impossibly long legs and a thick body. But it was the blue eyes that caught your breath—eyes that were far too aware for such a little baby. He looked at you as though he was somehow staring through you and into your soul. Nico was going to run New York one day, and I already pitied anyone who stood in the kid's path.

I reached forward, and those blue-steel eyes appeared to glance between my face and my hands before the infant finally outstretched his little arms.

"God!" I shuffled him from side to side to get a good grip. I wanted this. I wanted someone to look at me the way my brother looked at his wife.

I wish I may, I wish I might… Please, please keep Apollo from freaking the fuck out tonight…

"I'm only his favorite when my breast is out." Bella giggled at my back.

"Sienna." Alexei approached a moment later. "My uncle's returned with our… belongings."

The man in question walked in the room with Adrian—his right hand—at his side and a veil of dark hair behind him. Nikolai shook my father's hand and thanked him again for his hospitality. Adrian nodded and then ordered their men to patrol.

"This is my niece, Mila."

The Russian doll, often compared to Snow White, stepped forward. With her black hair and light eyes, her porcelain skin fit the bill. She was both beautiful and *sweet*, according to Alexei. Which was a rarity for someone in her position.

"Hello." Mila's saccharine voice was laced with a thick Russian accent as she spoke in broken English. "Thank you... having me."

Everyone took in the petite girl, their eyes landing on the bundle she was cradling against her chest. However, I was frozen in place as my mind was throttled back to a particular night at *Danza*.

"You do realize you don't always have to be a dick, right?" I watched Natalia storm out of the room after having been dismissed from her duties.

"I sent her home to avoid potential concerns for the fetus's health," Apollo stated, his nonchalance further demonstrating just how clueless the man was.

"Baby. Normal people call it a baby." I sipped my drink before turning my glare on him. "And the reasoning was sweet but the delivery was... dickish."

I didn't even know what I was doing here. What I was expecting from a man whose sense of compassion was as foreign to him as a mother's love. How could I ever hope that he could understand, accept me and my choices, when he didn't know what it meant to empathize. There was no future for us. I should have seen it that night at the club, when Natalia's child was nothing more to him than a medical term.

A condition, a concern, an ailment...

I was snapped back to the present when a shrill cry filled the foyer. Mila looked at me, her eyes wide and pleading for help. The sound was as unmistakable as my looming betrayal. And I only prayed they didn't kill me as each lie was unraveled in front of us. I didn't have to say anything as Mila lifted the now-awake baby towards me. His honey-brown eyes were an exact replica of his father's.

"This is my son. Salvatore." I straightened my spine and faced the awaiting onslaught.

The room erupted with commentary, but it all melted into the background. My head was filled with a crackling static as Apollo approached, reaching a tender finger out to his son. Sal was quick, latching on to it with his chubby hands and bringing it to his mouth. My son was also big for his age—a sure sign that he'd rival his father in height and width.

"Salvatore means savior in Greek." Apollo refused to look at me, his usually locked-down expression a myriad of contradictions as he stared at our son. However, there was one emotion I recognized and it was the pain I saw in his eyes.

"He was my savior in my darkest times." I smiled down at my precious boy, the light of my life. When I peered up again, I noticed that Apollo was finally looking in my direction.

His gaze dropped back to Salvatore when he spoke. "And now that responsibility will fall to me." When I didn't seem to immediately grasp his meaning, Apollo added, "I will be the one to save you when you feel lost amidst our shared darkness. I will protect you both. You're mine."

I faltered when those honey-brown eyes that matched my son's pinned me in place. There was a fire flickering beneath the surface, but every time I took comfort in its warmth, I was left to burn…

So, instead of surrendering to his pull, I squared my jaw. "What you'd label a fetus, see as a burden… I call a child, a gift. *I* belong to no one and *he's mine*."

CHAPTER 20
ROMANO BIANCHI

She was back in New York.

I had eyes on everyone who came and went from the compound. It had been months of nothing. My *alliance* with Mario was pushing the envelope and I could tell both of his daughters' disappearances were weighing on him.

Good. He deserved to suffer.

"Mario," I greeted as I held the phone to my ear, the noise drifting into the background as the sound of a door clicking in place filled the receiver.

"What is it, Romano?" he demanded on the other end of the line. The bastard was barely paying attention.

"We had a deal. I know she's back, so when are you handing her over?"

The man had dug himself into a very deep hole, one he couldn't climb out of alone. He knew I wasn't going to back off. He had used my men to protect Sienna after Octavia was taken. He used my resources to handle a few side issues that were threatening his family and his city. He owed me.

And that was a very dangerous predicament. For him.

"She just walked through my doors, Romano. You can't be fucking serious—"

I cut him off. "I am very serious. Dead. Serious. In fact."

His labored breathing was the only thing that indicated he was still listening.

"You know what it means to go back on our deal. I have the resources, and the desire, to fucking destroy you and everything you love."

"Do not fucking threaten me." There he was. The man Mario Agostino used to be before his world started crumbling around him.

"Facts are just that. Facts. I can and will destroy you if you don't hand over your daughter." And then I went for the kill. "And *the fact* that you haven't told your son tells me you're losing hold of your city. Your lies are catching up to you, Mario."

If Lucky knew the deal his father was brokering behind his back and the reason why, he wouldn't hesitate to start a war. Or send his little dog after me—especially because of the psychopath's penchant for my future wife. But like the throne of Philly, when I saw something I wanted, I *took* it. And marrying Sienna would be a nail in her father's coffin. She'd belong to me.

"I have some things to deal with. I'll be in touch." Mario was losing his composure and I couldn't help but feel pleased.

"Deal with what?" I mused. "Do tell, Mario. Do you need *more* help?"

"Boss." Romeo stepped to my side and I muted the phone. "He's got the *Bratva* onsite."

I grinned before unmuting the call. "Past sins aren't enough, Mario? Now you have to break every code in the book and get the Russians involved?"

The string of Italian expletives that shot out in response told me he thought I wouldn't know.

The soft click of heels walking into my office had me turning in my chair, my eyes landing on the dark-haired beauty standing just past the threshold. She was an incredible sight. So different from the meek girl I'd plucked from her former life. I'd created a siren, one who was a perfect replica of the image in my mind. I told her she'd be happy with me and that was part of the seduction. She said goodbye to her past all on her own. And she stayed because she liked the power I offered her.

I snapped my fingers and pointed to my lap, holding a finger to my lips as she approached. Her hips swayed naturally when she walked, and her breasts rose and fell with each even breath, while her submission heightened my pleasure. This bomb I'd drop on Mario would be the *final* nail in his coffin and I couldn't wait to watch him choke on the reveal.

"The clock is ticking, and when the bell chimes, I will take what belongs to me." She squirmed in my lap as I added, "And no one will protect you, your city, or the people you love." I ended the call before he could answer.

"I missed you," she whispered against my chest and my lips tipped up into a smirk.

"Did you?" I lifted her chin, forcing her to look at me. "We're taking a little trip that may require my attention." Her pout had me smiling wider. "Look at this porcelain skin. You're like a little doll. Precious and breakable, but I will protect you."

"Will... will you be gone long?" The concern I heard in her voice should be alarming, with the knowledge that I'd broken her down to nothing. But she'd put herself back together even stronger than before.

"A bit."

She sighed, her eyes welling with tears.

"But before you know it, we will leave New York together."

"Good." It wasn't a secret she hated this city and had come to love mine.

"Okay, go now." I helped pull her to her feet before giving her ass a slight pat.

"Sir, we have a whole other issue." Romeo leaned in and whispered the latest intel he'd received.

"A kid? You're sure?"

He nodded.

"Nothing's changed. Get the men together. We're leaving." I

stormed around the desk, snatched the girl's arm, and tugged her against me. "I need you."

Goose bumps prickled every inch of her exposed skin as I spun her around to press our chests together. I held her still, my palms cupping her jaw as she peered up at me with those large doe eyes of hers. I took note of the desire I saw in their depths, the sensation somehow heightening their intense color. Blue-steel… just like her father's. My teeth clenched at the comparison, before I dropped my mouth to hers, my tongue parting her lips until all thoughts of Mario Agostino were erased.

Then I pulled away, twisting her body and holding her at my side with my hand on the back of her neck. Using my free arm, I swiped everything off my desk, forced her chest to the wooden surface, and yanked her dress up. I slowly tugged her panties down her legs before spreading her wide. The soft material was soaked with her need for me, her *need* to *please* me. I stroked her folds, enjoying the soft whimper that escaped her plump lips. She was always ready for me. One command and she complied.

"Look at you. Perfection. Smooth, flawless skin and the tightest pussy I've ever felt. You're mine… say it." My hands shook as I freed myself from my pants.

"I'm yours." She'd barely finished speaking before I was buried deep inside her.

"That's right." I pumped into her harder, the desk scraping the floor as it moved with us. Her fingers turned white as she gripped the smooth wood with all her strength. "If only Daddy could see his little princess like this. With me."

Just saying it aloud had my balls tightening while she continued to moan beneath me. As I fucked her harder, her walls clenching around me, I smiled at my reflection in the mirror. I was a fucking street rat, a nobody who'd crawled out of the gutter. Who'd taken over one city and was moving on to the next.

New York, here I come.

CHAPTER 21

APOLLO DELUCA

I *belong to no one and he's mine…*

She felt it acceptable to hide this truth, not just from me but from her entire family as well. There wasn't a single physical trait that belonged to Sienna, except the boy's smile. The rest of his prominent features were mine without argument.

She still believed she could outrun me—I saw it in her eyes—but I'd never allow it again. Especially now.

The longer she'd been away, the more certain I'd become that she belonged to me. And our son just solidified that fact, regardless of her argument. She acted as though I'd abandoned them, left her to do this on her own. When, in reality, she'd chosen her path. And *my choice* was taken from me.

I couldn't fault her though. I wasn't exactly father material. Even now, it was difficult to distinguish between this strong sensation of ownership and anything that could be deemed paternal in nature. Females differed greatly in this aspect. Before and after giving birth, a woman's mind changed. Gray matter decreased in certain parts of the brain, then increased postpartum. This pollarding of neurons helped refine what society called maternal instincts, specifically the desire to nurture and protect their young.

I watched as Sienna's eyes continuously followed the boy, our boy, *my* boy…

And for as livid as I was, I was also momentarily stunned. Sienna Agostino had always had a penchant for storybook endings and romantic fairy tales. Something I never saw myself able to give her. But I did, in my own way. He was her soul mate. Our son. He would be the man I never could be. And I would be there to ensure as much.

My mind quickly returned to the very first time I took Sienna, and the many times after. We hadn't once used protection. The boy was several months old, and even if the eyes didn't give him away, the timeline certainly would. There was no doubt in my mind, despite the fact I had no scientific findings to validate my conclusion.

My body was releasing an overwhelming amount of cortisol. The steroid hormone was stress induced, the same reaction that initiated a person's fight or flight response. And where I'd always been one to muscle my way through any number of predicaments, I now found myself frozen. Unable to properly assess the situation. While everyone else seemed to move around me as if I didn't exist.

The staff bustled Nikolai, Alexei, and the Russian girl to their rooms as the rest of the Agostino family crowded around us. If there was one thing Italians loved, it was the progression of the bloodline. Their mouths were moving, their limbs animated as they appeared to fawn over the boy—my boy. But it all sounded like white noise to me. My throat was closing up, long repressed memories of a childhood I'd left buried with my guardians flashing in my mind, as the room seemed to narrow and go black.

It felt like only minutes had passed—my eyes had just closed— when a heavy boot made contact with my side. I acted on impulse and bent inwards, attempting to shield myself. I refused to give him the satisfaction of making a noise.

I opened my eyes to see Cara had moved farther into the basement, hiding in the darkest corner. But her light-gray eyes were staring at me —they harbored a brightness that drew too much attention to her. She needed to close them; she shouldn't watch. They filled with unshed tears as she pushed to her feet. I tried shaking my head, telling her that it wasn't worth it.

But this time felt different and maybe she felt it too. He was out for blood. Something snapped inside me when I saw Cara take a hesitant step forward. I wasn't worth her protection... wasn't worth the pain she'd suffer at his hands. When she ignored my silent pleas, I relented and Michael got exactly what he wanted from me.

"Ow!" I faked a cry, garnering his attention enough to pause his foot midair.

"You little shit." He smiled down at me, but there was only hatred curling those lips. "Shut the fuck up."

Time itself stilled. Cara retreated to the shadows as he pulled his foot back again. I watched it coming, staring at the steel toes of his boot still coated in my blood. When the tip made contact with my head, darkness descended immediately and I too was finally at peace.

"Apollo." Sienna's soft voice, her touch, brought me back from the abyss. Grounded me in the present and rescued me from a past I couldn't change. A past I wouldn't allow to taint my son.

The room had emptied and Sienna was the only one standing in front of me. She was chewing her bottom lip as she watched and waited, with a mixture of concern... and fear in her eyes. But not the kind of fear I'd come to recognize in others. It wasn't fear for herself. Her well-being. It was fear for me and mine...

The brain was an impeccable organ. Something that sought to both protect its host, while simultaneously causing its inevitable destruction. It could repress memories, just as easily as it would force them to the forefront of the mind to wreak havoc on one's ability to effectually cogitate.

I shook my head, as though that could somehow reset my cognitive abilities.

The boy. Salvatore.

He had a name. I had to remind myself, to fight that urge to somehow keep him at a distance while also never letting him out of my sight again. I had to navigate all these conflicting thoughts as rationality seemed to fight against some primal part of me. I had no natural inclination to be a father, no desire or need to procreate. It wasn't who I was. Who I thought I could be. This, whatever it was, was something else. Because he was already here and he was mine...

Sienna took my hand and I followed alongside her as she guided me to the backyard. The silence was tangible between us, clinging to the air like unfiltered tobacco until it was evident she couldn't stand it anymore.

"Do you hate me?"

"Yes." It was the truth. "You've always been a pestiferous little girl, nipping at my heels for attention. You should be proud, seeing as you finally got it. In full force."

She swiped at her tears, her tone now as steeled as her spine. "I left to protect him from us both. From who we are—who we become—when we're together. And to heal so that I could be better." She didn't wait for the response *I didn't have* as she stalked farther into the garden, putting as much distance between us as she could, but not before she threw one last parting shot over her shoulder. "And I'd fucking do it again. Anything for *my* son."

She'd protected him. Like no one had done for me. And I had no doubt this woman would jump in front of a bullet for our boy. Would watch the world burn to see him rise from the ashes. It was the purest form of her willingness to self-sacrifice I'd ever witnessed firsthand. Sienna Agostino had always been destructive in nature. But this was something different. This was unconditional love, an emotion I never thought I'd recognize, let alone understand. And, fuck, if that didn't make the insidious organ inside my chest beat faster. Harder.

After giving Sienna a few moments to come to terms with what was inevitable, I sought her out. We each remained lost to our own thoughts as we wandered Isabella's gardens. We were together, yet so far apart at the same time.

"Sienna? You okay?" Alexei's voice filtered through the air, causing my lip to curl in irritation and the muscles in my hands to flex and tense.

Sienna tried to grab my arm, but her brief moment of hesitation was to the Russian's detriment. My fist made precise contact with his nasal cavity. The posterior dilator naris muscle twisted with the severed bone, which allowed for an audible crack, as the lower lateral cartilage took the impact. I watched as his blood vessels erupted, sidestepping the tidal wave of bodily fluids, as I brushed the red now staining my hand across the front of his jacket.

"*That* was warranted."

He didn't respond, his silent acceptance melting between us. Sienna tapped me on the shoulder, and I stood frozen to the spot as she cocked back her fist and slammed it into my nose, the force behind the blow enough to induce bleeding without fracturing bone.

"It wasn't, but *that* certainly was," she gloated. "I'm fine, Alexei. Head inside. Bella can patch you up."

"Right…" The Russian bastard disappeared without another word, his fingers pinching the bridge of his nose and his head tilted back to hinder the flow.

I closed the distance between us, tugging Sienna to my chest as drops of red rained down on her flawless skin. "You know, studies show that the propensity for violence is an inherited trait…"

"Then I fear anyone who dares to cross my son's path." She ground her teeth with each word, her obstinance taking the reins and refusing to relent.

"Our son," I corrected her.

"I don't need you, Apollo." She leaned forward, pressing her lips to my ear before adding, "The girl I used to be, the girl you thought you knew… she's gone. Want to know how I know?"

My skin pebbled, my every nerve ending responding to her pheromones as my fingers itched to touch her. She was tempting me, and I forced a nod to keep her from pulling away.

It was the response she wanted.

Sienna smirked, her hand tracing down the length of my torso before suddenly grabbing my dick, her tight grip forcing my jaw to clench. "She's gone because I buried the bitch." Then she placed a chaste kiss to my lips, squeezing once more before letting go, so that she could pivot on her heel and turn her back on me.

Fuck. Me. She'd just tempted the beast, tugged at his leash just to force him to sit at attention at her feet. And the bastard longed for her next command.

"You can't fix me, you know. Any more than you can fix yourself. We are two fucked-up pieces of the same goddamn puzzle. We shouldn't work, shouldn't fit, but we do."

This had her pausing midstep, spinning back around, and stomping in my direction again. Good. I needed her fight. Her rage. Her retaliation.

"I was never supposed to feel anything, but every day with you was the purest form of agony, Sienna. And I need the pain. Because without it, I feel nothing."

"Am I supposed to empathize with that? Should I apologize for loving you to the point it almost killed me? Is that what you want? Will it make you feel better, Apollo?" Her anger was radiating off her in waves of toxic energy. I could almost taste it in the air.

"I'm the last person who would ever try to advise you on how to regulate your emotions, Sienna. However, that's not really what you want from me, is it?" My tongue traced along her ear, down her jaw, until my breath brushed across her lips. "No, what you want has nothing to do with what makes me feel better and has everything to do with what makes *you* feel better. You're the same spoiled princess I've always known you to be, no matter what you try to tell yourself. You like the power you have over me, the control. You get off on the fact that you tamed the one beast no one else could. That you and you alone can send me spiraling. Don't you, Sienna?"

I didn't give her the opportunity to answer, exploring her mouth while her unique flavor exploded on my tongue. The receptor proteins along my taste buds throttled my nervous system, sending satisfying impulses directly to my brain.

"You may think that girl is dead and buried. But I think she's been reborn." I rested my forehead against hers. "I can't love you the way you want. But we can hate each other until our dying breaths."

I felt her sharp intake of air, the sudden rise and fall of her chest, before I heard her audible gasp. My eyes searched hers but Sienna wasn't looking at me. Her gaze was focused on something over my shoulder as her hand fumbled along my waistband, her fingers reaching for my gun. I shoved her back, catching her wrist, but it was too late. She fired. Two shots. Right next to my ear as I dodged to the side, my senses scrambled amidst the chaos.

A high-pitched sound over 120 decibels could puncture the eardrum. A gunshot ranged anywhere from 140-175. Loud enough to not only disorient you and delay your body's reaction time, but also cause permanent damage.

Fortunately, I was keen enough to intercept when I saw the fucker behind me go down. The gun dropped to Sienna's side. I stepped into her space and took hold of her wrist. She ignored me, grabbing the gun that was just out of reach of her latest victim.

"Who the fuck sent you?" Sienna questioned, kicking him once for good measure. "Your boss is dead. I killed him." She raised the barrel and took aim. "And you can fucking join him."

"Wait." Lucky was approaching, Nikolai not far behind him. "Answer the question," Lucky demanded, but the bastard was losing his fight.

I shoved my boot into the would-be hitman's ribs, rolling him onto his side and pulling his wallet from his pocket. Just like before, the city and state matched those of the men we encountered in Sienna's apartment.

Gio Moretti might have been dead, but Romano was coming for her now.

"What is it?" Sienna asked, knowing there was some unspoken conversation being shared between us. "Seriously? I was sick to my stomach, terrified that you'd hate me for *my* lies and *my* secrets. I forgot how much yours have ruined this family." She turned to look at the man at her feet. "*Vai all'inferno.*" Sienna's body barely twitched as the gun discharged, forcing Lucky back.

"Fuck! Sienna, *puttana pazza!*" Lucky wiped the blowback from his face. "Get someone to clean this shit up."

Two of our men stepped forward, but Nikolai pushed them aside and ordered his guys to handle it instead.

"Have you always been such a pussy?" Sienna asked her brother, and everyone paused at her words. "Just a little bit of blood, *il diavolo.*" She grinned at his deepening scowl.

Lucky opened his mouth a few times as he looked back and forth between us. "You two, figure your shit out." Then he gestured in our direction before storming off.

My chest heaved as adrenaline coursed through my veins. I looked to the sky, needing a moment to collect myself as an image flashed in my mind. A glimpse of the pain I'd felt when I couldn't find her. The atrophy her absence had caused. And I refused to allow that to happen again.

"You're done running, Sienna. Both you and Salvatore."

And then we attacked each other like animals, freed from our self-imposed cages and absolutely ravenous.

There had always been a power she held over me. No matter how much I wanted to deny it, it was there. She kept my soul on a leash, and each time I wandered farther into the darkness, she pulled me back. She wouldn't let it consume me.

Her legs dropped from my waist and she tugged me to the ground, nestling us between a group of rose bushes. She gasped and I noticed how one of the thorns had scraped her cheek, a thin line of red pooling across her flawless skin. I snapped a rose from the branch and used its soft petals to collect the blood.

Sienna moaned as the flower dragged across her skin, before tugging me flush against her once more. Rose forgotten, I dropped to my elbows and allowed one single kiss to say all the things I couldn't.

Our bodies melded together, obliterating all the unspoken tension that hung between us. This was the push and pull that made the chaos between us seem… right. It was what made me realize so many things I'd avoided before. Sienna Agostino wasn't just my ruin; she was my salvation. And as much as she tried to argue otherwise, I was hers.

Rain started soaking into my shirt, through to my back, but I didn't care as I pulled her dress over her head. Her moans of pleasured mixed with the thunderous sky as the heavens let loose upon us. But neither god nor devil could stop our unsanctimonious union. It was the perfect symbolism for our tragic story.

Passion and destruction amidst the chaos.

I released her flesh from my teeth and unbuttoned my slacks, barely getting myself free as I fought for my next taste of her. The moment I was buried inside her, Sienna threw her head back and cried out. Our bodies were soaked through to the bone, and each forward thrust had her back sliding through the mud.

I wasn't even breathing anymore, as I watched on as she fell apart at my hands while burying myself deeper and deeper. The storm thrashed above us, but it was nothing compared to the sounds of her moans and my grunts.

I flipped her over, resting Sienna on her knees as she lifted her ass in the air, and shoved her face against the cold, wet grass. The rain was increasing with my thrusts, as was the symphony of skin slapping skin, the animalistic fucking sending us both over the edge and bringing us back to the present.

We righted ourselves with no words spared between us, taking a moment to adjust our clothing, before I tucked Sienna against my side and guided her back inside the compound.

We heard Bella's labored breathing before she entered the room, her arms attempting to contain the screaming child. She dumped the boy in Lucky's lap and flopped onto the sofa, releasing an exhausted sigh as everyone else seemed to chuckle at her plight. Isabella was cradling Salvatore against her chest; however, my son seemed to notice his cousin's distress and joined in on the high-pitched wailing.

Sienna picked him up and I tugged her to me as she soothed our boy into complacency. And it was then that I had a sudden revelation. Whatever this unspoken bond was between us, it made me whole. There was no Sienna without me. Her fire dwindled when she didn't have me to spark the flames. And there was no me without her. She inspired me to do better. Be better. And she kept my demons at bay as much as she incited their fury.

"I can't handle this." Bella was the first to break the silence, her eyes flicking to us with tears brimming her lash line and her chin wobbling. "It's about time." She shook her head, her comment clearly meant for me as she rose to her feet, collected Nico in her arms, and stormed off to tuck the boy in bed for the night.

"Nico is…" Isabella stopped to glare at her son. "Well, he's his father's son and giving Bella a bit of a hard time when it comes to complying with routine."

Sienna squeezed me tighter, her words directed at her brother. "I feel bad for her—I mean, one of you is bad enough."

"Easy," Lucky warned before his eyes landed on Salvatore. "I'm your Uncle Lucky, little one." Our boy grinned at him in return, and Lucky paused and cleared his throat. "I wouldn't expect your son to be so… approachable." He laughed at my responding growl and then the room froze, the air thick with tension until Lucky's face broke out in a smirk and everyone appeared to breathe again.

Isabella took Sal and left the room as Sienna slumped against me, clearly overcome with exhaustion. "The body?" I asked, changing the subject to one I understood far better than fatherhood.

"Handled." Nikolai stepped forward, as Alexei turned a glare in my direction.

"Problem?" I raised a single eyebrow in question, my eyes fixed on the Russian. Alexei's demeanor darkened before his uncle held out an arm to halt the bastard's approach.

Nikolai gripped his nephew's wrist. *"Ne seychas."*

"Ya v poryadke, dyadya." Alexei shook him loose and lifted a finger in my direction. "You're only breathing because she wants you to be."

"As are you. But I can't promise it will stay that way for much longer." My grip on Sienna was punishing by this point as she struggled to hold me back.

"Dostatochno." Nikolai corrected his nephew, effectively silencing our respective pissing match, and motioned for everyone to sit. "We need to discuss this deal Persephone bartered."

"I just don't understand any of it," Sienna muttered, looking up at me. "We're missing something."

Octavia was a victim of psychological warfare. She was taken as an act of war. Killing her would have been devastating but turning her against them, against her family, it meant their destruction. There was no coming back from it. And that had been their intention all along. Not to end Mario, but to eviscerate him from the inside out.

"The mind does what it needs to do to protect itself when forced to endure high stress situations. Her reality's skewed." Sienna's tears racked her body as I continued to speak the words no one wanted to hear. "If I were looking to punish someone, I'd send them back a shell of their daughter. Death is one thing. It's easy. People mourn and move on. But when the body's there, breathing but never truly living, there's hope. Even when there's not. And that's the real torture. The never being able to grieve properly, watching someone die a little more each day, without ever burying them."

We all turned at the sound of approaching footsteps as the truth seemed to choke the room.

"You look well, Sienna." Romano grinned as he crossed the threshold with his two guards at his back.

"I told you the fucking deal was off." Mario pushed to his feet, the room giving him their full attention.

"Language. I hear there are children in this house," Romano scolded and the implication seemed to thicken the air. He knew about my son. And his words were as much a power play as they were a threat.

"What is he doing here?" Lucky looked to his father.

"Your old man made a deal and I've come to collect." Romano's glare landed on Sienna, forcing me to pull my Glock from my holster. "I also expect compensation for the guys you killed."

"Your men were looking to hurt her. Why?" I hissed between clenched teeth, my barrel raised and my sights aimed center mass.

"Hurt her? They were there to protect her." He waved a hand, silently ordering his men to stand down. "There will be no bloodshed as long as everyone complies. A deal is a deal. Right, Mario?"

"Things have changed, as you seem to be aware," Mario countered. And despite all the double talk, everyone appeared to know those "things" were my son and the fact trying to take him from me would incite more than just bloodshed. It would mean all-out war. Beyond anything either city had ever seen.

"I broke barriers when I became the head of Philly. My mother was Irish, you know, and I was the first of my kind. So, you see, something as insignificant as an illegitimate child isn't a concern. You signed Sienna over to me, Mario, and I'm here to claim what was promised." Romano didn't flinch, his hands tucking into his pants pockets as he rocked on his heels defiantly. Clearly unaffected by all the weapons trained on him.

My body was vibrating, as I wavered between what I wanted to do and what I knew I shouldn't. He was calling my son insignificant. It was a challenge meant to send me spiraling, and even as I knew as much, it was a struggle to contain my rage.

"Get out before I do something we'll both regret," I growled in his direction, as Sienna clung to me with a misguided belief she could somehow hold me back if my leash snapped.

His two guards stepped closer to his side, and Romano raised a palm to halt their actions a second time. "Do you really want a war? Because I'll give it to you, and I can't promise who will and who won't end up as casualties. I mean, you know better than I do how often sons pay for the sins of their fathers."

Another threat against my boy, and my rage was boiling beneath my skin. I could feel it and it wouldn't be long before we all burned. "Don't make threats you have no intention of keeping," I ground out. "Because if you expect to leave here in anything other than a body bag, you'll drop your unfounded claims on my family and get the fuck out of our city."

"*Ours?*" he parroted. "Funny, didn't know a stray dog owned anything." Then he turned to Mario, uttering a single word, "Tomorrow," before storming out again.

"You used my pain against me. Leveraged my weakest moments to bend me to your will and push me to Philly." Sienna's dead, even tone filled the space. "Whatever happens, I want you to remember you did this, Daddy."

No one could look her in the eye, knowing each had played a part in everything that was to come. Even me. Especially me.

"Sienna…" Mario knew he'd failed both his daughters, but that knowledge came too late. "He'll never give you what you need." He nodded in my direction.

"None of you know what I need! You all just assume you know me better than I know myself." She paused, her eyes flicking between everyone in the room. "I'm not your fucking puppet, and much to your dismay, you'll never control me again. None of you will." She pushed to her feet and stalked towards the door.

"You will not walk away from this family." Lucky's arrogant tone had Sienna's shoulders pulling back and her heel pivoting to face him.

"Me? You don't want me to walk away, dear brother?" Her eyes narrowed in on him. "Each of you have turned your back on me time and time again, favoring everyone over me. And, suddenly, I'm the one who's the problem?"

"Sienna…" Lucky and Mario said in unison, but she continued to speak over them.

"I'm. Not. Done." She was eerily calm, her penetrating gaze stopping on each one of us again. "I was hunted. I was beaten. I was *raped*. Or did you forget that?" Her trembling hands were the only signs of her distress. "I overcame all of it. For me. For my son. None of you have the fucking right to ask anything of me. Let alone demand it. Now, goodnight. *I* will bring my sister home tomorrow."

The room remained quiet, each of us staring at the ghost of the woman Sienna left in her wake. She might have been out of sight, but her statement remained. Haunting us as surely as a fallen soldier haunted the battlefield.

"Handle this *shit*," Lucky hissed at his father. "You're destroying this family. We can't afford a war from both the west and the south. Not if you want any of us to survive it."

The patriarch looked at me, then back to his son, but I had nothing to say. Whatever bones Mario Agostino had buried long ago were resurfacing and worse than that, his decisions were rash. He'd lost control over his family and soon his city.

"And this?" Lucky motioned to the spot where Sienna had stood moments ago. "I hope I don't regret approving of it." He sighed before turning on his heel and following his sister's shadow.

And I wasn't far behind them.

CHAPTER 22
SIENNA AGOSTINO

I had to be dreaming.

I rolled over and the scent of Apollo surrounded me. I stretched my limbs, wincing at the delicious pain that overcame my muscles and clenched my thighs. Our little escapade in the rose bushes was his way of apologizing. Then the time in the shower and once again against the bathroom counter were my punishments.

But I was certain there was much more to come. I didn't care.

I love you held no meaning. Not anymore. I wasn't so naïve as to believe happily ever after existed after all this time. Not for us. I didn't need those words. Those lies. They were immaterial when it came to a real relationship between two people. I didn't want a romanticized love story. I wanted real. I wanted the raw emotions. The agony and the pain.

Apollo and I weren't going to ride off into the sunset on some white horse. I was going to yell, curse, and push his buttons just because I could. And when he had enough, he'd punish my body and I'd enjoy every delectable second of it.

No, I didn't need the words. I *needed* the actions. And his more recent ones told me everything I needed to know. His heart beat constant and strong under my palm. It beat for me and his son. I knew nothing about us was going to be easy, but that's what made life worth living. As long as he stopped fighting this thing between us.

I showered quickly, lost in my own thoughts of what today would bring. Octavia was coming home. All because of Nikolai's dedication to his nephew and Alexei's dedication to me. Then there was Persephone. She was some sort of avenging angel. The sort this fucked-up world needed and she'd kept her promise to me. However, something told me she knew more than she was letting on…

I straightened my hair and pulled it into a high ponytail. My smokey eyeshadow made my eyes pop and I added two diamond rings to each hand. I chose a strappy pair of blood-red soles with black metallic studs on the toes. My Dolce & Gabbana maroon and black lace bodycon dress fit me like a second skin, but the high slit on the thigh allowed me to move with ease. I slipped on a few mandatory accessories and headed downstairs. I refused to appear anything other than immaculate and posed, while knowing my reputation preceded me.

My heels echoed against the marble foyer as I entered the kitchen.

"Little overdressed, aren't we?" Alexei looked me up and down, clearly entertained.

"As if there is such a thing, Alexei," I fired back before bending at the waist and placing a kiss on Sal's head. He was seated in his highchair as I moved towards the island, stopping when Apollo tugged me to him.

He gripped my face between his palms, dropping a hand to my lower back and pinning me against him. He stroked my cheek and placed a tender kiss on my lips. It was soft yet somehow made my knees weak, threatening to crumble to the floor. I smiled at the feel of his arms around me.

And then he ruined it.

"Go change." The background noise around us died as everyone waited for my response.

"As if one night would somehow make me listen." I kissed him once again and made my way to the bacon on the counter. "Honestly,

Apollo, it's like you don't even know me." I laughed a little louder than necessary to drive my point home.

I was not. The One. He knew better than that.

"Morning." Mila walked into the room and Marco stopped moving, his eyes glued to the Russian doll in a silent stare down.

This wasn't good.

This girl was one toy my brother didn't need to be playing with. Luckily, his stomach took that moment to turn and he barreled out of the room—no doubt purging his liquid dinner. I looked to Al, who rolled his eyes before glancing at the girl curiously.

Nikolai watched his niece, his face deceptively blank. "Shall we go over the plan once more?" He motioned for us to enter the family room.

A mixture of Russian and Italian enforcers lingered in every corner, all here for one purpose while creating an alliance no one anticipated. Their plan was simple but mine was just that... *mine.*

The cars would pull up and I'd step out and motion for Octavia. Once she was safely tucked in our SUV, I'd open fire on every mother-fucker within range.

"I'm serious, Sienna. Stick to the goddamn plan." Lucky's tone held no room for argument and I was in too good of a mood to respond. Or listen.

"Are you going to be a good boy for Nonna?" I cooed at Sal, laughing when everyone cringed at his excitement. "That's my boy." I kissed his head and inhaled his sweet baby scent.

"You'll be the man of the house until we return." Apollo stepped to my back, his voice soft but no less commanding as he spoke to our son as if the infant could understand him. "That's a serious job, but I know you can do it."

Sal seemed to stare at him, as if somehow absorbing the weight of his father's words. My son was smart, too smart for his own good. I could only hope it didn't get him into trouble one day.

"Hello. I'm staying behind, remember?" Marco scoffed while wiping at his mouth with his sleeve, but the room started to empty as everyone headed to the front door, ready to bring Octavia home.

"Answer my call." Nikolai held Mila's wrist. "First ring. I want to know you're safe, and if anything goes down, I want you prepared."

The girl nodded, her eyes wide and innocent, and it tugged on my heartstrings. She'd been swallowed by a world too cruel for her, destined for ruin from the start. Alexei told me her story, all the horrific details of their childhood. The man carried a guilt unlike any other for leaving his baby sister behind.

I was about to pivot on my heel when something about Mila's body language caught my attention. The moment Nikolai left and she was free of familial eyes, her posture shifted and she popped a hip. That sweet, submissive demeanor was gone as she tossed a piece of gum in her mouth and flipped her hair over her shoulder with a smirk that told me more than her demure words ever could.

Who was this *girl?*

She turned to look at me, her eyes cold and dead as though they could stare straight through me before her glare landed on my brother. She watched him exit the room with something similar to mischief— but far darker—dancing behind her pupils.

I met our men outside the compound, Mila and Marco following to see us off.

"Be safe, do you hear me?" My mother leaned in to kiss me with Sal firmly planted on her hip.

"*Prommeti, Mamma.*" I kissed her cheek, then Sal's, before heading to Apollo's car. Until Mila's cry had my—and everyone else's —head spinning in her direction as she stumbled into Marco. She was gripping his lapels, my brother doubled over and groaning. At first it seemed innocent, but then I got a good look at his face.

Oh, no.

"What the fuck?" Marco shoved away from the girl, Nikolai and Alexei charging his way. "You little bitch." He lunged forward but not before our Russian allies stepped in front of him.

"What is the meaning of this?" Alexei hissed while Mila threw herself into his arms.

"He... he...." She wiped at the tears streaming down her face. "He too close. I no see. It an accident and he yell." Her broken English only added to that look of innocence.

"Chto on skazal?" Nikolai asked, his eyes never leaving my brother even as I tried to step between them.

My mom had disappeared inside with Bella and the boys. Apollo pulled me back, tugging Marco to his side in an attempt to alleviate the tension. But it didn't matter. The moment Mila opened her mouth, every Russian gun cocked in unison.

"On nazval menya russkoy shlyukhoy," she cried into Alexei's shoulder as he started shouting to his men.

"You called her a Russian whore?" Apollo asked, his eyes flaring with the question as he directed it at my brother.

"Fuck no! She ran her mouth. All I said was—"

"Enough. We don't have time for this," Lucky interrupted, stepping to the side with Nikolai before speaking in hushed tones. The discussion was obviously heated, Lucky's arms animated, but somehow we were able to avoid bloodshed.

Marco growled as Mila practically ran past him into the house. He waited a beat before slowly following after her.

What the hell was going on with my brother?

Everyone separated and piled into the cars, heading off to their respective locations in order to get my sister back in one piece.

The ride was as silent as it was tension filled, which did little to ease my frayed nerves. Octavia was the biggest part of my heart, a part that had been gone for far too long, and I desperately needed her home. Lucky and Al rode in the front of the armored SUV with Apollo and me in the back.

I was missing something. Some small detail. And none of it sat right.

Was this a setup to kill us all? Was Octavia even alive at this point? Or was the plan always to kill her in front of us?

"Breathe." Apollo wrapped his arms around me, giving me some of his strength when mine waned.

"Sienna…" Lucky stared at me through the rearview mirror, his eyes glued to mine in silent warning.

"I know what I have to do," I assured him. I didn't need the constant reminders.

"Then do it." My brother was a piece of work. He might have been the king but he wasn't mine. New York could be damned for all I cared. I was only here because my son deserved a father and I deserved my own form of happiness.

"This is it. I know what you're thinking, so don't," Apollo whispered in my ear before tilting my chin up and forcing me to look him in the eyes. "I need you safe." He kissed me slow and sweet, with a tenderness I wasn't prepared to receive.

"I just want her home." I bit down on my cheek to stop the sob from escaping. "And for whoever took her to pay."

"I know and they will. But there's a right way to do things." The gentleness of his touch didn't match the threatening undertone of his words. "Get her, get in the car, get out. That's it."

The car pulled into the meeting spot and a chill went down my spine. A Cadillac SUV was already parked at an angle, waiting for us. I sat forward in my seat, knowing I couldn't see through their tinted windows but needing eyes on my sister anyway. I could feel my nine digging into my hip, like a silent reminder that I needed to be the one to end this. My palms itched. I wiped them on my thighs to avoid doing something stupid before the time called for it. My thoughts were racing a million miles an hour and I could barely breathe, let alone think.

"Sienna." Apollo's harsh tone had me turning in his direction. He was watching my face almost as if he could see inside my head.

Who was I kidding? He definitely could.

"Don't," he annunciated the single word but there was so much more behind it.

Though I couldn't help but goad him. "Don't what, Apollo?" I huffed, crossing my arms over my chest and glaring at him.

"You thrive on the chaos. As much as I do if not more. I accept it. I accept you as you are, as you accept me. But now is not the time. We have a son to consider. This isn't just about us anymore."

My arms dropped to my sides. I hated to admit it but he was right.

Even if I refused to acknowledge it aloud, choosing to stare out the window again instead.

"You're mine. At first, I thought it started when you spread those pretty little legs for me. But maybe it's always been that way. Now let's get this over with and go home to our son."

My chin wobbled, my heart stalled, and my damn core clenched all at the same time. I nodded, unable to articulate what it meant to hear him finally say these things to me.

"About fucking time," Lucky muttered, earning himself a punch to the shoulder from Apollo.

"Jesus, she's silent. Tell her that shit more, will ya." Al grinned from the front seat, and I slapped the back of his head.

"Go get her." Apollo kissed me again before leaning over to open the door.

I stepped out of the car, the potential crime scene laid out in front of me. The Russians were hidden in the tree line surrounding us. The open space was vast, and the cheerful sounds of birds chirping would've made it beautiful if not for the promise of blood thickening the air.

I had no idea how I was going to get out of this without pulling my gun. I tugged my dress down a little and closed the door. No more than two hundred yards away was a black SUV. The windows were tinted but if I squinted hard enough I could see two men in suits in the front seats.

Who were they? Did I know them?

It didn't matter. Once I got Octavia back, they were dead.

As I continued to stare, plot, and wonder, the door finally opened and my sister's chestnut brown hair blew in the breeze. She stepped out alone and it took everything I had in me to keep myself from running to her.

The nine concealed at my thigh was burning a hole through my skin and my fingers itched to draw it and aim. The woman in front of me looked like my sister, yet not. Something was different, but I couldn't put my finger on the change. She took a tentative step forward, leaving the car door wide open, only to stop and look back over her shoulder.

I inched closer, unsure what it was she was saying to whoever was in the driver's seat. My hand slid to my waist as I felt the heat of all the weapons trained on me.

"Octavia, come here," I shouted over the wind swirling around us.

"A moment, Sienna," the voice of a stranger responded. Gone was the soft-spoken, sweet little sister of mine. In her place was someone demanding and loud, someone I didn't recognize. Her tone was clipped and I still couldn't hear what she was saying, but her demeanor had shifted, her eyebrows drawn and her jaw clenched with obvious irritation.

"You wanted your revenge and you got it. You promised me this," she shouted into the car.

"Octavia!" I called out when she retreated towards the vehicle once more. She said something, slamming the door the next moment. "Octavia!" I tried again.

She kept moving, slowly and calmly walking towards me. Her head held high, with a confidence I didn't understand.

Who was this girl?

The entire family had been falling apart at the mere thought of her absence. We *expected* a damaged girl to return, not this… self-assured woman. Her dress was tight and revealing, unlike anything she wore in the past.

My little sister had become a veritable sex kitten, and as much as I loved to see it, I was concerned.

A shiny shoe finally stepped out from the driver's side of the car. The large man had to unfold to exit before raising to his full height. I pulled my gun from my side as the doors behind me opened. No. Fucking. Way.

"You motherfucker!" I immediately took aim, my hands shaking with the rage I could no longer contain.

"Sienna, drop the gun! Lucky, no!" Octavia raised her arms in a placating gesture. "I don't want another war. This is behind us. Please, let's go and be done with it."

She was pleading with us, but it wasn't fear I saw staring back at me. In fact, her eyes were blank. But I couldn't give in. Couldn't let him get away this easy. That whole family was fucking dead.

The bastard stepped forward, drawing his own gun as his men surrounded him. "I changed my mind," he shouted, and Octavia stopped moving to glance over her shoulder at him. "I'm taking you back."

"Like fuck you are!"

I felt Apollo step in front of me long before I ever heard him exit the car. The sudden explosion of rapid gunfire deafened my ears and rattled my chest. In the mere blink of an eye, Octavia was collapsing into me and Apollo was tossing us into the car.

This wasn't supposed to happen. We were supposed to bring her home safely. It was supposed to be my chance to kill the bastard who took her from us. Instead, he had other plans… He would take her from us, once and for all.

Gunfire continued to sound in the distance. My brother and Al jumped into the front, Apollo shouting commands as we all took off. Octavia stared at nothing, her eyes glued to the ceiling as she heaved in sharp, labored breaths.

I wanted to scream and beg her to tell me what they did to her. But part of me knew I needed to ask myself that same question. This was our fault. All of us. We'd done this to her.

I sobbed into her chest because I knew that even if she survived, my baby sister was dead. Octavia would never be the same again…

EPILOGUE
OCTAVIA AGOSTIN0

My heart raced as I thought about seeing my family once again. I wasn't the same girl who was taken from them. If they only knew who I was now and why I was coming back, they'd hate me. *I* hated me.

I was beyond thankful to be coming home but also didn't want my darkness to touch them. I was damaged, no more their *prezioso piccolo bambino*. My innocence was shattered, stolen from me, and in its place, a monster was bursting from the seams.

He'd stitched me up like his own little doll, using me to plot and scheme behind everyone's backs. And I hated that I had to follow his lead. I hated him. But most of all, I hated myself.

"Do as your told, little doll." I watched the car pulling up to us, doing my best to ignore his heat radiating against my side.

"Yes," I muttered in reply but the clearing of his throat had me speaking louder. "Yes, sir."

"Good." He patted my leg, and I was so used to it I no longer pulled away from him.

A part of me longed for his touch. For the tenderness he rarely showed me. The other part was disgusted that I allowed myself to believe any of the lies this monster told me. The car got closer and closer, matching the beats of my heart. This was it. This was the moment I'd die, betray my family, and bury my lies alongside me.

His two men in the front spoke into their radios, alerting the rest of the team of our arrival. He'd promised me so many things and in that same breath took them away. I hated that this had to be done but understood there was no other way either.

I used to think my family was untouchable, that our strength was unmatched. I was wrong, so wrong. It was all a façade that came crumbling down around me years before I realized what was happening. I was living in my own perpetual nightmare, a shell of the human being I thought I was.

"Go." His words were short, clipped. "Now, Octavia."

I swallowed around the lump in my throat and opened the door, the wind kicking up and forcing a shiver down my spine. My sister stood in the distance, looking as formidable as ever. She seemed happier, a glow about her that made me question several things. I knew about my nephew. They kept me abreast to the updates on my family—one of the many forms of torture I'd endured. And I so badly wanted to meet him, but it wasn't a luxury I deserved.

I glanced over my shoulder once more, staring into the eyes of the man who ruined me, his team watching my every move. A growl from the back seat had me turning my back on him and taking a step closer. I leaned into the door.

"I know what I'm doing. We had a deal." My voice sounded stronger than I felt, and his pleased smile had my heart beating a little faster in my chest.

God, I was pathetic.

"We do, little doll. Hurry up before I change my mind." He eyed me in a way that told me exactly what he was thinking. I slammed the door in his face, the metal barrier doing little to diminish the sound of his booming laughter.

With each step closer to my sister, I felt myself lighten. The door opened behind me and my steps faltered, knowing all hell was about to break loose. My brother, Al, and Apollo stormed from the car, charging towards Sienna with their eyes on me. I could hear the gun cocking at my back and knew his men were also at the ready. I turned and glanced over my shoulder, and the bastard was smiling back at me.

"You wanted your revenge and you got it. You promised me this," I yelled at him.

Many emotions ran across his face and I knew this was where I'd meet my maker. This was where he'd destroy my family with one pull of the trigger. And he was a dead eye behind the sights, never missing a single target. My family was shouting and moving closer. I knew he'd aim for my sister first. He knew how much she meant to me.

"I changed my mind." I paused midstep at the sound of the first shot, my body jarred by the blowback. Pain. That was all I felt. My family started firing as more of his men emerged from the tree line and I was dragged to the car. He'd told me time and time again that he wanted to ruin me, my family, my name. He'd build me up just to break me down. But he promised to leave my mother and my two nephews alone, if I just followed his orders. It broke my heart but he forced my hand.

So I agreed. Before he killed me.

EPILOGUE
SIENNA AGOSTINO

I didn't think any of us were prepared for the shitstorm that became my sister's rescue mission. It shattered the family in so many ways. I didn't want to think about it. I couldn't even begin to tell you the details that would give her story the justice it deserved. As the saying went, it was her story to tell and I wanted no parts of it. I had my own messes to clean up after all.

But life with Apollo—after everything we endured together, far more than what was painted between these pages—was picture perfect. My own version of it. A twisted fairy tale. But it had to be that way. Do you really think if it were easy, I'd still be here? I was a glutton for punishment (still am) and there was no other way for me. For us.

Apollo grew into his own version of fatherhood. His natural inquisitive nature had him studying his son like a puzzle he was trying to decipher and the two were peas in a pod. I went from Sal's favorite to nothing more than a backup to his dad. And his father, well, Apollo was still an asshole. It didn't matter what it was about, we fought tooth and nail. Just because we'd finally gotten to a place of understanding didn't mean things were all unicorns and glitter.

I was still peeling dried blood from his skin, laundering Brioni suits covered in entrails, and stitching him up on a regular. We'd fight the entire time and then we'd make amends between the sheets, too sated to continue the argument by the time we were done. Then I'd piss him off all over again the next day. It was a vicious circle. And I was not too proud to admit that sometimes I'd do it just to watch him lose control. It was so goddamn hot.

But we were figuring out this parenting thing together. Apollo was very hands-on with Sal, seemingly methodical in the way he approached our son. I knew, without a doubt, that he'd lay his life down for either of us. And it was almost *sweet* to watch the way he smirked when he taught Sal something new. The kid was far too big and growing more each day, while his vocabulary was that of a middle-aged man and nothing like that of a toddler.

Again, his father's son.

Then there was the sex. I didn't need a four-letter word to finally understand how Apollo felt about me. No one could touch or even look at me wrong without being on the receiving end of his glare. Was it healthy? Hell no, we were off-the-charts toxic, but it worked for us. We fought, he stormed out to help my brother step into his new role, and then he would come back home to me after.

His silence was all I needed as he pulled me close and held me tight. I loved this man and I loved how much he cared for our son. In the beginning, I'd told him all I needed was him. Apollo would never change. It wasn't in his nature. But no one knew him like I did. And in his own way, he knew me better than I knew myself too. At least parts of me. He was the monster who'd moved out from under my bed and into it, while he liked to call me his angel, claiming he'd clipped my wings to prevent me from leaving him again.

EPILOGUE
APOLLO DELUCA

Vexatious. Maddening. Bothersome. Down-right fucking irritating. So many different adjectives, all with the same meaning. *Sienna.* They described the mother of my son, the woman in my bed, and the cause of the pain in my chest. She was all those things and more. But above all else, she was *mine.*

I'd made a promise the day she walked back into my life with my son in tow. I'd protect them. She'd always had my loyalty because of her last name, but my devotion came with the boy who shared mine. Salvatore had so many parts of his mother, but as each day passed, I saw the good parts of me in him too.

He was emotional, a bleeding heart in his own way, but he was smart and attuned to everyone in the room. He watched, dissected, and adapted. He didn't start walking; my son took off running, wreaking havoc alongside his cousin Nico. The boys were inseparable and constantly getting into trouble. Lucky and I were often pleased with their antics. They pushed themselves far beyond the limits you'd assume children their age were capable of. They were quick learners and had an eye for chaos that their mothers had a hard time harnessing. In the end, they were kids enjoying a very extravagant life.

Bella and Sienna were concerned over their immediate bond and it gave us a glimpse of the future of New York. But it was Lucky and Bella's second child who truly troubled them. Mario exhibited many of the same personality traits as I had, with his lack of empathy. They were keeping an eye on him, but their attentions were misguided. The boy was detached but his protective instincts were unparalleled. New York had no clue what the next generation was going to bring them. No one did.

"Well?" Al poked my side, motioning towards Sienna, who was standing in the vineyard yelling at Sal and Nico for whatever recent trouble they'd found themselves in.

"Would you presume you were born this irksome, or was it something you grew into?" I inquired, amused at Al's obvious irritation as he stomped away.

"Get on with it." Lucky nudged me.

"Salvatore!" My son froze, turning to look at me over his shoulder as I approached. "What did I tell you?"

He laughed, looking at his mother expectantly.

"What?" She watched both of us, her eyes narrowed with suspicion as our son dug into his pocket before pulling something out. It took Sienna a moment to realize what she was looking at.

If I had known a little piece of white gold with a diamond attached would silence her, I probably would've done it a lot sooner. Everyone in the city, in our world, knew exactly who Sienna Agostino belonged to. Her last name had always came with the weight of her father's strength and power. However, mine would elicit something else altogether. Fear. And it was time to do right by her.

"Nothing with you has ever been simple. There isn't a single uncomplicated part of you." I pulled her flush against me. "I think I've known for longer than I care to admit that you belong to me. Faults and all. Marry me." It wasn't a question. It was a command, but I expected a response nonetheless.

"And you belong to me, *psychotic tendencies and all.*"

I raised a brow, urging her to elaborate.

"Of course, I'll marry you."

I lowered my lips to hers to quiet her before she could say more, or push me into another argument. She went to open her mouth and I raised a hand to cut her off. "Do *not dare* to even think about it." I slid the ring onto her finger and kissed her once more.

For a woman who was so against using her family name to her benefit, choosing to work for everything she earned, she sure as fuck kept giving me issues when it came to changing it. Marriage she was fine with. Her not-so-subtle hints told me what she wanted from me, what she had been waiting for, and I obliged. But other traditions—like dropping her maiden name—gave her pause. That being said, relationships were about give and take, or so she liked to remind me, and I wouldn't concede on this. She didn't need to be an Agostino anymore. Deluca would suit her far better.

She was my darkened angel. My beacon in the bleakest of times, and I was ready to ensure it stayed that way. Because an angel couldn't fly without her wings. And this ring, catching the sunlight from where it presently sat on her finger, ensured Sienna Deluca's wings would be forever clipped.

About the Author

Corporate sales by day, closet romance novelist at night—Dahlia Reign has always had an unparalleled taste for dreamy alpha-men. In her youth, Dahlia had journals by the stacks that she used to jot down her innermost thoughts; subsequently, turning them into romantic stories. Now, years later and with her picturesque alpha-man at her side, she's taken the literary world by storm. Her man, her pittie and an overactive imagination mixed with her bleeding heart—she's set off to tell the world her stories. Buck up and grab a bandaid, shit's about to get heavy.

www.TheDahliaReign.com

facebook.com/authordahliareign

instagram.com/authordahliareign

tiktok.com/@authordahliareign

ALSO BY DAHLIA REIGN

<u>Agostino Crime Family Series</u>

Contracted to the Devil: Book One

Clever as the Devil: Book Two

Beautiful Deception: Book Three

And Twice as Twisted: Book Four

<u>La Reina de Escorpiones Duet</u>

Infinite Sorrow: Book One

Endless Deceit: Book Two

www.TheDahliaReign.com

www.ingramcontent.com/pod-product-compliance
Lightning Source LLC
Chambersburg PA
CBHW070507300726

48975CB00007B/2363